Author photo © www.mattchristie.com

Vina Jackson is the pseudonym for two established writers working together for the first time. One a successful author, the other a published writer who is also a city professional working in the Square Mile.

Also by Vina Jackson

Eighty Days Yellow
Eighty Days Blue

An Orion paperback

First published in Great Britain in 2012
by Orion Books Ltd,
Orion House, 5 Upper St Martin's Lane,
London WC2H 9EA

An Hachette UK company

3 5 7 9 10 8 6 4 2

A CIP catalogue record for this book
is available from the British Library.

ISBN (Paperback) 978 1 4091 2779 6
ISBN (Ebook) 978 1 4091 2778 9

Typeset at The Spartan Press Ltd,
Lymington, Hants

Printed in Great Britain by Clays Ltd, St Ives plc

The Orion Publishing Group's policy is to use papers that
are natural, renewable and recyclable products and
made from wood grown in sustainable forests. The logging
and manufacturing processes are expected to conform to
the environmental regulations of the country of origin.

www.orionbooks.co.uk

Eighty Days
Red

Vina Jackson

I

Running

My feet beat time with my heart.

Central Park was sheathed in white. Despite the relative calm within the park, I was constantly aware of the sprawling city that spread out around me on every side, like a huge open hand with a patch of countryside clutched in the middle, buildings pointing upwards like dirty grey fingers surrounding the pristine blankets of snow rolling out across the lawn.

The snow was still fresh, powdery, and I could feel it crunch lightly beneath my footsteps, cushioning my landing. The absence of colour in the park amplified all of my other senses, so that I could feel the dry, freezing cold air brushing my skin like the touch of some icy supernatural being. My breath steamed out in front of my face like wisps of smoke and the cold air burned my throat.

I had run every day for a month since discovering Dominik's book in Shakespeare & Co., on lower Broadway. I'd read it hurriedly, in the rare, snatched moments when I found myself alone in the house, wary of Simón's watchful gaze.

It had been a strange feeling reading Dominik's work. The heroine was so much like me. He'd included some of the conversations that we'd had in his dialogue, described scenes from my childhood that I had related to him, about the smothering nature of life growing up in a small town and my desire to get away from it. He'd even given her red hair.

And I recognised Dominik's voice throughout the text as clear as a bell. His particular turns of phrase, references to books I knew he'd read and music he liked.

Two years had gone by since we'd broken up. We'd had a terrible misunderstanding and I had allowed my pride to get the better of me and walked out on him, something I still regretted to this day. When I'd gone back to his apartment to try to clear the air he was gone. I had peered under the crack in the door and seen an empty room and mail piled up on the floor. I hadn't heard from or of him since.

Until that day when I'd been shopping for running shoes in Manhattan and discovered his novel in a bookshop window. Curious, I'd flipped it open, and been shocked to find that despite our tempestuous relationship and the sour nature of our parting he'd dedicated it to me: 'To S. Yours, always.'

I hadn't been able to think of anything else since.

Running was my way of beating the feelings out of my body. Particularly in winter, when the ground was covered in white and the streets were quieter than usual. In winter, Central Park was like a snowy desert, the one place that I could escape the cacophony of the city for an hour.

It was also a chance to give myself some thinking space away from Simón.

He was still leading the Gramercy Symphonia, the orchestra where we'd first met.

I'd joined the string section three years ago, playing the Bailly violin that Dominik had gifted me. Simón was the conductor, and under his tutelage my playing had improved immensely. He'd encouraged me to go solo and introduced me to an agent, and I was at the point now where I'd had a few tours and released a couple of records.

Our relationship had been professional, though admittedly flirtatious at times. I knew Simón was in love with me, and I did little to discourage his feelings, but nothing had happened between us until my row with Dominik. I had been touring at the time and hadn't had anywhere of my own to go. Simón's apartment near the Lincoln Centre with the built-in rehearsal space had seemed an obvious option, easier and more practical than a hotel.

But then Dominik disappeared, and a couple of nights with Simón had quickly turned into a couple of years.

I'd drifted into it happily enough. Simón was an easy person to be with and I was fond of him, loved him even. Our friends greeted the idea of us being an item with immediate enthusiasm. It made so much sense, the young virtuoso conductor and his up-and-coming violinist. After spending years either determinedly single or with someone that my friends and family suspected wasn't the right man for me, I suddenly fitted in.

I felt accepted. Normal.

Life slipped by in an ongoing sequence of rehearsals and performances, recording studios, the excitement of having my first album released, and then another. Cosy parties, Christmases and Thanksgiving dinners spent with friends and relatives. We even appeared in a couple of magazine articles listed as New York's musical golden couple. We'd been photographed in Carnegie Hall after a concert, standing hand in hand, me resting my head on Simón's shoulder, my curly red hair mingled with his thick dark locks. I was wearing a long black velvet dress with a low back.

It was the dress that I had worn for Dominik the first time that I had played for him, Vivaldi, *The Four Seasons*, at the bandstand on Hampstead Heath.

Dominik and I had struck a deal. He would buy me a new violin – my one at the time having been wrecked in a fight in Tottenham Court Road tube station – in exchange for a performance on the heath, and another more private performance where I had played for him entirely nude. It was a brazen request from a stranger, but the idea of it thrilled me in a way I couldn't explain at the time. Dominik saw in me something I had yet to see in myself. A wantonness and desire that I hadn't even begun to explore. A side of myself that had since brought me both pleasure and pain.

And true to his word, Dominik had replaced my old, battered violin with the Bailly, the instrument that I'd had ever since and still played at all of my gigs, though I had other spares for rehearsing.

Simón had wanted to buy me a new one. He favoured modern instruments with a cleaner tone and thought that I should try for a change, something crisper. I suspected that he just wanted me to be rid of all the parts of Dominik that still flavoured my life. Certainly I'd had enough offers from musical patrons and instrument manufacturers that I could have replaced the Bailly ten times over.

But Dominik's gift felt like home to me. No other instrument had the same tone, the same ideal weight that rested in my hand, the perfect fit beneath my chin. Playing the Bailly inevitably brought Dominik to mind, and thinking of Dominik made me go into that place that I went where I played at my finest; a mental disappearance act, my body taking over from my brain and my mind retreating into a waking dream where the music came alive and I didn't need to play any more, just experience my dream while my bow hand moved across the strings for me.

A woman stared at me in surprise. She was dressed in a heavy jacket with the hood pulled tightly around her face to ward off the cold and was pushing a bright blue pram with a heavily bundled child inside. A fellow jogger kitted out head to toe in bright yellow thermal gear with reflective stripes gave me a knowing glance as he passed.

Simón had bought me running clothes for Christmas, amongst his other gifts. Perhaps as a sign that he planned to stop nagging me to join a gym instead. Simón hated my jogging in Central Park, especially in the early mornings or late evenings. He quoted statistics about female joggers in Central Park and how likely they were to be attacked. Apparently, most likely when blonde, wearing a ponytail and running around 6 a.m. on a Monday. That almost entirely ruled me out, I'd told him, as I'm a redhead and never out of bed at 6 a.m., ever, but he still nagged me.

He'd given me a pair of designer thermal gloves and matching long trousers, shirt and jacket, and the most expensive pair of running shoes on the market although I'd just bought myself a pair.

'You're running on ice, you'll slip,' he'd said.

I wore the shoes to keep him happy, though I replaced the white laces with red ones for a splash of colour. And I wore the gloves. But most days I left the thermal jacket at home. Even in winter I preferred to run wearing just a singlet. It was viciously cold at first. The wind bit into my skin like a bed of nails but I soon warmed up, and I liked the feeling of the fresh air, and the cold wind which encouraged me to run faster.

By the time I reached home again my skin would inevitably be bright red and sometimes my fingers swollen despite the gloves, as if I'd been burned by the cold.

Simón would take me into his arms and kiss me to warm me up, rubbing my bare arms and shoulders until my skin hurt.

He was warm in every way, from his coffee-coloured skin, courtesy of his Venezuelan heritage, his big brown eyes, his thick curly hair and his big body. He was nearly six foot two and had been very gradually putting on weight since we moved in together. He was by no means fat, but eating dinners together and sharing bottles of wine on the couch over a DVD had taken him from lean to burly and the slight padding on his body gave him an additional sense of softness. His chest was covered with a thick mass of dark hair which I loved to run my hands through as we lay in bed together, after making love.

He was overtly masculine in his appearance and deeply affectionate in his manner. Our two years together had been like relaxing in a bubble bath. Falling into a relationship with him was like coming home after a long day at work and slipping into flannelette pyjamas and old socks. There's nothing like the company of a man who loves you utterly and without question. With Simón I was cared for, protected, soothed.

But I was also bored.

I'd managed to quell the undercurrent of dissatisfaction in our relationship with a barrage of hobbies. Working like a demon. Playing the violin as though each performance was my last. Running the New York marathon. Running, running, running, all the time running away but always going back home again.

Until I had read Dominik's book.

Since then I'd heard Dominik's voice in my mind almost constantly.

First in the words of his novel, as if instead of reading it I was listening to an audio book.

Then memories had risen up like a tide.

Our relationship had been coloured by sex, but not the frequent, affectionate sex that I had with Simón.

Dominik was a man with darker desires than your average, and being with him had been like having a light go on in my life. With Dominik I'd taken great pleasure in the realisation of fantasies that I previously hadn't dreamed of. He had asked me to do things for him that other people had not even whispered. It was not so much the adventurousness of it but his insistence that I allow him to use my body for his pleasure, submit to him in a strange game that was more mental than it was physical and in which we were both complicit, though it would seem to any outsider as though I was allowing him to rule me.

Sexually, Simón was virtually the reverse of Dominik. He liked me to be on top, and I spent most of our evenings together grinding against him from above, trying to prevent my mind from drifting away into daydreams of work and shopping lists, or staring at the glossy white wall behind the headboard.

My phone buzzed in my trouser pocket and I jumped in surprise, almost slipping on an icy patch. Few people had the number, and I didn't often receive calls. When I did they were from Simón or my agent Susan, and Simón knew that I was running, so was unlikely to call unless he wanted me to pick something up for breakfast, one of the sugary doughnuts that he loved to dip in his coffee from the deli on the corner of Lexington and 56th.

I hurriedly tugged off one of my gloves. My fingers were so frozen from the cold that I could barely grip the handset. It was a New Zealand number, though not one I had programmed onto the phone already.

I pressed the call answer button with some trepidation. I very rarely spoke to my family on the phone. We just weren't the type for frequent communication and preferred to email or use Skype. And it would be late in the evening over there.

'Hello?'

'Heya, Sum, how's tricks?'

'Fran?'

'Don't tell me it's been so long you don't recognise my voice, sis?'

'Of course I do, I just didn't expect to hear from you. What time is it over there?'

'Couldn't sleep. I've been thinking.'

'Don't make a habit of it.'

'I want to come and visit you.'

'In New York?'

'I'd prefer London to be honest, but any port in a storm. I'm getting bored of Te Aroha.'

Those were words that I had never expected to hear

coming out of my older sister's mouth. She stuck out like a sore thumb in our home town, Te Aroha, and didn't strike me as a small town person at all, but despite that she had lived there her whole life, nearly thirty years. She'd been working at the local bank since she left high school. Twelve years or so in practically the same job. She'd started as teller and moved up to team leader and then financial advisor, though she hadn't had any formal training besides that which was offered in-house. I was the only one in my family who had gone to university, though I'd dropped out after the first year.

I could picture her easily. It was a Saturday morning for me so would be late Saturday night for her. She'd be sitting in her cottage, dressed in denim shorts and a bright neon ripped T-shirt, eighties punk style, and fidgeting as she always did, running her hand through her short, cropped bottle-blond hair or wrapping a lock of her fringe around her finger. It was mid-summer there so probably hot, although her old house was draughty and Te Aroha always seemed to have a chill in the air, as if the entire town lived in the shadow of the mountain.

'What's brought all this on?' I asked her. 'I thought you'd be there for ever.'

'Nothing lasts for ever, does it?'

'Well no, but it's a bit of a change of heart for you. Has something happened?'

'I'm not sure if I should tell you. Mum told me not to.'

'Oh for God's sake, you're going to have to now. You can't leave me hanging.'

I had slowed down to a quick walk and without the momentum of a run pushing me along the ice I was slipping with each footstep, and freezing cold without the heat of the heavy exertion to warm me. The fingers of my ungloved hand were bright red from the cold and beginning to throb.

'Fran, I'm in the middle of Central Park and the temperature is sub-zero. I need to start running again and I can't run and talk so spit it out and I'll call you back when I get home.'

'Mr van der Vliet died.'

She said the words softly, as though she was gently releasing a weapon.

'Your violin teacher . . .' she added, filling the silence between us.

'I know who he is!'

I stopped completely and let the ice in the air wrap itself around me like a steel blanket.

Fran was silent at the other end of the phone.

'When? What happened?' I finally managed.

'They don't know. They found his body in the river, where his wife died.'

Mr van der Vliet's wife had died the day that I was born. She had been driving through the Karangahake Gorge on her way home from Tauranga when her car's wheels had slipped in the rain and she'd misjudged one of the tight corners and collided with a truck coming the other way. The driver of the other vehicle had been fine, not even a scratch, but Mrs van der Vliet's car had flipped and plunged over the side of the treacherous road and into the river. She had drowned before anyone had been able to reach her.

'When?' The word stuck in my throat like a mouthful of cotton wool.

'Nearly two months ago,' Fran whispered. 'We didn't

want to tell you. Thought it might upset you, affect your performances. Mum and Dad didn't want you to drop everything to come home for the funeral.'

'I would have come back.'

'I know. But what difference does it make? He'd still be dead, whether you were here or not.'

Fran, like most of the other New Zealanders I knew, was practical and pragmatic. But her hard logic didn't stop the vice-like sensation that was gripping my heart.

Mr van der Vliet would have been in his eighties now, and I didn't think he'd ever got over the death of his wife. But quiet and unassuming as he was, he'd been like a rock in my childhood. His voice, still thick with a Dutch accent despite having lived in New Zealand for most of his adult life, would be gentle but firm as he corrected my grip on the bow or praised me for a successful performance.

I'd learned most of the craft of violin playing by watching him. The way that his tall and painfully thin body became so alive and graceful when he took up an instrument. He played as if he had stepped through a door into another place, becoming a different man altogether, with none of his usual awkwardness. I'd tried to mimic the way he seemed to live the music and soon found that by closing my eyes and absorbing the melody with my body I could play far better than I could just by reading from a sheet.

Mr van der Vliet was not the reason why I had begun to play in the first place. My father and his vinyl records had to bear responsibility for that. But Hendrik van der Vliet was certainly the reason why I kept at it. He had seemed such a stern man on the outside, yet had a streak of softness that came out occasionally and I'd spent most of my childhood and teenage years doing everything that I could to elicit his rare praise by practising and practising until my fingers were raw.

'Summer? Are you still there? Are you OK?'

Her words were like an echo.

'Fran, I'll call you back, OK?'

I pressed the end call button and zipped the phone back into my trouser pocket without waiting for her to respond.

I put my earphones into my ears and turned the music up loud. Emilie Autumn's 'Fight Like a Girl', something that Mr van der Vliet would have hated. He had always pushed me in the direction of classical music and was disappointed when I had dropped out of my music degree and moved to London.

My mind filled with images of his face underwater. Had he had an accident? A heart attack, coincidentally in the same place as his wife died? I doubted it. I had never known Mr van der Vliet to have so much as a cold, I couldn't imagine him being ill. It must have been deliberate, but he didn't seem to me like the type to jump. That seemed too spontaneous. He'd choose to go in a manner that was definite, with every moment of his passing firmly within his control. He would have walked in.

I could see it like a film unfolding in front of me. He'd have worn his Sunday best. Perhaps the suit that he wore to the concert I played in the Te Aroha secondary school assembly hall, when I'd visited a couple of years ago on my Antipodean solo tour. A white shirt with a dark olive-green waistcoat, trousers and jacket. He'd looked like a grasshopper, his limbs folded up uncomfortably to fit within the confines of the small wooden chairs that had been laid out in the hall. His skin as thin as paper, as if he might rustle in the breeze like a leaf.

He would have just walked in, and relaxed. He must have done it late at night or early in the morning, before the river filled with holidaymakers, bushwalkers and children with their inflated tyre tubes intent on riding the current that ran all the way to Paeroa where the Ohinemuri River met the Waihou.

Mr van der Vliet must have been one of the only people in New Zealand who couldn't swim. He said that he had never wanted to learn, always preferring the comfort of dry land even in hot weather. With his total absence of fat tissue he would have sunk to the bottom of the river like a stone.

By the time I reached home tears were running gently down my cheeks. I was saddened by the news of Mr van der Vliet's death, but more so by the fact I hadn't known about the funeral, hadn't had a chance to say goodbye and thank him for everything he had done for me.

Simón was sitting on one of the stools at the breakfast counter reading the paper, his long, thick hair framing his face like a curtain. He was wearing a pair of old ripped jeans and an Iron Maiden T-shirt, revelling as ever in an opportunity to dress informally, out of the confines of his conductor's formal suit and tailcoat which I thought he looked great in – like a cross between a werewolf and a vampire – but which he hated, thinking it as constricting as a straitjacket.

He turned as I entered the room and was on his feet, wrapping me in his arms immediately.

'Fran rang,' he said. 'I'm so sorry, baby.'

I leaned against him and buried my head on his shoulder. He smelled the way he always did, like nutmeg and cinnamon, the fragrances that perfumed the cologne he'd been wearing for as long as I had known him. It was a rich, woody odour, a smell that I had begun to associate with comfort along with the feeling of his tight embrace.

'I didn't think she had our home number,' I said, dully.

'I gave it to her at Christmas.'

Simón was much more family oriented than me. He fought with his siblings like cats and dogs, and his parents too on occasion, but he spoke to them all at least once a week. My family and I had a happy enough relationship but I could easily go six months without hearing from them.

I looked up and kissed him. He had full lips, and most days a smattering of stubble on his jaw. Simón responded to the touch of my lips, kissing me firmly and pulling me gently towards the bedroom, running his hands up under my running shirt as he did so and tugging at the thick clips on my sports bra.

He had learned one of my peculiarities, there was nothing that I wanted more when I was upset – providing it wasn't with him – than sex. I knew this was a strange form of comfort specific to me and perhaps only a small minority of the female population. Sex grounded me in the same way that nothing else did, and it was the one thing on earth, second perhaps only to playing my violin, that made me feel at peace.

Now, he pulled my running trousers down and slid his finger inside me. A familiar bolt of pleasure ran up my spine in response to his touch.

'I should have a shower,' I protested. 'I'm all sweaty.'

'No you shouldn't,' he said firmly, pushing me onto the bed. 'You know I like you like this.'

It was true, and he tried to make a point of it, often. Simón liked me the way that I was, however that was, a fact that he reiterated often by waking me up with his head between my legs or by pouncing on me when I returned from the gym.

He was a passionate man who loved making love and he did everything that he could to please me, but we had different tastes in the bedroom. Each of us preferred not to be in charge.

Simón wasn't a dominant man and I missed that hint of ice, the firmness of Dominik's touch, and other men like him. I wanted to be tied to the bed and have someone have their wicked way with me. Simón had tried, but he had never been able to reconcile himself with the idea that he might genuinely hurt me. Even in jest, he said, he couldn't hit or restrain a woman, and that ruled out spanking, one of the things that I most enjoyed.

He was a good man. I knew that pulling me on top of him was much more his style than the reverse, but that he was doing it this way because he knew I preferred it. The fact that I had spent our entire relationship with a nagging feeling of unfulfilment was a constant source of guilt, like a wound that wouldn't heal, an itch that I couldn't scratch.

I wanted more than anything to be the kind of woman who would be happy with all of the usual things. I had even more than the usual things. Not just a good man but a wonderful man, both of us with good friends, good health and successful careers to boot. But still, a voice whispered in my ear that the life I was living wasn't the life that I wanted, or the life that suited me.

Simón wanted to get married and have children, and I didn't. It was the only thing that we had truly disagreed on and never been able to resolve, and I felt a stabbing sensation of horror each time I saw him glancing into a jewellery store window at the engagement rings, or smiling at a toddler that he bumped into on the street. All of the things that would make him happy and contented for ever were the things that terrified me, and in the dead of night when I wasn't distracted by work or social occasions or running in cold weather, I felt as though someone had attached an iron weight around my neck, or had hung a halo above me that was so heavy I couldn't keep it in the air. I sometimes felt as though I would be crushed under the weight of my own life.

Two weeks passed, and my dreams were filled with crashing water and the sound of Dominik's voice.

I woke up in the mornings with a start, as if I'd been dragged from sleep by a lion.

Despite my fears and worries, time passed, as it always would. I ran every day, rehearsed, attended soirées with other couples, mostly on the musical scene. But I felt purposeless, like a ship without a rudder, as though my life was gradually dissolving into nothing one moment at a time.

Fran continued to call at odd times of the day and night. She was checking up on me I thought, in her own way. We'd always been close but neither of us was overtly emotional and most of our conversations only lasted a few minutes. She was still set on leaving Te Aroha. Had handed her notice in, she said, to her work, and she was applying for her UK visa.

We had UK ancestry so were lucky in that respect. My grandparents on one side were Ukrainian, and on the other, English. We were pioneers, travellers on both sides. It ran strong in our blood, the desire to be on the move to places unknown.

'You're not coming to New York then?' I asked her one night, after she'd told me that she had booked her flights to the UK.

'I think London is in my blood. Anyway, I can't get a US visa.'

'You can live with me, you don't need to go searching for work. Come as a tourist.'

'Don't be ridiculous. You know as well as I do that I wouldn't last a minute if I wasn't earning my own keep, any more than you would.'

'Fine. Come and visit me though?'

'Of course. Come and see me in London?'

'Sure. I'm due a visit.'

The more I thought about it, the more I missed it. Cold weather, the gloom of old buildings, streets leading here, there and everywhere, pathways running like tentacles throughout the city, not the square blocks lining avenues rigidly like they did in New York.

I'd been back once since I'd been dating Simón but only for a flying visit, as we were both working. I kept in touch with Chris, my best friend who I'd met when I first moved to London. His band, Groucho Nights, were just beginning to make it. He and his cousin Ted, the band's guitarist, had come across Viggo Franck, the lead singer of The Holy

Criminals, at a party one night and they'd hit it off. Subsequently, they'd been offered a spot opening for the famous rock band at the Brixton Academy, the sort of gig that bands like Chris's spent their lives dreaming about.

Chris and I had actually met in the front row of a Black Keys gig at the same venue. I'd gone on my own as I didn't know anyone, and we'd bumped into each other as we both leaped to catch the lead singer's guitar pick. Ever the gentleman, he'd let me have it, and I'd bought him a drink after the show to thank him. We'd bonded over the fact that we were both new in London, and we were both string musicians. I played violin and he played viola, though he'd switched to guitar as his main instrument to appeal to the rock crowd. I had played the odd gig with his band, when the vibe was right to include a violinist.

I decided to give him a call. It would be late in London, but Chris was a musician, he'd be up.

His voice was bleary.

'Don't tell me you're asleep. Not very rock star of you.'

'Summer?'

'The very one. What's new?'

I could hear the rustling of blankets as he sat up, presumably still in bed.

'We got the gig.'

'With The Holy Criminals? Amazing. Did you have to sleep with Viggo Franck to get it?'

'Don't be stupid.'

'So what's he like?' I probed.

'Viggo?'

'Of course Viggo. I don't fancy the drummer, that's for sure.'

'Oh you'd like him. All the girls seem to. I don't really get it. But hey, that's the trouble with being the nice guy, isn't it – always the friend, never the boyfriend. It's the bastards who get it all.'

'Simón's a nice guy,' I said, teasingly.

'Yes, he is.' His tone became suddenly serious. 'But are you happy with him?'

I paused, unsure of how to phrase it. How could I possibly admit to anyone that I was considering breaking up with the nicest guy in the world because he was too nice?

'What's up, Summer? You never call just for a chat.'

'I don't know. I've been out of sorts. My violin teacher died. Mr van der Vliet. I don't know if I ever told you about him.'

'Yeah, you did. He was getting on a bit though, wasn't he? He had a good innings. And he was proud of you.'

'I think he might have killed himself.' The words came out in an awkward rush.

'Oh. God. I'm so sorry . . . Are you OK?'

'Not really . . . I . . . I don't know what I am. I just wanted to hear the sound of your voice.'

'Well, I'll be here for you whenever you need me, you know that.'

'Yeah. I know. Good luck with your gig then – is it soon?'

'Next month. We'll miss you though. It's never been quite the same without you there.'

'Oh, rubbish.'

'No, it's true. You added something. Hey, maybe we'd all be already famous if you hadn't left.'

*

When I got home that night, it was late, and Simón was up, waiting for me, sitting at the breakfast bar, his long legs crossed at the ankles. He was hunched over and staring at the bench, though he didn't have a newspaper in front of him. Something was sitting on the counter. A book, but it wasn't open. Dominik's book I realised, with a prickle of horror, as I got closer.

He didn't leap out of his chair to greet me, as he usually did. He looked as though he was cloaked in a heavy veil of exhaustion.

'Hello,' I said, breaking the ice.

He looked up and smiled at me wanly. His eyes were warm but he had the look of a sick horse that sees its owner approaching with a shot gun.

'Hey, baby,' he said. 'Give me a hug.'

He opened his arms wide and I stepped into his embrace. He was crying. I could feel the shuddering of his chest against his shoulder and my neck was damp with his tears.

'What is it?' I asked him gently.

'You're still in love with Dominik.' It was a statement of fact, not a question.

'We haven't seen each other for two years,' I replied.

'But you don't deny that you're in love with him.'

'I . . .'

He gestured to the book on the table.

'It's about you. Another place, another time, but it's still you.'

'You read it?'

'Enough. I'm sorry, I know I shouldn't have been looking in your things, but you haven't been yourself. I was worried.'

'It's OK. I shouldn't have kept the book.'

I'd tried to throw it away, knowing that there was always a possibility Simón would find it. It wasn't that I didn't trust him. But he had this way of clutching after me as though he knew that I didn't belong to him somehow, as if he was always trying to find proof that I didn't really love him. I did love him, but it was more of a deep affection than a romantic love.

He took my chin in his hand and brushed a lock of hair from my face.

'This is never going to work,' he said.

'What do you mean?'

A dull ache began to spread through my chest.

'We want different things, Summer. I love you, but you'll never be happy with me. And I'll spend the rest of my life trying to catch hold of something that I never had.'

'Don't be silly,' I protested, a hint of panic finding its way into my voice. 'It's just a book, it doesn't mean anything. We can talk it through, find a way—'

'I want to have children, a family. And you don't. You know what they say: a bird and a fish might fall in love, but where will they build their nest?'

I sputtered, trying to find a reason to disagree with him, but there was none.

'I spoke to Susan,' he continued.

'You told my agent you're going to break up with me before you told me?'

I could feel my face turning red, anger bubbling up inside in the absence of tears. I balled my hands into fists and pressed them against his chest. He took hold of my wrists and held me against him.

'Of course not. I was just suggesting that you need a break. I can see you're getting bored, frustrated. Even the best musicians need a holiday, a change.'

I couldn't argue with that either. I'd been playing the same tunes over and over for years now, even wearing the same dresses to my concerts. It was becoming old. I was getting tired, jaded. Even the album we'd just recorded of South American tunes hadn't had my heart in it. That was his homeland, not mine, and though I could imagine the country that Simón told me so much about in the melodies that I played, I didn't have the passion for it that I had for the New Zealand composers, or even the rock songs that I used to play with Chris when I jammed with his band in bars and pubs in Camden. I suppose that's the problem when you begin making money from something that you love. Music had become my career, and gradually, my job, and I was beginning to tire of it.

'You want me to move out?'

'No, I want to keep you by my side for ever. But that's not going to work for either of us,' he said prosaically. 'I'm taking a break myself. Going back to Venezuela for a fortnight to see my family. My flight leaves in the morning. I'll let you decide what you want to do.'

We made love again that night, and then again, in the middle of the night after he woke me up with a savage kiss at three in the morning and fucked me with a ferocity he had never shown before. We spent the few hours before his flight tangled in each other's arms, talking and laughing like old friends.

'If only it could always be like this,' I said, as he

untangled himself from my limbs to begin getting ready for his departure.

'I don't think we've ever been right for each other,' he said. 'I just didn't want to admit it. We like things the same way . . .'

I watched him dress, pulling his ripped jeans straight on without bothering with underwear. His thick brown hair covered his face as he fastened his belt and adjusted the silver skull that adorned the buckle. His muscles flexed as he pulled a tight white T-shirt on over his chest, hiding his thick swatch of chest hair from view. He added a silver feather pendant on a chain, one that I had bought him for Christmas the previous year, and fastened it around his neck. He loved clothes, and consequently was the easiest man to buy gifts for that I had ever known.

I wrapped my thighs around his waist as he sat down on the edge of the bed to pull on his snakeskin ankle boots with the red soles.

'You can't hold on for ever, you know,' he said, 'I'll never get my shoes on.'

He gave me another long kiss outside the taxi he'd ordered to take him to the airport, embracing me until the driver began to look impatient.

'Don't be a stranger. Keep in touch.'

'I will,' I said.

Then watched as the car pulled away and took Simón out of my life.

I trudged back into the apartment and sat back down at the breakfast counter. Dominik's book was still resting in the middle of the bench. I picked it up and flicked through it again, skimmed through lines about the red-haired heroine who had evidently experienced no shortage of lovers in Paris. Dominik and I hadn't managed to stay living together. Domestically, we were wildly unsuited. But sexually we were a perfect match. And whilst that seemed a ridiculous and terrible thing to build a relationship on, maybe that's just who I was. You can try to escape your nature, but it catches up with you in the end.

'To S.

'Yours, always.'

I wondered if he still thought about me. If he'd just been too unimaginative to pull a story from the ether and been forced to rely on a thinly fictionalised biography in order to get the feminine voice right, or if he just couldn't get me out of his head, as I couldn't banish him from mine.

Oh, Dominik, how is it that you managed to still have a hold on my life, two years and a million miles away?

I rested my head in my arms and began to cry, tears falling onto the pages and rapidly soaking in until they began to shrivel.

Thirty minutes later I picked up my phone and dialled.

Somewhere in Camden Town, a phone rang.

Chris answered.

'Jeezus, Summer, we don't speak for ages and then you call twice in a week?'

'I'm coming to London. I'll be on the next flight.'

'Great,' he said, audibly perking up. 'You'll be just in time for our gig. Maybe I can even talk you on stage again.'

'Just like the good old days?'

'Better,' he replied. 'Much better.'

2

The Simple Art of Procrastination

'So what are your plans for today?' Lauralynn asked.

'Procrastination, of course,' Dominik answered.

'No surprise there then . . .'

She was sipping from a tall glass of milk, standing up, gathering her stuff, ready to depart the house for a day's rehearsal. Yesterday, she'd left her cello at the rehearsal studio as she often did. It was a bitch to carry across London by public transport, and the building in which she and her fellow musicians in the string quartet practised had 24-hour security.

Her black leather boots reached all the way up to her knees, the rest of her long legs sheathed by skin-tight jeans disappearing at waist level in the comfortable folds of a shapeless grey sweatshirt. She looked anything but a classical musician and even less of a chamber music expert.

Dominik couldn't help finding Lauralynn sexy for all seasons. Some women had it, others didn't and she had 'it' in spades. One who turned heads at the flick of a smile. The fact she preferred women when given the choice just made her more exciting.

Lauralynn's tousled blond hair was pinned up to fit into her motorcycle helmet. One of the first things she had done after Dominik had agreed she could stay at his house and she had formed her quartet from the sole remnant of her previous music college formation and a couple of new-comers, had been to treat herself to a new ride. A sleek and shiny second-hand black Suzuki GSXR 750. She'd had to sell the Kawasaki she owned back in Yale before returning to the UK, presumably unable to ship it back. Dominik didn't know where she got the cash, but Lauralynn never seemed short of money and had a particularly cavalier attitude towards it. He didn't expect she made that much from the quartet's irregular performances and the assorted session work she got involved in.

She blew him a kiss and ran out of the door. The roar of her motorcycle's powerful engine followed quickly and then faded as the bike raced down the hill.

Dominik looked down at his plate. His final slice of toast sat there, forlorn.

He reflected on all the months spent with Lauralynn under his roof. They'd first met when Dominik was arrang-ing a very private performance in an underground crypt – a performance where Summer played her violin entirely naked, accompanied by a blindfolded Lauralynn and the string quartet she was a part of. Lauralynn had then turned up in Manhattan when Summer had been away and had given him a glimpse of other sexual possibilities. She had subsequently come to him following his return to London where they had become sexual partners in crime, and she had helped him banish the ghost of Summer.

He was alone in the vast house again, left to his own devices.

It was just him and the blank document on the computer screen. He knew, with a wave of self-loathing, that as the day progressed he would studiously align a thousand words or so there but would in all probability end up deleting most of them by evening.

Dominik missed his lecturing and teaching. He now thought it could have been a bad mistake to renounce his tenure on the back of the unexpected success of the Paris novel in which the tragic heroine had been so clearly inspired by Summer.

He had signed a contract for a follow-up book, but he was already several months late and well behind on the schedule he had pinned on his study wall.

On one hand there was the inevitable pressure of coming up with something that might match the inspired romanticism of Summer's book, as he now thought of it, but there was also the sad fact he had no proper ideas, and whatever came to mind he quickly dismissed as superficial or uninteresting. He needed a hook. A story. Characters. Surely he couldn't recycle the emotions that Summer evoked over and over again. If only because it hurt so much.

Following the break with Summer and his rushed return from New York, he'd completed the first novel in a rush of white heat, pounding away at the keyboard with music blaring around the room: a studied blend of the classical repertoire he had often heard her perform and the French *chansons* and American jazz of the early 1950s that formed the background to his unfolding story. Now, he even had the luxury of playing some of the former music in recordings that Summer had released in the intervening months as her own career had taken off, but it was of no help. It even had the contrary effect – most days putting him in a blue funk hearing the soaring crystal-clear sounds of the Bailly in full flight which unavoidably evoked the shades of her skin, the dark colour of her nipples and, deep down in the well of his memory, the taste of her sex. Once it had inspired him, now all it could achieve was to deepen his depression, his sorrow.

He had acquired the CDs she had released, the first of which was a scintillating recording of Vivaldi's *Four Seasons*, in which he could sense all her passion, her wild, wanton moods, but also her delicate sensitivity. He had read in a gossip column she was now shacked up with Simón Lobo, which had come as no surprise as he was the orchestra conductor on all of her recordings, and she had already been working with him in New York during the few short months Dominik and Summer had lived together in the Manhattan loft. The other CDs covered, respectively, the Tchaikovsky and Mendelssohn violin concertos, while the final one, which he had only come across in a store window the previous month, was devoted to improvisations on South American native themes, again a far from unexpected connection.

The CD box for the latter album was sitting open on the far left of his desk, next to a pile of research-related books and folders full of magazine cuttings and assorted notes, most of which he could no longer even decipher as his handwriting was all over the place and hurried. A photograph of Summer was spread across its cover, her face in soft focus and a hint of bare shoulders, the red flames of her hair like a deafening explosion of colour against a snow-white background and the thin black strap of a dress which he couldn't avoid recognising. The one he had bought her at the street fair on Waverly Place.

A wry thought passed his mind that in some stores where both books and records were available, some unknown buyer might accidentally purchase both his words and Summer's music as part of the same transaction, unaware of the ties that had once held them together.

Dominik sighed heavily, as if for an audience, and knew his mood was unlikely to improve if he played music right now.

Silence it would have to be.

The cursor on his screen blinked in and out of existence, taunting him.

After New York, Lauralynn had made it her job to put Dominik back on the straight and narrow. Without her encouragement, he would probably not have stuck to the task and completed his Paris novel, and would have effortlessly drifted back into his quiet routine of teaching and no-strings-attached seductions when the possibility arose.

She knew he was attracted to her and lost no opportunity to keep him on the boil sexually with her nonchalant attitude to nudity and sex. It was as if his arousal and interest was a form of fuel necessary for him to keep churning out the words and reach the end of his manuscript, without feeling sorry for himself and relying too much on memories of his times with Summer, even though the lead female character in his semi-historical book was undeniably based on the red-haired violin player.

'You need distractions, my dear Dominik,' she had said to him one evening, that playful glint in her green eyes a prelude to mischief.

'Do I now?' He knew her intentions were good, but part

of him still felt as if he was in mourning and it was much too early to go out playing again.

But Lauralynn would not take no for an answer and convinced him to dress up for the occasion, even jokingly rejecting his choice of patterned casual shirt as distinctly too middle-aged, getting him to wear a blue Tommy Hilfiger dress shirt with a button-down collar; something he was often reluctant to do unless the occasion was particularly formal, which he was quite certain this evening was not about to be by a long stretch.

'You won't regret it,' Lauralynn had said.

'I'd better not.'

Lauralynn was a woman with plans, and her tastes were deviant to say the least. He'd once joked she had a little black book full of names and addresses she could call on at a moment's notice to entertain her, just some like suburban Don Juan. But Lauralynn, with a broad, impish smile, had gleefully responded that this was not the case. She stored all the names and numbers in her mind, she declared.

'All carefully divided into columns,' Dominik suggested. 'Subs, slaves, swingers, cross-dressers, simple bottoms, switches, and whatever other categories an ignorant soul like me might not even be aware of. No doubt all pretty and sitting in a row, waiting to be picked off and played with?'

'Of course,' she had triumphantly confirmed. 'A girl must have a sense of organisation in these troubled times . . .'

'So what's on tonight's menu?' Dominik had asked her, as they waited for the minicab he had ordered earlier. It was still only late in the afternoon and parking restrictions in town would have made it awkward to drive his BMW into the West End.

'Just wait and see.' Her perfume swam across his face, a delicate blend of green notes and citrus. Lauralynn had an arsenal of fragrances at her disposal, each a distinctive weapon for different species of prey. When she openly hunted for other women, she went for sweet and musky, dark with aggression. Today's early evening, more nuanced, touch presaged a different sort of hunt, he guessed.

The meeting was in the basement bar of a pub on Cambridge Circus in the centre of town. Dominik had never been a pub person. The fact he didn't drink, purely for reasons of taste, didn't help, but there was something about pubs, the smells, the unclean, torpid air, that always made him uncomfortable.

'Couldn't you have arranged another place?' he'd asked Lauralynn as they descended the wooden stairs.

'It's where they felt safer to meet,' she said.

'They?' he enquired with an arch smile.

Her grin broadened.

'Just a nice, married couple, probably from the suburbs, so I thought suggesting your club or a posh hotel bar might put them off.'

'A married couple?'

'Nice, no?'

The basement was only half full and they quickly spotted the man and woman sitting nervously in one corner and, respectively, nursing a beer and an orange juice.

'Where did you come across them?' Dominik whispered.

'Online, of course. All the best people trawl for sex online, these days.'

Dominik had, but then that felt like another life now.

The man, likely in his mid-forties, wore a grey suit and

had probably come here straight from his office, while his younger wife, a pale-looking brunette with a fringe, wore her Saturday-night regulation little black dress with just an inch too many of cleavage on display. She looked up, acknowledging Dominik's presence, a faint smile of satisfaction on her lips, her eyes lighting up, as if reassured he was actually good-looking, having been prepared for rougher fare.

'I like your shirt,' she said.

'So lovely to see you both,' Lauralynn exclaimed as she extended her hand to greet their presence. Only the man reciprocated. Dominik followed suit. The man's grip was weak and damp and the woman just sat there, blushing slightly. The man's eyes were fixed on Lauralynn who was wearing a white T-shirt through which her hard nipples pressed, standing at attention. Instead of jeans, she had for the occasion changed into a figure-hugging pencil skirt. There was a sense of relief on the man's face, as if he had been worried that his internet interlocutor might actually have been a guy masquerading as a woman and he now breathed easier seeing that Lauralynn was truly female, and, Dominik guessed, identical to the photo she would have sent him. A nude one, he expected, aware of her developed sense of mischief.

Dominik assumed that his participation had been prefaced by just a summary description as he didn't believe Lauralynn stored any images of him, whether dressed or undressed, on her laptop. She had evidently advertised herself as principal bait, and he merely came as extra.

'Likewise,' the guy said.

They sat on the wooden bench, facing the couple across the pub table.

'So you're Kevin,' Lauralynn said, 'and you must be Liz?'

The young woman nodded. Surely not their real names?

Dominik just smiled at the two of them, hoping his appearance was in accordance with the unique selling points Lauralynn had no doubt promised the couple during their online contacts.

'And you are?' Kevin asked. 'You never told me your name in your mails.'

'Ah, are names really that important?' Lauralynn pointed out, dismissively. 'Just call us Him and Her, no?'

'Why not,' Kevin said. 'Can I get you drinks?'

Dominik remained silent. He still didn't know what Lauralynn had arranged with the couple. Were Kevin and Liz novice swingers? He thought so.

Kevin walked over to the bar to fetch the glasses.

'So what do you do, Liz?' enquired Lauralynn.

'I'm a secretary.'

'How interesting.' Lauralynn flashed her a flirtatious smile. 'So, this is your first time.'

The young woman nodded, her eyes turning to Dominik.

'His idea or yours?' Lauralynn continued.

'Hmm . . . both of us,' she replied, fidgeting in her seat.

'Come on, really?'

Liz nodded, but Dominik remained unconvinced.

The drinks arrived, followed by a moment of uncomfortable silence.

Lauralynn later told Dominik that this sort of situation was far from uncommon. Many men harboured the fantasy of seeing their wives or girlfriends fucked by another man, either out of deep-seated voyeuristic compulsion or the desire to be humiliated. This was what Kevin had been seeking on the online forum where he and Lauralynn had met. Maybe the fact that Lauralynn, another woman, would be involved and present, acted as reassurance, or perhaps it added an extra degree of humiliation to the scene.

Dominik was more uncertain as to what was in it for Liz.

The couple had agreed to get a room at a small hotel in nearby Bloomsbury which they finally repaired to after several further rounds of drinks, Liz having quickly graduated to alcohol. Lauralynn had evidently laid down the rules for the evening to Kevin before agreeing to the meeting, and he had presumably discussed all the details with Liz.

The set of handcuffs he had stored in the bedside drawer and which he handed over on arrival to Lauralynn were fur-lined. Pink fur. Lauralynn burst out laughing.

'Where the hell did you get those? An Essex sex shop?'

His face reddened. He hadn't expected the humiliation to also be verbal.

Liz, who had sat herself on a corner of the bed as soon as they had entered the narrow hotel room, kept on throwing enquiring glances at Dominik while studiously avoiding looking at her now somewhat fearful husband. She was slightly flushed after one gin and tonic too many, hurriedly gulped down at the pub to shore up her resolve before the action moved to the hotel room.

Lauralynn threw off her leather jacket and turned to Kevin who was still fixed to the spot.

'So, what are you waiting for?'

He looked uncertain, unsure of her meaning.

'Take your clothes off. Now!' she demanded.

His body was pale and thin. Lauralynn insisted he keep his black mid-ankle-length socks on. Thought it made him look more ridiculous. She ordered him to sit down and fixed the handcuffs to his wrists. She secured him to the room's lone chair and arranged it so that he faced the bed.

Liz sat, increasingly restless and nervous. Her knees held tight together, a bead of sweat forming on her forehead as she realised they had reached a point of no return.

'All yours, D,' Lauralynn said.

Dominik looked down at Liz.

'Come here,' he said quietly to the young woman. She rose. She was a whole head shorter than him.

He cupped her chin and brought his lips to hers. He could still taste the gin on her breath. And smell the shampoo she must have washed her hair with earlier that afternoon. A faint tremor raced through her body as they made contact. She stiffened briefly and then softened as the contact of his mouth relaxed her.

Out of the corner of his eye he could see a broad smile spreading across Lauralynn's face as she stood behind the chair on which she had immobilised Kevin and distractedly passed her long fingers through his hair, messing it about. This visibly made him even more uncomfortable as his side parting disappeared and he was reduced to being Lauralynn's wide-eyed plaything.

Feeling Liz's mental resistance melt as their tongues mingled, Dominik slid his hands slowly down her back to her buttocks, assessing the firmness of her skin and her response to his touch. Their mouths briefly parted and she sighed deeply. And closed her eyes.

Dominik's left hand searched for the side zip that would loosen her black dress.

'Allow me,' Lauralynn said, moving around them, leaving the captive husband, his now untidy hair crowning his dismay, a helpless onlooker shackled to the chair.

The zip was actually at the back of the dress, and Lauralynn positioned herself behind Liz and pulled the dress open, while biting playfully on Liz's ear, her mouth just inches from Dominik's.

The young married woman shuddered, sandwiched between them as she was.

Her husband's eyes were fixed on the trio, a curious expression of fascination on his face. How much had Lauralynn prepared him for this?

'Arms?' Lauralynn suggested and Liz raised her arms upwards and Lauralynn pulled the dress up, the cheap material brushing between the young woman's face and Dominik's.

Dominik stepped back. The young, pale-faced woman stood, face flushed, in her underwear and hold-up stockings.

'Let's see all of you,' Lauralynn ordered and Liz unclasped her bra and bent over unsteadily in her high heels to pull down her matching knickers. She kept the stockings on and Lauralynn did not insist she take them off.

Dominik looked down at her. Heavy thighs but a slim upper half with puffy-nippled breasts, a razor-shaped landing strip of thin hair prefacing her slit, a piercing in her navel, a silver crucifix circling her neck. Grey eyes bursting with questions.

An invisible weight came off Dominik's shoulders as Liz was revealed. The bodies of women had that effect on him, giving rise to a tsunami of tenderness. From an early age, he had been affected by the spectacle of women, from the moment he had swapped a couple of model cars at school for a pack of playing cards displaying voluptuous beach naturists at play and repose whose genitals had been carefully airbrushed, which made them appear more like Greek statues than flesh and blood. He had of course felt arousal, but the dominant impression had always been awe and wonder first. And remained to this day.

He would, he knew in his heart and loins, ever be a slave to the nakedness of women.

He was shaken out of his reverie by Lauralynn roughly taking hold of Liz's hair and pulling her down to the bed. She slipped her hand between the young women's thighs.

'She's rather wet, Kevin, I must say,' she said, glancing over at her immobilised husband sitting useless on the chair just a few steps away. 'So is this what you wanted, eh?'

Kevin remained silent.

She looked down at his flaccid cock.

'Your wife is going to be fucked by another man, and you can't even get hard! Pitiful . . .'

Dominik, witnessing her game, felt awkward. Was he now expected to undress and perform, knowing he was being watched rather attentively by the young woman's husband, let alone no doubt scrutinised by Lauralynn?

He remembered the time with Summer, when he had foolishly invited Victor to the house. The man whom he had mistakenly exhibited Summer to on a dreadful occasion and who had then betrayed his trust and seduced her after Summer and Dominik's parting, and exploited what Dominik still felt had been her grief. But somehow it had felt different, as he had blanked the other man out, so ferocious had his desire for Summer been on that fateful day.

Lauralynn stood and approached him, affectionately brushing a hand against his cheek. 'My gift to you, D,' she said. 'Do us all proud, will you?'

Dominik began unbuttoning his shirt, knowing all eyes were on him. 'It was all his idea, wasn't it?' he asked Liz. She nodded and he pulled her round so that she could no longer see her husband or follow his reactions.

She seemed lost and Dominik was assailed by a strong wave of desire for her.

He took her in his arms and kissed her again. This time, slowly, lazily, greedily. Making the whole ceremony of lust something essentially private, banishing the presence of others from the cocoon in which they now performed.

He completed undressing. Out of the corner of his eye, as he moved Liz further onto the bed in the best position to receive him, he caught a glance of Lauralynn's smile. A wordless form of encouragement from the mistress of ceremonies.

He parted Liz's legs wide, unveiling her, teasingly tested her wetness with his tip, before inserting himself, inch by maddening inch, an eternity at a time, in an attempt at making this vital moment last for ever, until he was fully inside her. Hot. Snug. He could perceive her moan already, the sound rising from the bottom of her lungs with every thrust of his within her, moving upwards to the pit of her throat. Heard someone's intake of breath behind him, Lauralynn or Kevin, it no longer mattered.

Dominik's strong hands took hold of the young married

woman's waist and gripped her tightly until their rhythms had come together in parallel unison.

There was a strange, passive behaviour to Liz, which failed to arouse Dominik. It was almost the opposite of submission and gave him no sense of dominance. There was an inert softness about her, a lack of passion and a quietness in her response. Lauralynn approached them, aware of the lack of sparks, and brushed a hand against Liz's warm cheek.

'Enjoy it. Let yourself go,' she whispered in her ear.

The young woman's body relaxed briefly and then she bucked, either provoked by Lauralynn's encouragement or by the combined effect of the endearment and Dominik's continued, energetic thrusts. She let out a sigh, and Dominik felt a stiffening within her softness, as she finally allowed her arousal to take control of her body and her mind.

Now oblivious to the situation, the surroundings and her nearby helpless husband, Liz threw herself back against Dominik's cock, inviting him into her, greedily embedding herself on him with studied rage as if she'd been denied pleasure with Kevin for ages immemorial and was now intent on seizing the day and pleasing herself.

Both Lauralynn and Dominik, witnessing the change now taking hold of her, smiled.

The room grew warmer.

Immobilised on his chair, Kevin watched in silence as his wife warmed to Dominik's thrusts, her movements becoming increasingly frantic as she impaled herself on him time and time again, her breath running short and her face contorting as waves of pleasure raced through her, increasing the flow of her wetness.

Her growing enthusiasm aroused Dominik and he took hold of her waist and orchestrated the rhythm of her reverse thrusts against him, feeling his cock grow even harder inside her, invading her, filling her.

There was a small cry, starting at the back of her throat, dying on the threshold of her lips, and she came with a spasm. Kevin went pale. Dominik wondered if this was this the first time he had witnessed his wife's pleasure.

After he'd come, ridding himself of the necessary condom in the room's regulation wicker bin, Dominik noticed how downcast Kevin was over by the wall, still shackled to the chair, uncertain as to whether this was the spectacle he had dreamed of (or feared)? And wondered how the couple would live with this memory.

Now subdued, Lauralynn unlocked the toy-like pink handcuffs and handed Kevin his clothing, while Liz rose tentatively from the bed, almost dazed, not so much as a result of Dominik's lovemaking, he knew, but at the realisation of what she had just done.

The couple were still slowly dressing in silence as Lauralynn and Dominik exited the room and found themselves in the gloomy darkness of the small hotel's main corridor, with its faded walls and indeterminate-colour carpeting.

Outside, the trees by the British Museum fluttered in a gentle breeze and Dominik began looking for a cab light.

'Ah, Lauralynn,' he said, as she zipped up her leather jacket against the cooler evening air, 'one day your sense of mischief will get us into trouble.'

'I know,' she said. 'But wasn't that little wife cute?'

'If you thought so, maybe you should have played with her instead,' he replied.

'It had occurred to me, but when I was negotiating the scene with her hubby, he was very insistent there should be no female interaction.'

'Really?'

'Indeed. Didn't you notice, when I passed my hand between her legs, how he almost jumped out of the chair? Some people are so prejudiced . . .'

'You are truly wicked, Lauralynn,' Dominik remarked as a cab pulled up.

'Better wicked than boring, I say.' She laughed.

Lauralynn's little interludes were all well and good but they made no difference when Dominik found himself back again facing the computer screen, attempting to summon the right words and ideas without being overwhelmed with thoughts of Summer. His memory was like a hard disk that was now so full of feelings and images, bursting at the seams, and was now incapable of processing further elements, redistributing them in equanimous fashion.

All the women he had known, Summer and the others who had come before her, were present, jostling for attention, for a sliver of kindness, and there was no way he could erase any of them. They were now part of him, what made him what he had become.

As soon as he wrote about one, in the hope that a stream-of-consciousness improvisation on her features, the colour of her eyes or the way she spoke or moved, might turn into the seed of a story, she morphed into another and then yet another and he lost whatever semblance of plot he was hanging on to.

He switched the computer to sleep mode, consigning his

half-written page to the multicoloured galactic explosion of his screensaver, and rose before stepping away from the desk.

Glancing at the window, he saw today's weather was grey but clear, with no signs of imminent rain, and opted for a walk outside to clear his mind.

The Heath was an obvious destination.

It was already mid-morning and joggers were by now thin on the ground, heavily outnumbered by childcarers with prams and buggies, trailing noisy charges, and pensioners ambling idly by the ponds, watching the ducks, feeding them in spite of the warnings not to do so. Past the second pond which expanded into a bathing area, Dominik took the first path and wandered in a daydream towards the narrow bridge connecting this part with wilder areas of the Heath.

This was what he loved so much about London; the infinity of places where within a few minutes' walk from a main road in almost all areas you could find yourself deep in a landscape of trees, sky shielded from view, a comforting jungle of greenery and nature. There was something almost clandestine about it that appealed deeply to him, a sense of privacy and isolation at the heart of the urban jungle. A place for secrets.

Dominik took a different direction, instinctively opting for the comfort of a winding, barely delineated dirt avenue where a thick canopy of trees blanked out the sky. A jogger came running towards him and he shifted aside to give her right of way on the narrow path. She briefly nodded in acknowledgment. It was a young woman in black leggings, wearing an incongruous pair of emerald-coloured satin shorts and a heavy dark-green sweatshirt. Her dirty-blond hair was held tight together by an elastic band and her ponytail bobbed up and down in her wake, accompanying in delightful synchronicity the rhythmic movement of her breasts despite the obvious constriction of her crop top. As she passed him, Dominik heard a thin melody straining through her headphones before fading as she continued her run away from him.

For some inexplicable reason, he wanted to know what she had been listening to. It felt important.

He stopped and sat for a moment on a felled tree trunk, allowing the fleeting memory of the young woman's breasts and the indolent rhythm of their movement to linger a while.

Had she been a nurse from the nearby Royal Free Hospital, a student maybe, a housewife, a banker, a shop or an office girl? The possibilities were endless, as a thousand fantasies raced across his imagination. 'Stop', 'Undress', 'Reveal yourself to me' . . . Not just having her undress, but getting her somehow to unveil what was beneath her skin, what went on in her mind . . . As he had once attempted with Summer. All so irrational. He quickly banished the thoughts from his mind.

He shrugged, rose and moved on. But the thoughts of Summer lingered. Her wariness the first time they'd met. His proposal, the private concert she had played here, just for him. The fire and passion that consumed her when she held her violin, saturating the Heath with her music.

The bandstand. He wanted to find the bandstand again. The place where Summer had played, a deeply ingrained image he just couldn't keep out of his mind. The landscape, the colours of the grass and the sky above, and the look of her face as she lost herself in the music.

Summer playing on the bandstand: his lost masterpiece.

Dominik made his way through the wood, saw a faint dash of unnatural colour in the distance. Movements. Figures beyond the thinning wall of trees. Stepping gingerly forward, taking care not to get his clothes caught in the outlying bushes, he emerged into a clearing. Children running around, bikes racing across a set of paths, the bandstand in the distance.

As he walked up the small hill that led to the concrete and iron edifice, he caught the initial drops of rain as the skies opened with a vengeance. Under the bandstand's roof, a rag-tag bunch of nannies, harassed mothers and unruly toddlers were gathered, indifferently watching the storm.

One of the mothers stood in one corner, her blouse unbuttoned, offering her breast to a baby. The small one's head was almost totally hairless and its scalp a delicate pink, its face all crunched up in a parody of either concentration or just sleep. Dominik watched them with deep fascination, couldn't keep his eyes away until the mother noticed him staring and gave him the dirtiest look she could summon. He was obliged to walk away, down the steps and into the clearing rain, angry at himself and annoyed by the fact he was now obliged to share the magic of the place with all these strangers.

Lauralynn had brought someone back with her the previous night.

Even though the bedroom she was using was on a different floor of the house, Dominik was kept awake most of the night by the noises the two women couldn't help themselves making: cushioned moans, sharp shrieks, muffled growls of pleasure or pain, indistinct words half whispered or cried out at peak moments, a whole curious symphony of unrolling lust.

He briefly caught sight of Lauralynn's guest as he came down to breakfast late the following day and the girl was on her way out. A goth-like waif, all dyed jet-black hair amateurishly cut in a short bob by a blunt pair of scissors, a fearsome silver skull necklace like a collar separating her head from the rest of her body, and a blur of faded tattoos snaking all the way down her right leg. He was glad Lauralynn had not invited him to join them.

Lauralynn, having escorted her friend to the door wearing nothing but a pair of French knickers and an unbuttoned man's shirt, returned to the kitchen and handed Dominik a mug of freshly brewed coffee.

'A new one?' he asked, taking the coffee.

'Yes. Picked her up at a gig,' Lauralynn said.

'She didn't look the classical type,' Dominik remarked.

'Nah. Rock 'n' roll, man. She was hanging with some guys I did some session overdubs for. Neo punks, whatever they call themselves. They invited me to see them play in Camden Town. She was there and, you know,' Lauralynn said with a lascivious smile on her full lips, 'one thing led to another.'

'The diversity of your tastes will always amaze me,' he pointed out.

'I'll try anything once,' Lauralynn said. 'But I knew she wasn't your type, so I didn't try and wake you.'

'You have all my gratitude for that—'

He almost spat out his coffee. She'd forgotten to put sugar in it.

'Careful there . . .'

'So what are you doing today?' he asked her.

'I have to be at the recording studio in Willesden from midday. I'm booked up for the rest of the week. The guys in the band don't seem to know what sort of sound they're after. The only reason they need a cello is that the bass player wants an "Eleanor Rigby" mood, or whatever, on the track.'

Dominik nodded, taking in her torrent of words.

'Easy money,' Lauralynn continued. 'I'm not complaining. I spend much of the time there reading magazines and I'm being paid for it at union rates. And you? Making much progress with the new book?'

Dominik hadn't listened to the Beatles' song in ages, and was unsure for a moment whether it did feature a cello. Or had it been a string section?

'Not much,' he admitted, his mind suddenly elsewhere, inwardly humming the tune to 'Eleanor Rigby'.

Lauralynn took the empty coffee mugs to the sink and ran the water over them before placing them in the dishwasher.

'If you're so uncertain about what you're writing, maybe you should let me have a look. I could help?' she said.

'Hmm . . .' Dominik feigned interest.

'I liked the Paris novel,' she added. 'A lot. Not saying it just because we're mates, you know.'

There was nothing he could decently show her yet. Unfinished scenes, thinly sketched lists of random characters, descriptions of places and things, sex scenes verging on the crude between faceless protagonists even he the author could not engage with. A fine mess, he was aware. As if the road map for the book had gone missing, the train it was travelling on still miles from the station.

'Hey?'

Lauralynn was watching him as he just stood there, his mind elsewhere.

'Snap out of it.'

'I'm sorry. You caught me daydreaming.'

'About the book?'

'I suppose so. Yes.'

'You could tell me about it, the story you're hoping to tell. Might help sharpen your focus.'

Dominik repressed a wave of irritation. She was a musician. She knew how to interpret, not to create. What did she know? Then he realised how unfair he was being to her. She was only trying to help.

'I don't have a story. A skeleton on which to hang the characters, the places,' he confessed. 'It just won't come. Whatever I conjure up is commonplace, done a hundred times before and no doubt better. I'm struggling. For a story,' he said.

'The story?' she repeated, her eyes widening as if she was only now realising the enormity of his failure.

'Yes,' he sighed.

He was saved by the ring of the front doorbell. From the kitchen window, he could see a red post office van – it was a postman with a parcel delivery. Probably more books he had ordered as part of his incoherent research.

'I'll get it.'

He rushed down the stairs and signed for the delivery,

not even bothering to look up at the driver's face as he handed the lightweight parcel over. A guide book to Berlin night life and a novel set there in the 1960s, which he'd impulsively acquired with the click of a button just a week ago when he had toyed with the idea of setting the new novel in the German capital. Which, by the following day, he had realised was a stupid idea, as not only had he never been to Berlin but didn't even speak German.

He set the brown cardboard box down on the floor next to the muddy trainers he had kicked off and abandoned there on his return from the Heath the previous day.

Lauralynn's tall and heavy cello case stood in the corner of the hall, festooned with labels, travel mementoes from hotels foreign and local, backstage passes and memorabilia she had assiduously stuck across its surface.

One of the labels was peeling off, he noticed, advertising the charms of the Royal e Golf Grand Hotel in Courmayeur. Where was that? Switzerland or Italy, he thought. When had Lauralynn ever been there? It was a ski resort and unlikely to have much of a music scene. Maybe he would ask her.

His curiosity awakened, he kept on staring at the gallery of labels adorning the cello case.

Ideas come out of nowhere. They make no sense. Drop unannounced in your lap. Ignore logic or sanity.

It was as if something had clicked.

The instrument. Its travels. The tale behind all those stickers, hotel labels, decals and the torn remnants of airline baggage tags.

There was his story.

The one that had been eluding him. As if he'd been blind all the time and ignored the obvious.

It didn't have to be about characters.

In the Paris book, he'd been writing about an alternate, imaginary version of Summer. Of a past world in which she was not a musician, had no violin.

This time, he could write about her instrument. The one he had bought for her.

The violin.

The story of a violin.

3

It's Only Rock 'n' Roll

'I always knew you were a dark horse,' Fran said in a smug tone.

She was leaning back on the car seat with her head nearly resting on Chris's shoulder.

We were speeding through London in the back of a black cab on our way back to the flat in Camden Town. I had moved in with Chris temporarily, just until I managed to find a place of my own. Fran was sharing my room until she found her feet, so things were cramped in comparison to the relatively vast apartment that I had shared with Simón in New York, but so far we hadn't had any major rows.

It was early on Sunday morning and the three of us had been to celebrate our single status at the Torture Garden Valentine's Ball, which had surprisingly been Fran's idea.

She'd been helping me unpack and had found a photograph that I had forgotten I even had, of me and my old friend Charlotte at the first fetish club I'd ever been to.

Dominik had been my first dominant lover, but it had been Charlotte who had initially introduced me to the fetish scene, and with her by my side I had experienced my first spanking, and witnessed other fetishists at play. We'd lost touch after a party had turned out badly. She'd hit on

Dominik and I hadn't been able to control my jealousy, and though I bore her no hard feelings now, I hadn't been in contact with her since.

The picture, which brought back fond memories, had been taken by one of the club's roving photographers, and Charlotte, in one of her kinder moments, had had a copy printed and given it to me. In the shot, she was wearing a bright yellow latex dress with pink lightning bolts running down each side of her waist. It was more of a tunic than a dress, and cut so low at the front that it exposed half of her nipples.

I was more modestly dressed, in a pale-blue satin corset, frilly knickers and a top hat. We were standing out on the deck of the boat that had hosted the party, both laughing at a private joke, my top hat at a jaunty angle giving me a mischievous expression.

'That looks a fun party,' Fran said, picking up the picture.

'Oh, it was nothing,' I replied, keeping my voice even and hoping that she would drop it and move on.

But Fran was both perceptive and persistent, and she kept asking questions.

Under her insistent pressure, I told her about the club, leaving out the details of how I had received my first ever spanking under the watchful eyes of Charlotte and the club's dungeon master.

'I'm going,' she announced. She picked up her iPad and tapped some keys, bringing up their website. 'Ooh,' she said, 'they have a Valentine's thing on tomorrow night. Looks more like an anti-Valentine's thing. Perfect. I fucking hate Valentine's Day.'

'Honestly, I don't think it's your kind of party.'

'How would you know what my kind of party is?' she bristled. 'We've barely seen each other for five years.' She pursed her lips together and ran her hand through her cropped blond hair in a gesture that brokered no argument.

Chris was standing in the doorway, surveying the proceedings. 'If you're going, I'm coming with you.'

'Surely you have to rehearse?' I said. His big opening night show with The Holy Criminals was the following Saturday night.

'We've got plenty of sessions planned. I'm not letting you out of the house dressed in your underwear without a bodyguard.'

'Fine, then,' I said reluctantly. Knowing Fran as I did, she'd go without me if I refused. At least this way I'd be able to keep an eye on them.

Fran had disappeared the next day to find outfits for her and Chris at the Portobello Road Market. She'd returned with her eyes shining and her arms full of bags of clothes, and proceeded to dress a very reluctant Chris in a vintage three-piece groom's suit which she then covered with stage make-up to mimic the effect of someone who had been killed on his wedding day and stepped out of his grave a hundred years later. She went matching, in a ripped-up wedding dress, with her hair gelled into a quiff which gave a strange punk vibe to her vintage zombie look.

'I hate pin-up girls,' she sniffed, when I suggested doing her hair in victory rolls instead.

I was wearing latex for the first time; a skimpy sailor suit outfit that I'd hurriedly bought from a chain store online that offered express delivery and arrived in the nick of time.

I'd been too embarrassed to ask for help to get into it, so had lubed myself up in order to button up the tight vest jacket and matching blue and white striped hot pants, and was now feeling sticky, uncomfortable and paranoid that I would catch on something and tear the delicate rubber apart, leaving me naked on the dance floor.

When we arrived, Fran had seemed at home immediately, bouncing from room to room, eager to explore each cranny of the venue, an old theatre which was filled to capacity on one of their biggest nights of the year.

She glared at Chris, who was surveying the crowd with wide eyes. 'Some rock star you're going to make,' she said, 'if you find this lot shocking. I bet Viggo Franck has a dressing room full of naked women. Men too, probably.'

'Don't you start,' Chris groaned. 'I think every woman I've ever met has rung me since the posters went out, asking for a backstage pass.'

'He's not my type,' Fran replied, 'but I reckon he's right up Summer's street. She always makes a beeline for the bad boys.'

I blushed. Viggo Franck was half Danish and half Italian, and The Holy Criminals, already well established in Europe, had risen seemingly from nowhere in the UK to become a massive hit almost overnight when he'd been pictured tumbling out of a hotel in Chelsea with not just one, but three women, including the granddaughter of a Conservative politician and a young actress who had made her money from Disney-produced family-friendly romcoms. Viggo was immediately tarred with an almost god-like womaniser status while the women had been flamed in the press, which had generated even more news coverage when feminists had been up in arms about the sexual double standard evidenced in the media.

As a result of his sudden success, The Holy Criminals had been accused of selling out, and Viggo's once indie underground status had been abandoned in favour of a stadium-filling mainstream audience. According to Chris, Viggo had managed to maintain his street cred amongst fellow musicians by gaining a reputation for promoting struggling small-time bands.

He'd met Chris at a party where they'd been hanging out with Black Hay, another band we used to share the stage with occasionally, who'd just been taken on by The Holy Criminals' record label.

'Well,' Chris said, 'I did get you two backstage passes so I guess we'll soon find out.'

Fran whooped. 'No wonder you haven't come home, Sum,' she said. 'London is way too much fun.'

One of the club's photographers asked if he could take a picture, and before I could step away, Chris and Fran had agreed and both leapt into fearsome monster poses for the shot.

I pulled my sailor's hat down to cover my face just as the flash went off. Being a minor celebrity with a conservative fan base had made me more worried about my public image.

'Are you sure you're OK with having your picture taken?' the photographer asked, noticing my reticence.

He sidled alongside me to show me the shot, standing close to avoid having to lift the camera strap over his head. He had a wide smile and friendly eyes, lined with dark eyeliner, which matched his outfit of a latex shirt in a purple so dark it looked black, and wrist cuffs in the same colour that reached almost to his elbow, gladiatorial style.

'No, it's OK,' I said, peering at the image on the lens. It was a good shot. Fran and Chris were unrecognisable in their thick make-up and I could have been one of a dozen girls in my sailor suit with my hat obscuring almost all of my face, just a lipsticked grin visible and a flash of my red hair bright against the white paint on Fran's shoulder.

'Email me if you change your mind,' he said, handing me a plain black business card with just his name printed across in white, simple font. Jack Grayson. The name sounded vaguely familiar.

'Stop flirting, would you,' Fran complained. 'We want to go and dance!'

Jack was already a few feet away, taking another picture, his tall body curved into a slight crouch and the big SLR covering one eye and half of his wide smile.

We headed off to find the music, passing by the dungeon on the way. Fran peered inside quickly, but seemed uninterested in the goings-on within.

'Each to their own,' she said with a shrug, without giving it a second glance.

Listening to the soft moans and swishing of floggers landing on skin, I wished that I wasn't with my sister and my best friend.

It had been a long time since I'd worn a rope harness or felt a hand against my arse in anything more than a gentle smack during lovemaking and I missed it. I had made a deliberate effort to cut myself off from the scene after I'd broken up with Dominik and then got together with Simón. It wouldn't have been fair on him to keep that side of myself alive, I'd thought, if we couldn't make it work together. So I'd pushed those feelings away in the hope that if I ignored them long enough, they'd disappear.

The fact that I had been unsuccessful in my attempts to banish the fetish scene and its effects on my body and mind was obvious. The noises emanating from within the darkened corners of the dungeon, the whistling of a whip through the air, the thud of a palm onto a buttock, the groan of submissives being put through their paces, made my thoughts race and my hands shake. I was immensely turned on by my surroundings, and I wasn't sure if I could make it through the rest of the evening pretending otherwise.

I knew that Fran would be safe with Chris, and I was entirely comfortable alone, so I would be able to slip away for a short while to enjoy myself.

'Hey, I'm going to get some drinks, meet you guys on the dance floor, OK?'

'OK,' Fran yelled back. 'We'll be here all night!'

They disappeared into the crowd, leaving me to my own devices.

I considered a return to the dungeon, but dismissed the idea as the equipment had all been in use, and I actually wasn't sure that my outfit would survive a flogging, or that I'd be able to get out of the latex hot pants without tearing them.

Instead, I followed a set of stairs up to a large, dark and unnamed room, my heels catching dangerously on each uneven step and threatening to send me tumbling.

It took my eyes a moment to adjust to the light. I was in the balcony of the converted cinema, which still featured the original fold-down seating. I moved into a row and settled onto a perch, taking advantage of a chance to ease out of my uncomfortably high heels.

A short film was playing on a loop. Flashes of naked bodies, in sometimes extreme and fetishistic poses, appeared onscreen, casting a glare on the other partygoers in the room.

After a moment, a woman slipped into a seat in the row ahead of me, her partner trailing behind her. She was one of the prettiest women I'd ever seen, almost certainly a model or an actress. She had an oval face, straight, short blond hair and blue eyes so pale they were close to grey. Her make-up was muted, and she was dressed in a latex nurse's outfit which fitted her like a second skin and wasn't even close to tacky. It had probably been designed for her, rather than picked off the peg like mine.

Her partner was clad all in black, in jeans and shirt, his only hint of fetishwear, despite the strict dress code, a mask that covered his eyes. He might have looked ridiculous, but for the confident slant of his shoulders, rakishly messed hair and the company of such a beautiful woman – all factors that suggested a devil-may-care attitude rather than a tendency to dress badly.

She met my eyes as she entered the row, her full lips travelling upward in a half smile. There were empty seats all around me, but she'd chosen to sit less than an arm's breadth away.

I inhaled sharply and held my breath, wondering what would happen next, why they'd sat so close. They began kissing almost immediately, soft, gentle kisses, and at first I averted my eyes as they seemed so intimate together. This was no drunken moment of passion but a scene that they'd chosen to share with me.

I turned back to see him dipping his head, and her wriggling backwards so that she was lying over several of the small flip-down seats, with her legs open, one of them bent up by her side and the other down on the floor, giving her partner free access to caress her beneath her short rubber skirt, which he was doing with obvious abandon, with no thought to who might be watching.

My view of her was blocked partially by his head, now buried between her legs, but in the flash of the cinema screen I could see a vision of her bare legs, slim calves leading up to her smooth, silky thighs.

Before I knew it, I was leaning closer, and wondering what would happen if I touched her, if I joined in. I wasn't sure what I should do. Lean forward and tentatively brush her arm? Ask for permission? But while I was wondering, I turned my head to glance at her face and saw her staring at me, her expression fixed in a look of total arousal, though she wasn't as lost in it as I imagined I would have been in her place, but rather she seemed to be making a deliberate effort to maintain eye contact with me.

He evidently quickened the rhythm of his licks, as she began to lose control, and grabbed my hand, squeezing my palm and pulling me forward until I was leaning over them, close enough to kiss her, close enough to feel the softness of her skin brushing against mine.

She moaned, and bucked beneath me as an orgasm coursed through her, and then she let go of my hand, and relaxed into stillness.

Her partner lifted his head, and stroked the side of her

face with his fingertip. I waited quietly for them both to recover, though I was now so aroused by the situation that I was finding it difficult to sit still.

She turned her head to look at me and smiled.

'Thank you,' she said.

'You're welcome,' I replied, though I felt a little foolish under the circumstances. There weren't any words to acknowledge the intimacy of the encounter that wouldn't have sounded contrived or silly when spoken aloud.

He gave me a slight nod, his expression unreadable beneath his mask.

The pair stood and then disappeared into the night.

I sat still, alone on my seat for a minute or two, regaining my composure, wondering what to do next. I was still immensely turned on, but I didn't feel right about leaving Fran and Chris to their own devices for too long. Just as I was making my mind up, I heard Fran coming up the stairs behind me.

'There you are! We looked everywhere. What are you doing sitting up here alone?' Her tone of voice was wondering rather than suspicious. I doubted that Fran would ever even imagine the sort of scene that I had just witnessed.

'Just taking a break. It's crowded out there.'

'Come on then, you're missing all the good tunes.'

I followed them both back into the party, though the image of the woman's face as she came didn't leave my mind, and my fantasies were only exacerbated by the sexual vibe in the air and the sheer number of attractive people in the crowd, particularly the men who had either dressed the part, in military jackets, or who had that certain confidence about them, a demeanour that reminded me of Dominik.

*

As I slipped into bed after our night out, the thoughts in my mind became ever more persistent.

Visions of men wearing long boots and carrying riding crops flittered across my mind and turned darker and fiercer, until I saw myself kneeling on a stone floor with a gag in my mouth and my wrists tied behind my back, not with rope but metal cuffs attached to a long, thick chain which ran along the floor behind me, meeting a bolt on the far wall. I was completely naked, and totally smooth. Someone had shaved my pubic hair. I had two nipple rings, both stinging as though I had been pierced only hours earlier. A heavy door swung open and I heard footsteps, slow, deliberate, coming closer. I couldn't see the person but sensed that it was a man. He neared, but I couldn't make him out in the thick gloom, just a pair of legs clad in black suit trousers with a sharp crease down the centre standing directly in front of me. I heard the sound of a belt unbuckling and a zipper being pulled down.

In my dream, I desperately wanted to feel the man's cock, but he stood just out of reach. I twisted my arms in their sockets and wriggled my hands, trying to free myself but it was no good. My mouth hung open slightly as I longed to feel the penis breach my lips, caress my tongue and hit the back of my throat. My lips were dry and I moistened them with my tongue. I tried to stand, but realised that my feet were shackled as well.

'Do you want something?' said a voice in a mocking tone.

It was Dominik.

I woke with a start. My lips still felt dry, and my hands

shook as I picked up the glass of water on my night table and took a mouthful, spilling liquid down the front of my singlet as I did so. I normally slept nude, but not with my sister in the room. She was lying on her back with her mouth half open, snoring softly, her face and hair streaked with bits of white powder, so she still looked a bit like a corpse.

Neither Fran nor Chris mentioned our night out again. This fact rankled with me. Attending a fetish club for the first time had been such a big deal in my life, like a landmark that separated the person I was before from the person I had become. That other people saw it as just a night out left me vaguely irritated. If the part of my life that I thought of as my 'dark secret' had become mainstream, then what did I have left?

Without my gigs to keep me busy or the often frantic social life that I had maintained in New York in classical music circles, I was at a bit of a loose end. Fran, who had always been incapable of sitting still for more than a few minutes, had begun looking for a job in London almost the moment she landed, and had taken on some casual bartending work, so she was out most evenings and slept during the day. Chris spent most of the week rehearsing with his band.

'Why don't you come down?' he suggested. 'Watch us play. The guys have been asking about you.'

He gave me an address for a studio off Holloway Road. The place was sleek, manned by a security guard and a complex alarm system, and full of hi-tech equipment. The last time I'd seen the place that Groucho Nights were renting, it was a mouldy basement with a padlocked door in an ominous-looking alleyway near Camden Lock barely big enough to swing a cat, never mind fit a band inside. I knew that Chris's uncle had lent the band a bit of cash to help them get on their feet, but I didn't realise that it was enough to afford a place like this.

'Wow,' I said when I arrived, 'you guys have gone all out, just for me.'

I walked over to Ted and gave him a kiss on his cheek, ruffling my hand through his hair.

He batted me away playfully. 'Don't touch the hair.'

'Seriously, do you always dress like this for rehearsals?' I asked.

Ted, who played guitar and sometimes the harmonica or kazoo, was from Boston. He and Chris were cousins, and looked so alike they could have been brothers. They were about the same height, with brown eyes and thick, curly brown hair. Ted had started growing his out and frizzing it up so that it was almost an Afro, and he was kitted out in tight red drainpipe jeans and a black waistcoat. Chris was made up to match him with the same outfit but in reverse, red waistcoat and black drainpipe jeans.

Ella, on drums, had dyed her once-blond poker-straight hair fire-engine red, the colour of a postbox, but she was otherwise unchanged. She was originally from Hull, and the only English member of the group. Ella was long-limbed with a boyish figure and muscled arms. When I'd last seen her, she had a half-finished jellyfish tattoo on her chest which had since been filled in with bright shades of pink and blue, tentacles snaking down like map lines under the neck of her singlet that made it hard not to stare at her chest. She dressed like a trucker, in men's jeans and shirts, a look that I found singularly appealing on a woman.

'Viggo might be dropping in later,' Chris replied.

'Really? He hangs out with the common people? Doesn't sound much like a rock star to me.'

'Maybe it makes him feel normal,' Ted said. 'Though I wouldn't really call him normal.'

'He owns the place,' Chris added. 'Did you think I'd be renting something like this?'

I parked myself down on one of the leather beanbags scattered inside the studio as they began warming up with a couple of slower tracks. I'd brought my violin along with me just in case he wanted to jam, for old time's sake, but I left it tucked out of the way for the time being.

They had just finished warming up when the door swung open. I noticed Chris's hand falter on the fretboard, but he carried on playing.

'Don't stop, sounds great.'

Viggo was carrying a tray of coffees, balanced precariously in one hand. He was holding a pair of sunglasses in the other, although I hadn't seen a sign of sun for a week. I leaped up to hold the door for him.

'Oh, thank you, darling,' he said in a husky voice. 'I'd shake your hand but both of mine are full, so I'll have to kiss you instead.'

He bent down and kissed my cheek, brushing his lips across my ear as he did so in a gesture that was both bold and totally inappropriate for a first meeting.

'I'm Viggo Franck,' he said. 'Pleased to meet you.' He had one eyebrow raised in a gesture of flirtation.

'Summer Zahova,' I replied, with a curt nod. 'Can I take those?' I gestured to the tray of coffees. I was parched.

'Of course. Don't drink them all at once.'

My hands shook as I picked up one of the cardboard cups, without an S for sugar on the side. I was trying to act normal, but in truth wasn't much accustomed to meeting celebrities. There'd been a few in the classical music world, of course, but they were a different breed altogether, mostly introverts, and not my type.

None of them were like Viggo Franck. He was dressed in black jeans so tight that I thought he might have got them from the women's leggings section. They were low slung, and revealed an inch or so of flesh on one side of his midriff underneath a ripped white T-shirt. He was thin rather than muscled, with surprisingly pale skin considering that he was half Italian. I guessed he took after his Danish side. He had high cheekbones and full lips framed by closely trimmed facial hair, halfway between five o'clock shadow and an actual beard. His hair was very dark brown, almost black, and quite straight but teased into fullness.

It was immediately apparent to me why women chased after Viggo. Sexual energy radiated from him in waves. Even with his dark glasses on and nondescript, rough clothes, he was the sort of person who you would look twice at in the street. Or at least, I would. He leaned against the wall with one foot on the floor and the other on the wall behind him. I sat back down on the beanbag again, and tried not to stare at him.

Chris and the band were full tilt now into their fastest number, and oblivious to our presence in the room.

I looked up and caught Viggo staring at me, his lips raised in a half smile. He sauntered over.

'Mind if I join you?' he said. He was sitting down, wriggling onto the beanbag alongside me before I had a chance to tell him yes or no, and despite the fact that there was a two-seater sofa alongside us that was unoccupied.

'Sure,' I replied, maintaining a hint of ice in my tone, though in truth the warmth of his body alongside mine and the flash of his torso had sent a thrill up my spine.

I jumped as hot coffee splashed onto my arm, my cup tipping suddenly as he settled into the bag.

'Shit, I'm sorry,' he said. He tried to pull the bottom of his T-shirt up to dab at it, but the material wouldn't reach, so he pulled it over his head and mopped it up.

I stared at his chest. His skin pale, with a faint line of dark hair covering just between his breastbone. His nipples, small and dark. The small fold of flesh that had appeared on his stomach when he sat down, a result of the unflattering position we were both folded into. I wanted to reach out and touch him, to run my hand over the softness of his skin.

'There you go,' he added, before pulling the shirt back on again, ignoring the faint coffee stain that now marked the fabric.

His eyes ran over my body, then alighted on my violin case, leaning against the beanbag.

'Are you a new member of the band?' he asked.

'No, I used to play with them occasionally, jam, but I'm more of a classical music performer these days.'

'Show us then, I like to see an instrument.'

'The violin? Sure.'

I leaned down, unbuckled the Bailly from its case and handed it to him.

He ran his hands over the body of the violin, gently caressing the burnished wood.

'Do you play?' I asked, curious at his reaction. His eyes,

previously so flirtatious and focused on me were now entirely fixated on my instrument.

'Not the violin, no,' he replied, without lifting his gaze. 'Though, believe it or not, I was classically trained in piano. Where did you get it? It's a particularly beautiful instrument.'

I blushed, remembering Dominik, and the unwritten contract that I'd entered with him in order to keep the Bailly.

'A friend gave it to me,' I said.

'Really?' he responded, catching my gaze now. 'Must be a close friend. Do you know where he got it from?'

'You're presuming my friend is a "he".'

'Yes I am. Where did he get it from?'

'I'm not completely sure, to be honest. A dealer, I think. It came with a certificate. The last owner was called Edwina. Edwina Christiansen. But I don't know anything about her. I did Google her once, but no luck. Are you a collector? Or in the market for something new?'

'No, no. Just curious. I like pretty things.' He handed the Bailly back to me, letting his fingers linger against mine as he did so.

'Why don't you play it for me?' he asked.

'Now?'

Chris was just coming into the final chords of the last song the group had on their set.

'Yeah. Play for me.'

Naturally, I could have declined his request, as I'd brought the violin along in the hope that I'd get a chance to play a song or two with Chris and the band. But Viggo was essentially sponsoring Groucho Nights. I wanted to stay on his good side for their sake.

Viggo stood up and applauded heartily as Chris and the band reached the end of their last song.

'Good shit,' he said. 'Now, I want to hear the violin. One more piece?'

Chris was sweating with the exertions of his set, but smiling broadly.

'Yeah, course, come play, Sum.'

I picked up my violin and stepped alongside him.

'Just improvise,' he said, bursting into one of the folk tunes that we used to play together. Ella abandoned her drums so she wouldn't drown me out and waved a pair of maracas about instead. It wasn't my best performance, but the rhythm came back to me as though I'd played it yesterday.

Initially I felt a little self-conscious playing for Viggo, particularly as the rock numbers were outside my normal repertoire, but within a few minutes I had forgotten he was there entirely, I was so lost in the rhythm of the music.

It wasn't until I opened my eyes at the end that I noticed his gaze was fixed firmly on me as I played, but rather than undressing me with his eyes as Dominik had, his focus was entirely on my violin, almost as if he were admiring me in the way that he would admire a piece of art.

*

The difference between the two men, and their gaze as they watched me play, lingered in my mind as we returned to the flat.

Chris was jubilant, and didn't seem to notice that I was distracted.

'I want to do that every day for the rest of my life,' he said with a flushed face as we piled into a taxi. 'Especially if you're around to pay for us to get cabs everywhere.'

I'd got used to travelling by yellow cab in New York, and had lost the energy for carrying instruments on the underground. I had plenty of money saved from my recent tours, and the albums were by now all producing tidy royalty cheques. Susan, my agent, had sent me a few sternly worded emails to find out what I was up to, though I was sure that Simón would have told her that I had moved out and was taking a break for a while.

Truthfully, I'd barely thought of Simón, or New York, since I'd left. I slipped so easily back into my single life in London that the past couple of years were like a dream. I missed him at times, when I thought about it. Missed having someone in my bed next to me, and the security of a full-time relationship, but most of the time I was just relieved to be free.

I thought about Dominik more often, in my waking life and my dreams. I wondered whether he had someone else, a girlfriend, and if he had abandoned his dominant tastes in bed in order to sustain a more regular relationship, as I had, or if he'd found another submissive woman to tie up at night.

Towards the end of the same week, we found ourselves in another taxi, this time on our way to the Brixton Academy for the actual show. Chris, Ella and Ted had gone ahead several hours earlier to assist with set-up, which was being supervised by Viggo's band's road crew, and to carve out enough time for a soundcheck, so it was just Fran and me coming behind.

Chris had assured me that we had both been invited to the after-party that Viggo was apparently planning to celebrate the opening night of his tour in London. He had rolled his eyes when I quizzed him. 'What do you *think* Viggo said when I told him you had a sister over for a visit?'

'Ugh,' I replied. 'He can think again if he thinks that's happening.'

'I'll be keeping my eye on both of you.'

'You'll be too busy with the three hundred models he's probably ordered to bring his drinks.'

'You know me better than that. Bikini-clad dancing waitresses aren't my style.'

Fran laughed and he glanced over at her with a grin.

As Chris and I had first met at the Academy, we both had a lot of affection for the place. It was a little gloomy without an audience in it, and the space on the inside was smaller than I remembered. Hard to believe that four thousand people would be crammed in here in a few hours. The sloping floor was covered in stains and smelled like beer, but despite that the building had a grand feeling to it, a sense of history.

Out front, punters who had been lining up for hours were chatting good-naturedly, drinking cans of beer and smoking cigarettes. A fair few of them, I was gratified to hear, had come to see Groucho Nights. Chris had accumulated quite a following. They stared at Fran and me curiously as we flashed our passes at the burly, uniformed bouncers who were guarding the front doors and we were waved straight through. I'd gone fairly nondescript, in a denim miniskirt and my old cherry-red Dr Martens, but Fran drew a lot of attention, determined as she was to prove that she wouldn't be defeated by the British weather, and despite the cold, she was wearing the shortest pair of high-waisted denim shorts I'd ever seen her in. Her skin had turned almost blue in the chill.

'Hey,' she said, 'I'll be thirty soon and I hear it's all downhill from there. May as well get my legs out while I still can.'

I'd brought my violin with me at Viggo's request. He hadn't specified why, but I guessed that he wanted me to play for him at his party, after the show. I felt a little strange about the idea. Dominik had been the only person who I had performed for in that way, but for the sake of the band, if nothing else, I agreed. At least it would keep me in practice, seeing as I didn't have any gigs lined up. I left the Bailly in the Green Room, which was heavily guarded, but empty for now as The Holy Criminals were in their dressing rooms and Chris, Ella and Ted were busy sound-checking. We idled the time away in the top bar, before taking our places at the front centre of the stage as the first half of the show was about to begin.

Chris was like another person the minute he stepped out in front of the crowd. Day to day he had a shy, boyish air about him, but in front of a microphone he wore a second skin, the perfect image and demeanour of a rock star.

The group burst straight into one of my favourite tracks, 'Roadhouse Blues', all rolling riffs with a blues melody and Chris and Ted's husky vocals riding the sound like molasses rolling slowly down a whisky barrel. Ted pulled out his double bass for the second tune, 'Fire Woman', a song about hot love with more of a swing feel. It was a piece that always made the women in the audience go crazy, and tonight was no exception. Chris held the mic in one hand as if he was slow-dancing with a lover, his mouth open wide to catch the high notes.

'Hello, London,' he shouted out to the crowd, 'how are we tonight?'

They leaped and cheered in response.

'Would you like to meet our special guest?' He stared down at me in the front row.

More cheering. Maybe Viggo had agreed to make an early friendly appearance.

'What are you doing?' I shouted back, but my voice was lost in the screaming.

'My girl is here, over from New York,' Chris shouted. 'Give her some encouragement, people, get her up on stage.'

One of the roadies raced out hurriedly from behind the curtain with an electric violin, and plugged it in with a burst of feedback. I was relieved it wasn't my Bailly, as the sound would have been lost, even with the mic, but I hadn't played an electric for nearly three years.

I crouched under the rope that cut the mosh pit off from the stage. The two bouncers hoisted me up and Chris grabbed my hand and pulled me alongside him. I turned to face the crowd. The energy onstage was much wilder than I was used to compared with my demure classical gigs. The room felt hot and alive, tingling with noise and electricity.

'Just go with it,' Chris said, as he broke into one of the songs that we used to play together, 'Sugarcane', a folk rhythm with a short violin solo and double-string licks punctuating the vocals, a fat, dirty sound that I hadn't played since I first left London.

I stayed for the band's next song, enjoying the ebb and flow of the music rushing through me like a current, forcing myself to leave them onstage alone for their finale, a heavier rock number which reached a thundering crescendo on the drums.

Fran was waiting for me in the wings minutes after I made my exit, having pushed through the crowd and flashed her backstage pass and a smile at security so that she could congratulate me. She stared at Chris as the crowd went wild, and the lights swept over the band one last time as they left the stage, fingers of green and red light gleaming against the hard wooden floors.

'He's pretty good,' Fran said.

'Chris? Yeah, I know. He's like a different person when he plays.'

'So are you.'

'Really?'

'Just more confident, I guess. And I can see you all getting into the music, like you're high or something . . .'

'We're not. Always been very boring like that. Chris is massively anti-drugs, says he doesn't want to upset his creative flow by fucking up his brain cells.'

'Fair enough . . .'

I left her looking after our jackets in the wings, and headed off to hunt down a couple of drinks, taking advantage of the short break between acts. We didn't get that many big acts in New Zealand, and even then they always went to the major centres: Auckland or Wellington, sometimes Christchurch. Neither of us had seen that many gigs at home. Fran seemed content drinking it all in, and staring up at the Academy's starry ceiling which even after several visits to the venue still made me feel as though I was watching a show outdoors.

I returned just in time to see the stage lights dropped into blackness, save for a single red spot that lit up the centre of the stage. A trapdoor had opened and a cage was slowly rising out of it, with Viggo Franck inside, crouched over with his hands wrapped around the bars in a gesture of defiance. He raised his head and grinned as the cage reached level with the floor, and I was almost deafened by the high-pitched screaming of the women in attendance. Fake smoke bubbled across the stage and when it dissipated, the cage had disappeared and he was standing with his legs apart wearing virtually the same outfit I'd seen him in the other day. Low-slung black jeans, leather boots, a ripped T-shirt. If it wasn't for the fame, and that Casanova aura that hung around him, he could have been any guy in a pub in London, though definitely not the sort that you would introduce to your mother.

He was on stage for about an hour and a half with his band, building to a final crescendo with a track from his first album, *Underground*, a song with a screeching guitar solo in the middle which he played on his knees, leaning over backwards so that his head rested on his ankles. He reportedly practised hot yoga in a special sauna room in his mansion and my mind immediately wandered when he demonstrated his flexibility.

Fran elbowed me in the ribs after the show, as we headed off to find Chris and the others.

'You know you're going to be one of dozens, don't you?'

'You're presuming I'm going to sleep with him.'

'Well, obviously. Just so long as you know you're not the only one. Probably not even the only one today.'

'You think I should avoid him?'

'God no!' she said, grinning from ear to ear. 'How many chances does a girl get to fuck a rock star? Go for it. Just make sure he covers his loving, won't you.'

'I'm not an idiot . . .' I replied, remembering that the first time I'd slept with Dominik we hadn't used a condom. A stupid mistake that I hadn't repeated since. With anyone.

'No helmet, no ride,' Fran added, giggling as one of the stagehands hovering by the dressing rooms glanced at her and lifted an eyebrow quizzically.

The scene in Viggo's dressing room was quieter than I expected. He was sitting on a stool drinking a bottle of beer and Chris and Ted were relaxing on a black vinyl couch pushed against one of the walls. The rest of Viggo's band had gone out to track down some more drinks. The room itself was fairly stark. Walls painted white with A4 printed signs warning occupants not to smoke belied the ashtrays that rested on the dressing table. Ella was leaning close to the mirror, wiping off her make-up with baby wipes.

They applauded when we walked in. Viggo's gaze lingered on Fran's short shorts.

'Hey, our little star!' Chris said. 'They loved you.'

'They loved you guys, more like. Listen to it out there.'

A bunch of fans, most of them women, had gathered around outside and were shouting 'Viggo, Viggo', and occasionally 'Chris!'

'Chris isn't a very sexy name,' I said to him, cheekily. 'You should change it.'

'So everyone keeps trying to convince me,' he said, 'but it's too late now. I'd feel like a fool.'

Viggo put his beer down, grabbed my hand and pulled me towards him, so I was standing between his open legs. I was wearing a short skirt with tights, and could feel the scratch of his denim brushing against my legs. His touch hit me in a rush, like a glass of champagne going straight to my head, and I had to force myself not to fall straight into his arms.

'So, darling,' he drawled, 'did you bring your violin? Will you play some more for us later?' He rolled the word 'later' as though he was referring to something much more X-rated.

'I would love to,' I replied breezily, resisting the urge to press my body against his. It was one thing to hook up with an obvious womaniser in private, but quite another to do it publicly. I didn't want to be the butt of Chris and Fran's jokes for the next decade.

'Well,' he said, 'we should go.'

The crew had loaded everything into a couple of vans out the back, and arranged to take Chris and his band's stuff back to the studio where they'd pick it up next week, leaving us free to travel in Viggo's cars, a couple of fairly nondescript black sedans with tinted windows. He apparently drove a black 1987 Buick most of the time, but preferred to keep his anonymity after shows.

The cars pulled up to a gated complex in Belsize Park. It was about 2 a.m. by the time we got there, and the neighbourhood was deathly quiet.

'Loads of celebrities live on this street,' Chris whispered to me. 'And their unsexy names didn't do them any harm.'

'I see your point, but I'm sure plenty of people would disagree.'

'There's no pleasing some people,' he replied, rolling his eyes at me.

The interior of Viggo's mansion was nothing like I expected. No snakes in tanks, or aquariums full of nude women swimming as had been rumoured. The place was barer than bare, almost spartan, but for a few art pieces positioned to catch the light. A sculpture of a bird with its wings outstretched was suspended from the ceiling. A spiral staircase in pale timber and metal snaked up the centre of the room.

'Is that a Hirst?' Fran asked, staring at a long oblong painting, a white background covered with perfectly round coloured dots.

'God no,' Viggo said, standing a touch closer to her than I was comfortable with. 'What kind of person do you take me for?'

I stared at the painting more closely, noticing tiny m's painted in the centre of the coloured dots like sweets.

'Clever,' I said.

'Exactly,' Viggo replied. He was running his hand lightly up my skirt, brushing his fingers against my stockinged thighs. I shivered in response. 'I don't like things that aren't clever. Now, come upstairs with me, the show hasn't finished yet.'

The second floor was much more like I had imagined. The place looked like a harem, furnished entirely in deep-red and purple with chandeliers hanging from the ceiling, plush, gold-coloured carpet and an array of black leather couches in unusual shapes that I suspected were designed for activities that might be pictured in the Kama Sutra. In the centre of the room was a fountain, and in the middle of the fountain, a lifelike statue of a woman.

At least, I thought it was a statue, until she gracefully unfurled a hand and pulled a pin out of her long, blond hair which tumbled around her shoulders. She turned slowly to face us, revealing small bare breasts and totally smooth genitalia.

Her movements were subtle and beautifully executed, as far away from the stereotypical stripper as you could imagine. She had positioned herself in such a way that the water bursting from the fountain appeared to flow up her legs, stopping just as it reached the barrier created by her flesh. Next to her pussy was a tattoo of a tiny gun.

A dim memory began to echo in the recesses of my mind. The world was full of dancing girls, but I'd only seen one who moved like this, with an identical weapon marked into her skin.

It was the Russian dancer who had performed at the place, a private club in New Orleans that Dominik had taken me to. I recalled with a flush of humility and arousal how, after we had watched her impossibly erotic dancing, Dominik had instructed me to dance for him on the stage. I had done so, nude but for ruby-red nipple rings and a butt plug.

Luba.

She met my eyes and smiled.

4

The Angelique

The small shop in Burlington Arcade where he had bought
Summer's violin was shuttered, although it was already mid-
afternoon. Dominik peered through the glass door and
noticed piles of mail gathering dust on the floor on the other
side of the narrow letter box. A notice on the door redirected
enquiries to a telephone number which he noted down.

He rang it later.

There was no answer.

He tried again at hourly intervals.

Around ten in the evening he was just about to hang up
on his final attempt for the day, after letting the phone ring
for several minutes, when someone finally picked up.

The man sounded elderly and spoke in hushed tones.

'It's about the store in Burlington Arcade,' Dominik explained.

'You should get in touch with the letting agents,' the
man answered.

'That's not why I was calling,' Dominik said. 'I was once
a customer. Bought a violin there. I just had some questions
I wanted to ask . . .'

'We went out of business. I decided to retire. Just not
worth the bother any longer,' the man said. 'I don't think I
can help you.'

'Were you the owner?' Dominik asked.

The man's voice didn't sound at all like the assistant who had sold him the Bailly.

'I was.'

'I don't think we met. Your colleague sold me a beautiful instrument, but I'm now keen to find out more about its history, the previous owners . . .'

'Weren't you supplied with a certificate of provenance? He should have provided one.'

'I was. But the information proved quite sparse.'

'You can't expect me to remember chapter and verse on every instrument that went through our hands, surely?'

'I know. But I was just wondering . . .'

'Why?'

Dominik hesitated for one brief moment. How could he explain it? That he was clutching at straws? That he wanted Summer to come back into his life? That he had become a writer with nothing to write about?

'It's difficult to explain. The person I bought the violin for is—'

The other man cut him short. 'Was it the Bailly?' he asked.

'Yes,' Dominik admitted, surprised.

'Ah . . .'

'So . . .'

'Listen, it's late. Why don't you call me tomorrow morning; not too early though, and maybe we can arrange to meet up.'

'Absolutely. I'd love that.'

The shop's owner lived close to Dominik, in north London, his house a ramshackle cottage off a private road near Highgate Village. The front garden was overgrown, the lawn peppered with weeds, and rose bushes which hadn't seen a trim in ages. The front doorbell didn't work and Dominik had to repeatedly knock hard before he heard any signs of life inside.

The moment the man opened the door and peered at him, Dominik recognised him. Somehow the soft voice on the phone had made him think the man was much older than he actually was. He was, at worst, in his late fifties. He had seen him before. Twice, in fact. And each occasion was lodged deep in his brain.

He had been present at two of the most excessive parties Dominik had attended on the London scene during his wilderness months. More of a voyeur than a major participant, the man had usually faded away after his initial enjoyment of the woman who had volunteered to be at the centre of attention, and then had spent the rest of the evenings sipping a glass of white wine and watching the others – and Dominik – as they continued to play with and use the woman. Dominik had initially found the situation a little creepy, but by then the action in the room had taken over his attention.

The instrument dealer's rheumy eyes looked at him. There was no sign of recognition. He evidently did not remember Dominik. After all, the sights on display on those particular infamous hotel room evenings had been pretty distracting and more notable for bodies and body parts than faces.

'We spoke on the phone – I'm Dominik,' he introduced himself.

'John LaValle. Come inside.'

He led the way to the front room. A massive grand piano sat at its centre, its top littered with a mess of old, yellowing newspapers, partitions and broken-spined books.

LaValle showed him to an old leather armchair and sat himself down on the piano stool to face him. He offered Dominik a drink, which Dominik declined, and helped himself to a measure of Scotch from the adjacent liquor cabinet.

'Keeps me alert, you see,' LaValle said, pointing to his glass and the amber liquid stirring inside it before taking a few slow sips.

'You weren't at the store the day I acquired the violin,' Dominik remarked.

'No. A great pity. My colleague, who left my employment shortly afterwards, felt he could make a bit of a name for himself and please me by disposing of it. As a matter of fact, I had no intention of selling that particular instrument.'

'Oh. Why?'

'It was a collectors' item. Strictly speaking, worth so much more than what you ended up paying for it,' LaValle said. 'It had only come into stock a few weeks earlier through a lawyer in Germany disposing of an estate's assets, unaware of the violin's value or significance, and I was of a mind to keep it for myself, bring it back here. I felt it would be safer under this roof . . .'

'Safer?'

'It's an instrument that has a habit of getting lost.'

'Tell me more.'

LaValle ignored his question. 'But I gather it's no longer

in your possession. Did you intentionally purchase it for a third party?'

'It was a gift,' Dominik confessed.

'To Summer Zahova. A rather expensive gift, no?'

'How did you know that?' Dominik asked.

The older man rose, leaned over to the piano top and pulled a folded poster from the mass of papers lying there, unrolled it and, with a flourish, presented it to Dominik.

It was the poster that had initially been produced to advertise Summer's first solo concert. Cropped just beneath her chin and below her midriff, although allowing for a cascade of red curls to emerge like tentacles from the unknown space above, it showed her torso and stomach, her breasts artfully concealed by the body of the violin, its deep orange burnish contrasting with the pallor of her skin.

It was erotic and intriguing and had no doubt played a major part in attracting a sell-out audience to her performance, drawing a crowd to the venue where the face of the mysterious violin player would be revealed.

Dominik realised he never did try and obtain a copy of the poster at the time.

'I see,' he said.

'It's surprising that no one appears to have noticed at the time that the violin displayed in the photograph was the Angelique,' LaValle pointed out. 'It's so distinctive.'

'The Angelique? I was told by your colleague at the time that it had been manufactured by a French luthier called Bailly. His name appeared on the pegbox, beneath the strings.'

'Oh yes, Bailly was the man who created the instrument. But he made many such violins. It's just that this particular

Photo © www.mattchristie.com

one comes with a lot of history. An interesting man, our Mr Bailly. Very interesting indeed. Most violin makers, luthiers as you put it, were initially Italian, but Bailly was one of the few French artisans who carved a distinctive reputation for himself in this delicate trade.'

LaValle took a further sip of his whisky.

'I assume you're not a collector of vintage instruments, seeing that you passed the violin on to Miss Zahova, so I was wondering what is now your interest in it?' he asked Dominik.

'I just collect books,' he replied. 'That's enough of a pastime. I was just curious. I was thinking of writing something about musical instruments. A novel. And having been involved in this particular Bailly violin to a certain extent, I thought it could be a starting point for my research.'

'How interesting.' LaValle nodded.

'I'd love to know more. You've certainly whetted my appetite,' Dominik pointed out. 'You mentioned something about the instrument getting lost?'

'More to the point, stolen,' LaValle said. 'In fact, during the fortnight I had the instrument in safe storage at the store in Burlington Arcade, there were two break-in attempts. More than we'd experienced in the previous twenty years we'd been in business. Highly suspicious. Not that anyone knew it was there. We never advertised it, whether in store or in our catalogues. I'd barely had time to identify it after it came in from Germany. Whoever it was tampered with our alarm system, broke a few cabinets and locks but never located the safe where I had stored the Angelique. Unfortunately, the break-ins affected our insurance premiums, yet another reason for winding the business up a few months later, although by then you'd acquired the instrument. I'd been running it for too long, and was getting bored with the work. But don't let me bore you with talk of business rates and taxes . . .'

'No, I'm fascinated.'

'And Miss Zahova has it insured, I hope, and in a safe place whenever it's not being used.'

'I assume so. We don't see much of each other these days.'

'How sad. She appears to be a striking woman.'

'Oh yes.'

'But I know you are a man who appreciates women deeply. Something we have in common.' He smiled at Dominik, with a look of complicity. Of course he had recognised him. He had known all along.

'You knew—'

'Who you are? Naturally. I have a memory for faces.'

'Why didn't you say?'

'We all have our secrets, our dark places,' LaValle said dismissively. 'No one was hurt and much pleasure was enjoyed. Let other people judge . . .'

'Are you still . . . in contact with the group, the women?' Dominik enquired.

'No, everyone just drifted away in different directions after a time. No offence, but Miss Zahova would have made a wonderful addition to our parties. Did you ever think of bringing her along? I've always found that musicians make for the best submissives – no logic to it, more gut feeling – and—'

'I hadn't met her then. We met later,' Dominik interrupted LaValle.

'Shame.'

'So,' Dominik hurried to change the subject, 'tell me about the Angelique.'

Born in 1844, Paul Bailly was a man who suffered badly from wanderlust. He trained in the craft of violin-making in his hometown of Mirecourt in the French provinces and later in Paris with the famed luthier Jean-Baptiste Vuillaume and the legendary Jules Galliard.

A restless and romantic soul, Bailly had a particularly turbulent love life, and moved endlessly across France and later England. In Paris he met and fell head over heels in love with a young English au pair, Lois Elizabeth Hough, who was working for a wealthy French family out there.

He followed Lois to London when she returned, but their relationship didn't work out and he soon moved to Leeds. There, he worked for a local company manufacturing musical instruments, although no violin from this period bearing his signature has ever been seen, leading to speculation that he worked there on menial tasks and neglected his art.

After a time, Bailly was next heard of back in Paris in the 1880s, his most prolific period and one that was reflected in a series of exquisite instruments on which his reputation was established. It was also in Paris that he met Angelique Spengler, a woman married to a famous theatrical impresario, Hughes Caetano.

Angelique was an extraordinary beauty; in contrast with her rough and ready husband who controlled several Paris theatres and was said to have strong connections with the Paris underground sex trade. In all likelihood, political connections helped Caetano expunge anything illegal from the records. But his reputation was one of a fierce and jealous man. Rumour had it that he had acquired Angelique, straight from her convent education, as settlement for a gambling debt with her impoverished father.

How Bailly and Angelique met was uncertain. Possibly a concert. But when they did, sparks flew and they quickly became lovers. What with her husband's possessiveness and position in society, it was inevitable that the affair would eventually be discovered, and so it was. Bailly was set upon by thugs in the hire of the husband and badly beaten. The story goes that his right wrist was broken, and that as a result he never made any further instruments from that date onwards, and certainly no violins with his name have ever surfaced since that time.

Incensed by her husband's actions, Angelique succeeded in breaking into his safe, and with the stolen money, she and Bailly fled to America.

Caetano's reaction was swift as soon as he discovered where the fleeing couple were and some of his acolytes were despatched to New York where Angelique and Bailly were quickly located. Angelique was abducted while Bailly was out working, and she was never seen again. Some said she was executed and her body dumped in the Hudson, while others told a tale of revenge and degradation in which the once beautiful young woman was forced into sexual servitude, initially in Chinatown and later in Tijuana in Mexico. But, as LaValle said, these sorts of stories are passed from mouth to mouth over the years and can sometimes be subject to much in the way of disinformation, and truth is often the first to suffer.

At any rate, and maybe this was also a form of punishment in the vengeful Caetano's mind, Bailly was left unharmed, aside from the terrible anguish of having lost Angelique and worrying about her fate. In due course, Bailly returned to France but was never involved in the violin-making trade again.

'Fascinating,' Dominik said when LaValle had finished his story. 'But what about the violin you call the Angelique, then?'

'Ah,' LaValle said. 'This is where it becomes even more interesting . . .'

Some years later, a decade after the turn of the twentieth century, a violin bearing Bailly's name and no visible year of manufacture appeared in an auction at Christie's. Experts were puzzled. It was recognisable as Bailly's handiwork, but the wood used for its manufacture appeared to be of a different provenance than all the other instruments he was known to have been responsible for. In addition, the curves of the violin in question were ever so slightly different – more subtle, rounded, sensual one expert claimed, as if the way the wood had been carved into shape had been inspired by a woman's body. At which stage someone claimed the reasons for the discrepancy was that this particular instrument had originated during the time of Bailly's affair with Angelique and had been influenced by his love for her. It was unanimously agreed that this was the very last violin ever crafted by Paul Bailly. And so, for lack of any evidence to the contrary, a legend had been born and the violin acquired a name.

Which is where the story takes a more sinister turn.

The collector who won the auction for the Angelique later became one of the first English officers to be killed in the trenches in the First World War. Not an uncommon occurrence but for the fact that the next two owners of the instrument, the first inheriting it and then another purchasing it from the deceased's family, would suffer a similar fate. So far, just bad luck during the course of a bloody period of history. However, after the war had come to an end, the violin fell into the hands of a British family who all died in a house fire at their country estate – the instrument having remained safely at their London house. But when the beneficiaries of the estate came to retrieve it, it could not be found. It had been stolen.

The Angelique was next heard of in France. To compound the coincidences, the next owner was a Parisian politician and collector who died in the arms of his mistress within weeks of acquiring the instrument. It appears that, to compensate for the loss of a benefactor, the courtesan in question quickly grabbed the violin and other moveable items in her lover's collection and spirited them away before reporting the death and the body. The violin's whereabouts for the following ten years are unknown, but it next turned up in Germany, owned by a high-ranked army officer who became involved in one of the rare plots to overthrow Hitler and ended up hung on a meat hook for his involvement. The authorities impounded his belongings and the violin came into the hands of the governmental authorities. It was stored in a museum near Hamburg, which ended up being looted by the Russian Army.

The next time a record of the violin appears was in more peaceful times in the 1950s, where it was owned by the Christiansens, a well-to-do Hannover family, none of whom died an unnatural death over the course of three generations. The violin was passed from child to child, until it came into possession of Edwina Christiansen.

The name of the last proprietor of the violin, according to its certificate of provenance, Dominik remembered.

Edwina was the wild child of her bourgeois family, and by all accounts an outstanding beauty. During the 1960s she had come under the influence of an older man, an American, whom she had met in San Francisco. But their relationship was unconventional and very far from respectable. To cut a long story short – 'Maybe you could write it all into your novel,' LaValle had suggested – Edwina had been turned into his whore.

'What about the violin?' Dominik asked.

'It remained in Germany, while Edwina was in America. She just happened to own it; it had been passed on to her by her father. She actually never played it, or any instruments, at that.'

'What happened to Edwina?'

She'd ended up killing her American lover. The circumstances were murky and Edwina, at her trial, had been steadfast in refusing to answer any questions, and was sentenced to life imprisonment. The case had made newspaper headlines for a few weeks, if only because of the sordid backstory that was unveiled by the prosecution as much as the accused's spectacular beauty and sadness.

Disowned by her prudish family and alone in a foreign country, Edwina had not stood a chance.

She died in prison a decade or so later. Back in Germany, her relatives, embarrassed by the whole farrago, drew a lid over the episode and Edwina's belongings went into storage, with no attention to the Bailly violin. It was only when the building in which her affairs were kept was threatened by demolition a few decades after her death – the area it was sited in was pinpointed for regeneration – that distant relatives arranged for a lawyer to dispose of everything as he felt best.

'That was how I came into possession of the violin,' LaValle said. 'It was listed in the estate disposal catalogue as a Bailly, with no indication of its particulars, as the lawyer involved had no idea of either its history or its value.'

'And when you first saw it, did you realise it was the Angelique?' Dominik asked.

'Not initially. I'd acquired a lot of other instruments as part of the transaction and I knew I already had buyers for most of them, so I didn't give the Bailly too much thought initially. But when I did, I realised it was the instrument so many had talked about in the trade because of its un-common history. Now I don't believe in curses and all that, but I was thinking that I might actually keep it for myself, and not put it on sale, but before I had a chance to do so, that fool of an assistant who thought he was being clever, sold it. To you.'

'The Angelique.'

'Yes.' LaValle grinned. 'So, might I ask if the instrument has brought Miss Zahova any bad luck?'

Dominik considered his words carefully.

'Well, she's become quite famous since. Maybe others have been affected, though . . .'

LaValle looked him in the eyes.

'I hope you're not superstitious. It's just coincidences, you know. Although all these silly stories certainly give the instrument an interesting reputation. And beautiful objects do attract thieves, these days. If she were willing to sell, I'm sure it would manage at least five or six times what you paid for it.'

'I don't believe it's a question of money, Mr LaValle,' Dominik said, standing. 'But it's been a most interesting story. Thank you for your time.'

'I hope I've satisfied your curiosity,' the dealer said.

'Absolutely. You've given me much to think about. Truth can be stranger than fiction, can't it?'

'It certainly can,' LaValle agreed. 'And have you got enough material for your novel?'

'A start, I believe.'

Outside, the sound of the rain was like a tattoo on the Highgate Village roofs, but Dominik knew he now needed some fresh air to contemplate everything and decide what his next step should be, and whether he should warn Summer about the violin. He also knew that appearing out of the blue with silly stories about curses, thefts and dead lovers was not likely to endear him to her or make him welcome again.

In dreams came confusion.

Not helped by the sharp onset of a strong migraine which suddenly flared up with little warning, the tale LaValle had unfolded and the automatic reflux of memories of Summer, Dominik's night turned into a complicated jumble of emotions and irrational images.

He saw Summer as Angelique. In old-fashioned clothes he had never seen her wear before, images conjured up by old movies in the style of *Gone with the Wind* and Merchant Ivory. She wore a white crinoline dress, tight at the waist, and what looked like a bustier beneath compressing her breasts, squeezing them upwards to give the impression she was more ample than she actually was. She was sashaying across the newly mown grass of the Heath in her finery, and through the walls of sleep, Dominik could even smell the distinctive odour of cut grass. His vision cut to the clearing and the empty bandstand under a sky of pure blue, with the white stain of Summer in Angelique's dress ascending the stone steps. He stood a hundred yards away, an invisible spectator, rooted to the spot and unable to move.

A black violin case lay across a velvet-covered piano stool at the centre of the stand. In his dream, Summer as Angelique ran towards the violin, but out of a curtain of darkness, two men appeared to halt her progress, shielding her, blocking her way. They were dressed all in black. One had a moustache, the other a scar. Melodramatic operetta villains ticking all the clichés in the book.

Summer screamed, but Dominik, locked in a shell of silence, trying desperately to run towards the bandstand, to Summer, could not protect her.

One of the men slapped her, the other violently tore the top of her dress away from her body, releasing Summer's breasts, proud and fragile, her dark nipples emerging from the corset in which they were sheathed. It must have been a cold morning as even from where he stood, Dominik could see the goosebumps spreading across her bared skin.

The other man picked up the violin case and handed the Bailly to Summer. Her body shook with tears as she slowly brought the instrument to her chin, straightened, and adjusted its position. As she began to play, the first man, the one with the Mexican moustache, conjured a sharp knife seemingly out of nowhere and quickly slashed the dress at the waist, leaving Summer naked but for period white stockings attached to a similarly white garter belt that encircled her thin waist.

Under the gaze of her captors, she began to play.

Even though the dream was silent, Dominik imagined the music rising from her fingers and the dark orange wood of the instrument, flowing downwards like rivulets of rain, dancing, coming alive, floating upwards in minuscule cloud formations until it formed a halo above the bandstand, a rainbow of sounds that spread like a blanket over Hampstead, and then all of London.

In his sleep, the vision of Summer, now naked apart from the white garter belt and stockings, the forest fire of her pubic hair raging in the pale landscape of her body, and playing her Bailly with her eyes closed, lost to the silence of the music, made Dominik hard. He moved his hand down to his cock to verify his arousal. As if in response, the men on either side of Summer on the bandstand unzipped their own trousers and moved towards her, malicious intent dancing in their eyes.

Dominik wanted to rush towards her, to help, but in an instant the whole scene disappeared before his eyes and he was back in his bed, eyes wide open, awake. The collar of the T-shirt he had been sleeping in was damp with sweat.

It was a dream. Or a nightmare. Dominik took a sip from the glass of water by the bed. It was three in the morning and in the darkness of his room, visions of Summer, pursued by men, lost, alone and violated, her precious violin smashed to pieces on the ground, filled his mind.

*

Dominik and Lauralynn were sipping coffee at the kitchen table.

'Are you OK?' she asked him.

'Yes, why shouldn't I be?'

'I thought you had company last night. You were rather noisy.'

'Was I?'

'I swear I once heard you scream,' Lauralynn said. 'It certainly woke me up. I had to restrain myself from coming upstairs to check your bedroom.'

'No, I was alone, probably just some nightmare.'

'You were damn loud . . .'

'Sorry.'

'I must say you also look a bit rough this morning.'

'Just slept badly. Still suffering from a bad migraine.'

'Poor you,' Lauralynn deadpanned.

'Thanks for the sympathy.'

'My pleasure.'

Lauralynn emptied her cup, went for a refill, then walked with it upstairs to the room she had made her own, leaving Dominik on his own, a prey to reminiscences and a terrible feeling of foreboding.

He had mentioned to LaValle that he was not superstitious, but what remained in the dark corners of his mind of the bad dreams, and the images that had followed in their wake, now left him anxious. About Summer and the violin. Curses were something that happened in books, not in real life, surely.

But what if something were to happen to her? He knew he would feel responsible and wouldn't be able to live with it.

Should he warn her?

Contact her again after all this time? Disrupt her life?

He heard Lauralynn's phone ring in the distance. Her ringtone was a thumping piece of disco music so much at odds with her restrained cello playing. He tried to remember whether she was working today or would be hanging around the house. He felt like company.

He moved to his top floor study to check out the notes he had jotted down yesterday following his meeting with the instrument dealer. He wouldn't be able to use the story of Angelique, the Bailly violin, wholesale in his novel. He would have to embroider it, gather in a lot of historical details and weave an interesting set of characters around its story. But he knew it could certainly form the basis, the skeleton of a book. He enjoyed research and was aware that a lot would be required if he tackled a variety of periods, but that was also a challenge he would relish.

The one thing he would have to be careful about was to avoid any characters too similar to Elena, who had been Summer's recognisable counterpart in his Paris novel.

As much as he would have wanted to do so.

Writing about her was not only a form of exorcism but a way to keep her alive in his mind. Her flame, her features, her skin, her smell, memories he couldn't just let go. Even if it was all tinged with pain.

He sighed, shuffled the sheets of paper and pulled the laptop closer. He created a new document, his fingers hovering over the keyboard as he tried to come up with an appropriate title for the folder.

He was typing away half an hour later, now oblivious to

the rest of the world, when he heard the tap-tap at his study door. It was open, but Lauralynn was being considerate.

'Dominik?'

'Yes, what is it?' He looked up sharply.

'I didn't want to disturb you. It's just that something has come up.'

He pushed his chair back. 'What?'

'I just had a call,' Lauralynn said. 'It's my brother . . .'

'The soldier?'

His stomach tightened. After yesterday's violin stories, nothing would have come as a surprise today. But then he knew Lauralynn and her family had nothing to do with the Angelique. Coincidences only go that far.

'Yes, he's been wounded. It's not too bad. He might lose a finger, but they've saved his hand. A roadside bomb in Afghanistan.'

'I'm so sorry.' Dominik stood and moved over to her.

'One of my aunts rang. She's with him at the veterans' hospital, where he was repatriated to. It's in Virginia. I even managed to speak to him briefly, as she was by his bed. He's in good spirits.'

'That must be a relief.'

'It is.' Lauralynn moved further into the room and leaned against the desk. 'Anyway, I think it would be best if I went back to the States for a short while. He's the only close family I have, after all.'

'I understand, completely. Is there anything I can do?'

'No, not really. I've managed to book a flight for to-morrow. I'm leaving the return date open. Might stay a few weeks.'

'You'll always be welcome back. I won't install anybody

else in the spare bedroom. I promise.' He attempted a smile.

'It's an early flight from Heathrow. Can you give me a lift?' Lauralynn asked.

'Of course. It's the least I can do.'

'Thanks. You're a good friend. I'll find a way to repay you . . . Other than with money, of course.' Her eyes sparkled, ever so full of undisguised guile.

'I'm sure you will.'

She leaned over and kissed him on the cheek.

'I have to rush into town now and cancel some of my sessions and see if the guys in the quartet can manage without me for a while. We don't have any gigs in the near future so it should be OK.'

'We'll all be waiting for you when you get back,' Dominik said, already thinking about how it would feel being alone in the house again.

It wasn't a prospect he was looking forward to.

5

A Bitter Knife

I felt as though everyone in the room knew my secret. Viggo, Fran, Chris. And perhaps they would, if Luba chose to mention it, but she broke away from my gaze and continued with her dance, slowly moving back into stillness until the spotlight disappeared and the fountain was plunged into darkness and Luba with it.

'Wow,' Fran said. 'Maybe I'm not as straight as I thought I was. That was pretty hot.'

I waited for Viggo to say something, expecting that he would invite me to follow her with a recital of some sort, but he had his back to us and was already mixing elaborate cocktails at an extensive bar that ran almost the entire length of the room.

'Chris,' I asked, 'have you seen my violin? Did the runners bring it?'

'Yeah, I think I saw one of the roadies fit it in the back of the van. And they're more careful with instruments than they would be with infants. It will be with all of our other gear at the studio. Don't worry.'

'I just feel so strange without it by my side. Naked. Like wearing shoes with no socks on.'

'Just when I was about to accuse you of being melodramatic, you ruin it with an image like that,' Chris teased.

'And I didn't even need to bring it.'

I was beginning to feel a little lonesome without the company of the Bailly. Playing the electric one I had been handed had felt a bit rough, hadn't been the same. The sound almost mechanical, lacking warmth. Maybe I would give Susan a call and see if she could organise some gigs in London. I couldn't lie low for ever.

'We were going to bring it out for you to play, that's why I asked you to bring it along. But it was a stupid idea. The sound would have been totally lost in the mix, so we dug out the electric instead. You were great though, you know. You should play with us more often.'

'Well, I guess it would give me something to do.'

I glanced over at Fran, who was lying back on a black chaise longue with claws for feet and an arm roll in the shape of a panther's head, deep in conversation with The Holy Criminals' drummer, Dagur, who sat opposite her. He wasn't as popular with the female fans as Viggo, but he had a certain worldliness about him and an intense stare that seemed to have captivated my sister.

Chris sighed. I'd noticed his interest in Fran and their instant spark from the moment I introduced them, but I wasn't sure yet how I felt about it. My best friend and my sister.

'Chin up,' I said to him. 'There's always Luba.'

'Luba?' he asked, confused.

'The dancer,' I replied casually, realising my mistake instantly.

'How did you know her name?'

I tried to feign nonchalance, kicking myself for letting it slip.

As if by magic, Luba appeared in the doorway behind us.

'We met very briefly in New York,' she said to Chris, in a tone as soft and soothing as a lullaby, her accent a purr. 'I attended one of her concerts. I'm flattered that you remembered me,' she said, giving me a warm smile. 'Especially in such a different costume.'

She had changed into a flowing black gown which was made of such thin material, she may as well have remained nude. Somehow, though, she looked sexier half clothed, with the fabric drawing attention to the subtle curve of her breasts and hips. She was uncommonly graceful, more like a swan than a human being. She sat down on the couch next to me, and crossed her legs at the ankle. Her hair was so blond it was closer to white, and she had light-blue eyes that were almost grey. Her eyebrows were so pale and delicate they were practically invisible, giving her face a slightly alien appearance, though she was by no means unattractive.

'I'm Luba,' she said to Chris, leaning over me to shake his hand.

'Chris,' he replied.

'Oh sorry,' I said. 'I forgot to introduce you.'

Her skin brushed against mine as she brought her arm back to her side.

Women like Luba didn't usually arouse me in the same way that men did. My predilections, as a general rule, lay firmly in favour of testosterone. I liked height, body hair and muscles, and if I had been inclined to experiment, I had thought that a butch, dyke-styled girl would be more my type. Lauralynn, the tall blonde who had played the cello in Dominik's string quartet the night we first had sex, after I performed naked for him in the crypt he had hired for the occasion, had been the exception. She and I had nearly had a bit of a fling, or so I imagined. She was a domme, and dominant folk of either gender were always likely to push my buttons.

Luba did not appear to be a dominatrix, per se, but she had a quality about her which made my skin tingle and my blood pump faster. I felt hot and light-headed.

Chris did not seem to be suffering from the same effect. He was beginning to look bored, and headed over to the bar where Viggo was still flamboyantly mixing drinks.

Luba leaned in close, lifting my hair up so that she could whisper in my ear.

Goosebumps rose on my arms in response to her nearness.

'Your secret is safe with me,' she said.

'Thank you. I appreciate that.'

'I do ask for one thing in exchange though,' she continued.

'Yes?'

'I want to hear the story, about how you ended up in a place like that. And the man you were with.'

She was referring to the villa in New Orleans, where I had danced naked for Dominik in the early hours of New Year's Day, after Luba had performed at the same venue professionally.

'Dominik?'

'I suppose so, if that's his name.'

She smiled at me, baring a set of white teeth. Two of her incisors were slightly pointed, like a pair of very gentle fangs. I wanted to feel them scratching against my skin.

'Did he ask you to dance for him?' she continued.

'Yes,' I replied, 'though "instructed" would be closer to the truth.' I shifted in my seat, searching for a way to redirect the conversation. It wasn't something I felt comfortable talking about, but neither did I want to move away from Luba.

Viggo appeared between us, holding a mojito in each hand.

'I see you've met my pet,' he said to me, handing me a drink. He'd gone all out, decorating the rim with brown sugar and a wedge of lime. It was so full of crushed ice that there was no room for it to chink, and the glass was so cold it was almost painful to hold. I immediately thought of Dominik, and how much he hated ice in his Coke.

Luba made a strange growling noise in the back of her throat, and nuzzled her head against Viggo's leg.

She did have a certain animal energy about her, from the way that she moved down to the way that she spoke, in a soft purr. Her movements were sometimes birdlike, and other times feline.

'Have you seen my Bailly?' I asked him, suddenly. Thinking of Dominik immediately brought the violin to my mind.

'Your violin?'

I nodded.

'I think the roadies were looking after it earlier.' He was scratching Luba's chin as if he was petting a cat. She had her eyes closed and was smiling with pleasure. 'It'll be in my studio, don't fret. With all the other gear. I can lend you one if you want to play something; I have all sorts of spare instruments in the basement.'

'No, it's OK, I just miss having it in my hands. I usually

carry it around myself. Even to my own gigs. For some reason I don't like it to be out of my sight.'

'That's very sweet,' he replied.

'Luba?' he said, his intonation a question.

She growled in response.

'Would you find Eric and check that Summer's violin went in with the other stuff?'

She nodded, uncurled herself from his leg and disappeared to find the road manager who had been in charge of moving all the equipment.

'Thank you,' I said to him, feeling foolish and unduly paranoid.

'Don't thank me,' he replied, leaning in towards me. 'I just wanted to get rid of her.'

He brushed his fingers gently up the base of my neck and into my hair, wrapping them tightly in my curls, and pulled me against him. His lips tasted of sugared lime, from sampling the mojitos. He ran one hand slowly up my skirt, searching for the waistband of my tights. My body responded immediately, coursed with a searing pleasure that soaked me with desire as his hand moved higher.

I pulled away. 'Not in front of my sister,' I hissed, though she looked happy as a pig in mud, wedged between Chris and Dagur who were both vying for her attention. Fran could certainly look after herself, and I knew that Chris would watch her like a hawk if I was to disappear. Ella and Ted seemed to have just about passed out already – they were both sprawled on a faux animal skin rug staring up at the ceiling, which was decorated with luminous stars and planets like a miniature solar system.

'Oh, what a shame,' he whispered into my ear, 'just as I was hoping you were kinky.'

He stood up quickly and took my hand, pulling me up with him and out the door, up another set of stairs to an entire floor which seemed to be just his bedroom. The bed was the size of four beds pressed together, and the whole room was decorated in white, from floor to ceiling and everything in between, including the paintings on the wall which appeared to be just blank canvases. It was like walking into a dream.

Viggo's black jeans and hair clashed awkwardly with the pale colour scheme. His body stood out starkly against the furnishings.

He turned to face me and held my chin in both of his hands, then tugged my hair back until I moaned.

'You like that, don't you?' he asked, pulling until my scalp began to tingle pleasantly.

'Yes,' I whispered.

'Good,' he said, pushing me up against the wall, his hand under my skirt again.

'Stockings are much easier for this,' he said.

'It's too cold,' I protested.

'Not when I'm with you, it won't be. Stay there.'

He stepped back a couple of paces and rolled open the bedside drawer, picking up a small object in the palm of his hand. A condom, I figured.

Then he returned to me and bent his face close to mine so his lips brushed against my ear. He exhaled deeply, his hot breath soft as a feather against my skin. 'Don't be afraid, OK?' he said. 'I'm not going to hurt you.'

A knot of worry twisted inside my chest, then relaxed again.

He opened his palm to display a small ivory pocket knife. The blade appeared with a flick of his wrist. It glinted prettily in the light of the nearby table lamp.

Fear bubbled up inside me, and I prepared to scream, or run for the door.

'Shhh,' he said, running his finger over my lips.

My heart thudded inside my chest, but I felt locked to the wall, imprisoned by my own desire to find out what he was going to do next. Perhaps I was a fool to trust him, but nonetheless I did. He was eccentric, a bit of a bad boy, but not dangerous.

He crouched down and ran the tip of the knife blade up my legs, from my ankle to the gusset of my tights. Then he pressed the tip against the fabric a little harder, just enough to create a small tear, without damaging the skin under-neath. A small voice in the back of my head wondered how it would feel if he pressed harder, if he left a mark, a scratch, or even drew blood. I had a vision of my inner thighs, the skin pale, soft, pure, but for two long shallow cuts, one running down the centre of each leg, a red stripe that would throb for days but send endorphins rushing to my brain along with pain.

Another part of my mind recoiled in horror at the images rolling out in my mind but despite that, my underwear was damp.

Viggo pushed a finger into the hole to increase the size of the tear, and then took hold of the fabric of my tights with both hands and pulled viciously, ripping a hole that exposed my underwear and the tops of my thighs. I flinched. He pulled my panties to the side and ran the flat of the blade very delicately over my wet lips.

The touch of the knife was like a metallic kiss, cold and solid. My pulse was beating so fast I felt almost faint, in a heady mixture of terror and lust. It was like being on a theme park ride, that combination of fright, thrill and adrenalin making me feel as though my heart was pumping in my fingertips.

I heard a faint swish, as he flicked the blade back into place, and then the cold sensation again as he inserted the body of the knife inside me. I shivered and let out a low moan, but the handle was too small to do anything other than tease me. I needed more.

I buried my hands into his hair and shifted his head, pushing him closer between my legs.

'Lick me,' I said.

He complied, dropping the knife so it clattered to the floor and then moving his tongue against my clit in long, slow strokes. It was the first time I could recall that I'd actually told a man what I wanted of my own accord, without being made to beg, and the thrill of discovery gave me an even greater rush than the sensation that Viggo was producing with his mouth.

Though the pace he had chosen was steady, the rhythmic feeling of his tongue against me, slowly, calmly bringing me towards orgasm, was almost more than I could bear. Noticing my desire increase he pulled away playfully, making me wait, drawing it out.

I pulled him to his feet again and kissed him, deep and slow. He had extraordinarily soft lips which contrasted pleasantly with the scratch of his stubble. His tongue tangled with mine very gently. Viggo knew not to overdo a kiss. I took his bottom lip between my teeth and nipped.

'Oh,' he said, pulling his head away. 'I like you a lot. Come to bed.'

He took my hand and led me over to the mattress then sat down on the edge and turned to face me, running his hands over my arms and shoulders and settling around my waist, closing his legs over mine like a vice.

'Take your clothes off for me.'

'You're not going to cut them off too?' I asked teasingly.

'Denim is a lot harder to get through than nylon,' he stated, his eyes narrowing in a way that suggested that he wouldn't mind giving it a try just the same. However, I had no wish to have my clothes cut to bits, if for no other reason than I needed them to get home in.

I began to remove my clothes, hurriedly, asked teasingly.

'No,' he said, 'do it slowly. I want to watch you.'

His eyes lit up and he stared at me with the same fixated gaze that I had noticed when I'd been playing the Bailly.

My heart began to pound, in response to his commands, and my fingers shook so that I could barely grasp the button on my miniskirt and unhook it through the thick denim buttonhole.

I was pleased I'd put on a set of matching underwear; a pair of pale-blue French knickers and a matching bra set, nice enough to look good but not so risqué that it would be immediately obvious that I had left the house with sex in mind.

I unbuttoned my blouse slowly, feeling a little silly and self-conscious at the idea of doing a striptease, but my confidence increased as I noticed the expression on his face becoming more and more intense with each button that I undid.

He visibly inhaled and held his breath as I unhooked my bra, and then with my breasts bared, hooked a thumb slowly into my tights and began to push them down over my hips.

'Leave the tights on,' he said. 'And the boots. That's kind of hot.' I was wearing my cherry-red patent Dr Martens. Viggo didn't have any mirrors at all in his bedroom, though I guessed that he probably had a luxurious mirrored bathroom or perhaps a walk-in wardrobe nearby. I couldn't see myself, but I guessed that I must look like one of the Suicide Girls, naked except for a pair of ripped tights and red DM's.

I knelt down on the floor so I could unbutton his jeans and pull them off. He was commando, I discovered, when I managed to pull the tight denim down as far as his thighs.

His cock sprang up, fully erect. It was long and slim, like the rest of him, and perfectly straight, like something carved out of marble. He had trimmed his pubic hair so that the area around the base of his shaft was perfectly smooth. I was a little disappointed about that, as I prefer hair on a man. I like to run my fingers through it when I suck a cock, or feel it when I run my hand under a man's belt, like a promise of hidden secrets.

I gave up trying to get his jeans off.

'How do you get into these things?' I laughed, as he wriggled up the bed with them still on.

'I jump and pull,' he replied. 'There's an art to it.'

He grabbed my wrists and pulled me up onto the bed

after him and placed his hand firmly on my waist, indicating that he wanted me to roll over.

'On your knees,' he ordered.

By now I was so desperate to feel him inside me that I was in position almost before the instruction had come out of his mouth.

He moved down, I felt his tongue wet against my ankle, rasping. He began to lick upwards, slow and rough.

'Shh,' he said, as I began to wriggle at the ticklish sensation. 'Relax.'

I concentrated on blanking my mind, pushing away all the other distractions and just focusing on the sensations arising within my body. His movements were firm and thorough. His mouth travelled up my calf, pausing to lick the crevice on the inside of my knee, then continuing up the inside of my thigh, where I was certain that he must have noticed the wetness that I could feel was now seeping down my legs. My breathing began to quicken as his tongue neared my pussy, where I desperately wanted him to linger, but rather than stopping in the obvious place he continued further upward and began to lick my arsehole.

Dominik had done this once, in New Orleans, not long after I had danced for him on stage the day after we'd witnessed Luba's act. I remembered feeling embarrassed at this most intimate of explorations and attempting to wriggle away, and how he had put his hand on the base of my spine to hold me still.

I shook thoughts of Dominik from my head. He was long gone, and Viggo was right here, a hot man with a hotter mouth, and a rock star to boot. I might have been one of hundreds of women he'd made love to but I didn't care. At least he'd had plenty of practice.

I wriggled back further against him and spread my knees apart a little wider.

'Good girl,' he said. 'You like it the Catholic way, I take it?'

I remembered the shape of his cock, long and slim, perfectly built for anal sex.

'Yes,' I replied. 'If you start slowly.'

'I'll be gentle, promise. But I'm saving that for later.'

He reached over to his bedside drawer again and pulled out a box of condoms, a bottle of lube, and the biggest sex toy I'd ever seen. It was about a foot long, white with a blue ring around the ball-like attachment at the top, and attached to a plug, and an adaptor.

'Jeezus,' I said. 'What the hell is that thing?'

'You've never seen one of these before?' He smiled wickedly. 'You're in for a treat. It's a Hitachi magic wand.'

'There's no way that will go inside me,' I said, anxiety tainting my growing arousal.

'Don't worry, my pet. It doesn't go inside you.'

He slid off the bed and plugged it into an extension lead, and then into the wall, before flicking it on. It made a sound somewhere between a lawnmower and an electric grinder, and the ball on the top was vibrating so hard, it visibly shook.

'Relax,' he laughed, watching my response.

He resumed his position behind me and touched the head of the wand very gently against my labia. A wave of pleasure pulsed through my body like a lightning bolt. I felt as though I was going to come within seconds, a response that even with the most skilful lovers usually took a good thirty minutes of foreplay at a minimum to elicit from me. I gasped, and jolted forward in shock.

'Are you all right?' he asked, still chuckling softly.

I turned to look at him. He still had his jeans wrapped around his legs, inhibiting his movements, and a firm erection which he so far had not attempted to pleasure me with. His hair was backcombed into a messy bush with a few straight locks that fell over his eyes. He had a wolfish expression, good-natured and mischievous. I found it hard to believe that he had looked so savage, just minutes ago, when he'd been tearing a hole in my clothing with his pocket knife.

'Yes, it's just, I thought I was going to come. I never orgasm that quickly.'

'It's not like there's a moratorium on orgasms, darling. You're allowed to have more than one.'

'I've never had more than one. In one go, I mean.'

'Well then, all your other lovers ought to be ashamed of themselves.'

'I don't have any other lovers.'

'A girl like you? I find that hard to believe.'

I didn't have a chance to respond, as he flicked the wand on again and pressed it against me. He pressed lightly at first, until I relaxed against him, then he steadily increased the pressure. At first I felt an increasing warmth, as if all of my nerve endings had become radioactive, and then an orgasm ripped through my body like a wildfire, one huge burst of energy rushing in through the tips of my toes and out through my head. It was the most intense climax I'd ever had.

I couldn't speak. I collapsed on the bed in a heap, suffused in a warm glow, my skin alive to every brush of air or slight movement in the room.

'You get one minute's rest,' he said, 'then I'm going again.'

I lay silent for a few moments before I was able to gather my wits to respond.

'What are you, my personal trainer?'

'If that's what it takes. Sounds to me like you have some catching up to do.'

He began to stroke my buttocks gently, running his nails over my skin.

Viggo was true to his word. Within a minute, though it felt like only a few seconds, the whirr of the wand's vibrations filled the room so loudly I thought that the noise must be interrupting the party downstairs.

He pressed the head of the toy against me and again within moments a second orgasm tore through my body. This time, though, the pleasure teetered on the edge of too intense and I jumped, nearly hitting my head on the wall in my effort to escape.

'Stay still. Or I'll have to restrain you.' His tone was amused, but with a hint of steeliness.

'Seriously,' I pleaded, 'I can't take any more.'

'Yes you can. Hold onto the headboard.'

I gritted my teeth and wrapped my hands around the white metal border that framed the head of the bed. He didn't restrain me, but the power of his instruction, and that formidable pride which refused to let him win had kicked in and I locked myself into place as he made me come again and again.

By the time he let me rest, my body was twitching and my lips were swollen and bruised. I was sweaty and bits of my hair stuck to my face. I was overcome by a flood of exhaustion. The sky was beginning to lighten outside. Viggo didn't have any blinds in his white room; he must enjoy the light. A crimson-coloured sun was rising. It must be around 7 a.m., I guessed, meaning that we had been up here enjoying our party of two for about five hours. Neither of us had had a minute's sleep. Fran, under normal circumstances, would be awake by now – she had always been an early riser – but since she had been working in the bar, she'd become more nocturnal. The rest of the band were like bats, awake all night, and asleep during the day. So we had a few more hours to relax before anyone would expect to see us.

Viggo lay down next to me, tracing his finger gently from the base of my earlobe across my jaw and then along the curve of my neck. He lingered on my throat, increasing the pressure in the pads of his fingertips as if he was measuring my heartbeat. I shivered involuntarily in response. The journey of his hands continued, trailing over each of my breasts and around my nipples. His touch was so light he barely grazed my skin, but I was so wired from our previous exertions that the slightest contact made me twitch.

Eventually he reached the base of my navel, as far as his arms would reach while he was lying down. He snuggled into my back, drawing me close against him, and his cock, still rock hard, poked against my lower back. I tried to turn to face him.

'I'm sorry,' I said. 'I should really do something about that.'

'Plenty of time for that later,' he replied. 'I'm just warming up.' His voice trailed off into a sigh, and I felt his cock gradually soften against me. He was asleep in moments.

I followed him into dreamland shortly after, but not before spying, out of the corner of my eye, the pocket knife lying on the floor near the door. The blade was folded back into the handle, and the slice of silver from the back of the knife glinted in the light. It looked harmless enough, a pretty weapon, abandoned. But my last thoughts as I drifted into sleep were ominous, and I awoke a few hours later with the unshakeable sense that something was wrong.

My phone was buzzing in the pocket of my denim skirt which lay in a heap alongside my top and ripped tights, which I had removed along with my boots before we settled down to sleep.

It was full of texts from Fran and Chris.

From Chris: 'Are you up yet? We're cooking pancakes.'

From Fran: 'Wake up, dirty slapper!'

Both brought a smile to my face.

I slipped out of bed and slid open a few doors until I found an en suite. Viggo was still sleeping soundly, with his shoes on and his skinny jeans holding fast halfway down his legs. His dark hair was matted and spread out on all sides like a dark halo.

Freshly showered, I slipped back into yesterday's clothes, sans tights, and made my way downstairs to find the kitchen, led mainly by the smell of butter burning in a pan.

Dagur was standing over a frying pan deftly flipping rounds of batter to brown each side before sliding them onto a plate that was already stacked high with pancakes. He was shirtless, clad in just a pair of jeans with frayed slits under each cheek of his arse, revealing a hint of bare skin when he leant forward that suggested he was naked underneath. He had a tattoo on his back of a beautiful and rather feminine horse's head, a delicately rendered piece of art that contrasted with his thick, swarthy musculature. He was ripped. I hadn't noticed it last night. No wonder my sister had found him captivating.

Fran danced like a pixie around the kitchen alongside him, pulling open cupboards and drawers until she found plates, cutlery, maple syrup and all the other accoutrements to spread over the breakfast bar.

Chris, Ella and Ted were balanced on stools, poised with forks in hand waiting to tuck in.

They looked much fresher after their night's sleep than I felt.

'Morning. Did you lot find beds, then?' I asked with a forced brightness that I wasn't feeling.

'Some of us did,' Ted said, laughing under his breath and looking pointedly at Fran, who looked pleased as punch, not a hint of a blush on her cheeks.

Chris was sitting with his shoulders slumped, in the posture of a defeated man.

I didn't want to know what my sister had been up to, providing that she was happy, but neither did I want to see my best friend looking sad.

I stood alongside him and threw my arm over his shoulder, giving him a squeeze.

'Whatcha up to today?' I asked, hoping to distract him from the sight of Fran flirting with the handsome drummer.

'Back to the studio,' he replied. 'Need to clear up our stuff, get used to the idea of normal life again, and hope that the reviews are good. Or that we even get a mention.'

'Of course you'll get a mention. You guys were amazing, the crowd loved you.'

'Thanks, Sum,' he said, putting his arm around me. 'We've got a gig in Brighton next week, if you want to come.'

'Sure. I love Brighton.' I'd only been once for a weekend. Maybe another couple of days by the seaside would be just the ticket to bump me out of my recent creative slump.

'Has anyone here seen Luba? The dancer?' I asked, after we'd finished breakfast. I wanted to know whether she'd got hold of Eric, the roadie who had been in charge of moving all the gear.

'Not today,' Dagur replied. 'I thought she ended up in bed with you.'

I blushed as I realised what he meant, and that he was being completely serious. He had noticed then, the effect she had on me.

'No,' I replied. 'I haven't seen her since last night.'

'I'll check on your violin, Sum,' Chris said, anticipating my concern before I'd had a chance to voice it.

Viggo still hadn't stirred by the time the band disappeared to collect the gear and Fran raced to catch her shift at the bar. I almost went with Chris, but a nagging feeling in the back of my mind made me stay behind. I told the others I didn't want to leave without telling Viggo goodbye, and Chris and Fran both stared at me suspiciously.

'Not like you to be sentimental,' Fran said. 'Are you in love?'

Naturally, I protested vigorously, but the truth was I rather fancied Viggo. He had a humour and sense of mischief about him that I found attractive, not to mention his ability and desire to make me orgasm. That and a streak of arrogance which made him unpredictable, and I liked to be kept on my toes.

I settled into Viggo's vast and empty living room to check my emails and surf the internet on my phone while I waited for him to wake up, or Luba to appear.

There were two from Susan, both wondering what I was up to and advising me in no uncertain terms to get in contact with her so we could plan my future. One from Simón, a friendly update of his current circumstances. He'd lengthened his stay in Venezuela and the orchestra had taken on a temporary substitute. I had a pang of homesickness for him, for New York, and the life that we shared together. We hadn't been right for each other but I'd loved him nonetheless and I missed his affection, his company and his instinctive understanding of my career and the travails of a classical musician.

We were suited in so many ways that sometimes I wondered whether we could have worked it out, if we had tried harder, but he'd taken that decision out of my hands. In a way I was relieved. It had meant that I didn't have to make the choice, to admit to myself or to him that finding the right person to have sex with was more important to me than all the other qualities he offered in our relationship.

Short-term vanilla sex was lovely, and scratched an itch, but long term, I didn't want to commit to someone who didn't want to do the things to me that I craved. Dark things, dangerous and hurtful things. The sorts of things that Dominik had enjoyed so much.

Recurring thoughts of Dominik made me uncomfortable and restless, and I began to wander the room, running my hands over the walls and furniture to feel their textures, rough against my skin. I replayed the memory of Luba's dance in my head, and despite last night's countless orgasms and the feeling of my bruised and swollen labia I was aroused, again. But more than anything I missed my violin. I wanted to feel the Bailly in my hands, to wear out the mixed emotions that swamped my brain, with a song.

Viggo had said that he had a number of instruments in the basement. I didn't feel entirely right about going to investigate without his express permission. I'd never been one for snooping. But I wasn't prying, I told myself, just borrowing something that he'd said only twelve hours earlier that I was welcome to use.

After looking for a few minutes, I found the door that led to the basement and followed the spiral staircase downwards with some trepidation. You would think that he'd have been able to install a lift, but I hadn't seen one. There were two more floors below the entrance, art space and kitchen area where we'd had breakfast. The first was surprisingly light and airy, considering that it was underground. He must have oxygen pumping in, I thought, perhaps as a way to preserve the art on the walls. The room was like a gallery with a number of pieces tastefully distributed on the walls, and a couple of modern sculptures, more like installations in the middle. I knew very little about art, and didn't know whether the pieces were genuine or knock-offs, expensive or fakes. Some, I thought, seemed like a joke, an example of Viggo's unusual sense of humour. One was a small coloured ball suspended in the air by a fan blowing beneath it, so it appeared to be floating, untethered in space. It was situated in such a way as to entice the viewer to snatch it up, but there was an unspoken rule firm in my mind, the knowledge that one reveres art and doesn't touch it, that made me watch it closely from a polite step away without disrupting its trajectory.

The next floor down was a much darker room with, at its centre, a swimming pool. It was more like an indoor stream than a swimming pool. The water seemed to be fresh rather than chlorinated, and instead of the traditional rectangular concrete box of a regular pool, this one curved through the room and was laid with stones and surrounded by ferns and even a waterfall at one end.

So the rumours about Viggo having tanks in his house for women pretending to be mermaids were true after all. Luba was sitting on a stone next to the waterfall, looking for all the world like a mermaid, wearing a metallic swimsuit which was slick with water and stuck to her skin so her hard nipples were clearly visible through the fabric. Her long hair was wet and clung to her shoulders.

She smiled at me, but didn't say anything, as if she had expected me to find her down here all along and wasn't in the least bit surprised.

My eyes had adjusted to the dimmer light in the room, and I noticed that the walls in here were also decorated with art pieces, but here they were mostly scattered around the walls or hanging from the ceiling, seemingly at random, and the pieces were much wilder, and darker, I thought. Viggo had the bones of an animal's face, attached to a long pair of antlers, hanging over the door. There were carved figures of nymphs and grotesques, some sensual and some frightening. I lifted my head and looked up to see that he had a series of metal sculptures, presumably rust-treated, fixed to the ceiling over the pool, so that someone lying on their back, floating in the water, would be able to look at them. At the end of the room was another heavy door, the first I had seen so far that appeared to be locked. That must be where he kept the really expensive stuff, I guessed, and couldn't blame him for it. Security in this place seemed surprisingly low, considering the number of people he must have roaming around at most of his parties. His insurance premiums must be enormous.

One wall in this room was lined with a glass case, and in the case was the collection of instruments that I had been looking for. Viggo had guitars, wind instruments, violas and violins. Some were more modern and fairly nondescript, others looked immensely beautiful to my relatively untrained eye. The light wasn't good and I couldn't get close enough to make out any distinguishing markings or check the few violins for signatures.

The glass case, I saw, was unlocked, and I had to push away an almost overwhelming desire to open it, pick up one of the instruments and play something, but the presence of Luba made that seem an impossibility. I could not take something that didn't belong to me while she watched, even if Viggo had told me that I could. Right now, he was unaware that I was here.

Luba stood up, as gracefully as a fern unfurling itself, and stepped out from the stone by the waterfall onto the side where I stood, and padded over to me.

'He won't mind, you know,' she said. 'If you want to borrow something.'

She opened the door where the violins hung, and gestured towards them. 'He likes to collect beautiful things, but he's very free with them. Will you play something for me?'

I wondered if she was one of the beautiful things that he liked to collect.

I picked up one of the instruments and a bow, held it to my chin, and began to play. The sound was awful at first, and it took me a few minutes to tune it. But the tone was pretty, and the violin felt pleasant in my hand. It wasn't the Bailly though, and that recollection reminded me why I had been looking for Luba in the first place.

'Did you speak to Eric?' I asked her. 'Did he say if he'd picked my violin up last night?'

Before I could get the words out, Luba held a finger up to my mouth, and she ran her fingertip along my lower lip. Her touch made my heart beat wildly. She was soft and sleek and smelled sweet like sugar. She removed her finger, and replaced it with her mouth, pressing her lips against mine in a slow kiss. My tongue entwined with hers, and she pressed herself against me, dampening my body with her wet bathing suit. She slid her hands up the back of my neck, holding my head in place while she kissed me.

Luba was mesmerising, like one of the nude statues come to life, but with all the warmth of a human being. Her touch on my skin felt like electricity, and for the first time in my life, I really wanted to explore every part of her, a woman, not just out of a curiosity to try on bisexuality for a night but because she made my whole body feel alive.

'Let's go,' she whispered in my ear. 'There are more comfortable places for this.' She took my hand and pulled me out the door with her, and up the stairs, all five flights up to Viggo's room. Not for the first time, I wished for an elevator but the thought was lost in the vision of her arse wiggling attractively, framed by the wet fabric of her high-cut one-piece which was either one size too small or deliberately designed to reveal half of each of her butt cheeks.

Viggo was in the shower when we arrived on the fifth floor.

'Come on,' Luba said, mischievously, approaching the door to the en suite. 'Let's wish him good morning.'

He certainly seemed pleased, if not surprised, when we undressed and then opened the door of his oversized shower and joined him in it.

The cubicle was large, but it was still cramped with the three of us packed inside. Luba wriggled out of the way, pressing me firmly between her and Viggo.

He spun me to face him and bent his head down for a kiss, meeting my lips with his own as he tangled his fingers in my hair and Luba ran her soapy hands between our bodies, her breasts pushed against my back.

Viggo made no move to turn off the shower, allowing the water to course over us, so I felt as though I was drowning in his kiss. He moved his hands to pull my nipples fiercely, and I gasped in the shock of sudden pain, so at odds with Luba's light caresses.

She laughed softly.

'He is not always gentle,' she whispered, bending down so that she could speak into my ear. I refrained from telling her that I preferred it that way.

His cock was now pressing against my thigh, and I ached to feel it inside me.

I moaned, a sound full of need, barely holding myself back from pressing him inside me unprotected.

It was Luba who reached behind us and flicked the water off, and then led us both out of the shower and onto the bed, oblivious to the water dripping all over the covers.

She reached into the bedside drawer and threw him a condom, which he caught with such a practised flick of the wrist, that I wondered how often they operated as a two-some.

'Put the girl out of her misery,' she said in her slow, seductive drawl.

'Always happy to oblige,' he replied.

It was dark when I realised that I still hadn't spoken to Chris. Viggo was asleep again, tangled up on the bed with Luba. Her now dry white-blond hair contrasted vividly with his black locks.

That must be a good sign, I thought. Chris would have called me straight away if he hadn't found my instrument in with all the other stuff. I'd been worrying needlessly. Then I remembered, with a sinking feeling in my heart, that I had left my phone in the living room with the fountain in it, when I'd gone to explore the house, hours ago now.

I padded down the steps, a feeling of dread hanging around my shoulders like a dark cloud.

My phone sat on the arm of the panther chaise longue, just where I had left it.

I picked it up and tapped in the passcode.

It was Chris. Three missed calls, a voicemail and a text message.

'Your violin. It's gone.'

6

The Brighton Front

When he had still been lecturing, Dominik could rely on the comfort of some sort of routine, a pattern of hours divided between preparing his talks, the lectures themselves, tutorials, marking and the regular pilgrimage down from the greenery of Hampstead on the northern line to the point where he merged into the busy grey crowds of the centre of town.

Now that he had given up academia for writing, he felt himself adrift, with no fixed point in the middle of a sea of indecision, a slave to his keyboard and the dismissive glare of the computer screen as he scrambled not so much for inspiration but for the right words.

The long day lay ahead of him, its emptiness a deep well of temptations from the moment he achieved his daily target of pages. There were occasions when everything flowed and, always an early riser, he would reach that liberating point by mid-morning and would then treat himself to a late breakfast as a reward for a job well done. On other days, however, the work proved an uphill task, more full of deletions than new lines.

But he had always been a strongly disciplined person and he stuck to the task at hand, the oasis at the end of the long slog being the prospect of leisurely empty beaches of free time when he could read, watch movies on DVD without feeling guilty or, more often than not, explore the nooks and crannies of the Internet with a mixture of detached amusement or a measure of interest in the women he came across there.

With every name flashing across the screen, Dominik would replay the episodes in which other women with the same names, or other ones – they all had become a blur in his mind – had featured and which made him the man he now was. Christel, the German au pair who lived in an attic space and had been at least ten years older than him and for whom he had pined since the day she had taken a shower in his presence and hadn't minded his watching (or his hard on), and the weekend when he had run like a madman backwards and forwards from his base at the local Youth Hostel through the Vallée de Chevreuse in search of her. Or Catherine, who had the privilege of having been the first to break his heart when he discovered she had slept with another, the first in a seductive procession of Catherines, Kats, Cats, Kates and Kathryns. And then there had been Maryann, the American exchange student, whom you could do anything to as long as you didn't touch her breasts, followed by Danielle whose sexual appetites had initially scared him and whom he had shamefully deserted in her hour of need. Aida who sucked his cock like no other, with an appetite that was never sated. The list was a long one. Rhoona who wanted to be spanked. Parvin who insisted on keeping her top on as she was embarrassed by the roundness of her stomach. Rebecca who invariably cried when she came and fell into a deep-blue funk, until the next time when she promised she wouldn't, but of course always did.

And then there was Kathryn, of course.

After whom everything had changed.

The way her grey-green eyes had begged him to hold her neck tight as they fucked. The imploring for him to act rough and take her to the edge, to pin her arms down until his fingers left a deep mark on her wrists, to pull mercilessly on her hair as he took her from behind, to tighten the teasing hold of his teeth on her nipples. The constant mute demand to explore new boundaries.

There was a before and an after Kathryn.

And he had begun to assert himself more in the bedroom, or wherever the sex took place, dominating his lovers by instinct and inclination and discovering, much to his initial surprise, that so many women were not put off and even – like Claudia – welcomed this new side of him.

Which had led to Summer.

Dominik sighed and idly began clicking on some of the profiles on the contacts website he had out of habit summoned up from the long column of bookmarks on his laptop.

Willing victims or predators? Or just normal people, like him, subject to a spider's web of compulsions that warped their minds into perverse imaginings and compulsions?

He had long learned to navigate the words and thoughts that appeared between the lines of the profiles, becoming adept at recognising the flakes, the fakers and the jokers. He also made it a habit – snobbish, he knew, but the rule had seldom let him down – to skim over any profile or ads which were badly spelled or featured particularly bad grammar. He preferred his fucks to be literate, and if this elitist part of his character excluded a good proportion of the submissive women in search of domination, then he could live with it without too many regrets.

Lost in thought, Dominik was about to desert the shady dark alleys of the web when a window on his screen opened, indicating he had mail via his Facebook page.

A fan, it seemed, who had liked his novel and sent him a complimentary note. Even though the book had enjoyed a modicum of success, getting readers' letters was still an uncommon thing, and appealed to his vanity.

It was the usual guff about how she loved the story and identified with the main female character in which she saw a lot of herself. Dominik smiled. It was a comfort that people were still reading the novel. For him, it felt like so long ago now.

On the left of his screen, a green dot indicated the sender not only had the same email provider but was still online. He typed a message.

> Thank you for the kind words, Liana.

The response reached him immediately.

> Not at all, I really loved the story. Found it so
> moving. Wow, and now I'm talking to you . . .

Dominik was intrigued, and one thing soon led to another. He briefly considered the ethics of the situation and decided the relationship between a writer and a reader was above board, and had no similarities, moral or otherwise, with that between teacher and student. On the contrary, he reassured himself.

She was a young woman in her mid-twenties by the look of the photograph on her profile. If the image was recent, of course. She told him she had an office job in Brighton. The later photographs she volunteered to send him after a few days of generally innocent chats, had migrated to flirtatious and teasing, proving both explicit and restrained, lacking vulgarity despite their amateur nature. A flash of breast, a half moon of buttock with a hint of past bruises or marks, a fuzzy almost abstract composition which turned out on further examination to be a close-up of her red pubic curls from an angle which at first sight gave them the appearance of a seductive alien landscape. She continuously brought up the fact that she had much in common with Elena, his heroine, despite the differences in nationality, eras and circumstances. When Dominik asked her whether these heavy hints meant if she was submissive sexually, her answer lit up his screen.

Yes.

His heart jumped. Might this be a chance to start again. Do things right this time?

And you, Dom?

Maybe, he answered, teasing her. Hmmm . . .

He was normally suspicious when a woman was too detailed about her tastes, needs and cravings. The more they wrote about extreme sexual practices from bondage to restraints, asphyxiation, ropes, collars, degradation, humiliation or whatever was the flavour of the day, the more it indicated that they were in fact unlikely to go through with it when it came to the crunch. A more limited menu was classier and more authentic and true to life, he reckoned.

Liana was interesting. She kept on dropping heavy hints

but they were also tinged with a touch of humour and deprecation, and featured all the right elements to attract his attention.

They had been sparring live online and through emails for a couple of weeks already and Dominik was warming to the idea of an adventure. Somehow hoping not that this could prove the love of his life but that it might help once and for all banish the spectre and memories of Summer.

Do you have a face pic, pse

He had deliberately refrained from having his photo on the book's dust jacket, and kept his Facebook image ambiguous, preferring at the time a form of mysterious anonymity.

Maybe it would be at this stage that he lost her. Dominik had always disliked being captured by the photographic lens and there were surprisingly few pictures of him in existence.

He downloaded a rare image, a photo he'd had taken to accompany his application for the New York fellowship a few years back and pressed Send.

Yet again there was now a fifty–fifty chance that she would disconnect if he didn't fit her criterion for whatever reason he would for ever remain unaware of. Once she saw the man behind the writer.

He waited, his fingers hovering over the keyboard, his eyes fixed on the image he had called up of her bruised arse cheek, idly seeking patterns in the yellow, brown and purple stains of the bruise which he had blown up to full-screen size, colours indistinctly merging softly into each other. It now looked like a work of modern art. Enigmatic, random. Like a fuzzy cloud unforming and reassembling. A screen saver.

The response came.

Tasty. And should I call you Sir?

You flatter me. But no need to call me Sir. I'm not that kind of dom . . . it's not about words.

Good. I always find it ridiculous when so many guys demand to be addressed that way within a few lines when you haven't even met.

A girl after my own heart . . .

I think this could be the beginning of a wonderful friendship.

Dominik smiled.

The train rushed across the South Downs and as it approached the steel cavern of Brighton station, Dominik could smell the sea and hear the herring gulls fluttering above. It had been ages since he had last been here, using a conference as an excuse. On the only occasion Kathryn had been able to get away from home, her husband, and spend a rare couple of nights with him. Maybe that was why he had never come back. The memories. Not that they had seen much of the city – apart from walks on the seafront and through the Lanes, and rushed seafood restaurant meals – beyond the private world of their bedroom.

There was a big convention in town and most of the major hotels were full, but he had managed to get a room at a so-called rock 'n' roll boutique hotel called the Pelirocco on Regency Square. Every room had a different theme and he had been allocated one in which the decor evoked a camp boudoir, with pinks and reds the dominant colours and a panorama of female underwear in all shapes, sizes and compositions adorning the walls, replacing the more traditional paintings or prints. It was a bit overwhelming and not a bit incongruous, but it brought a smile to his face, bearing in mind the nature of his visit to Brighton.

They had agreed to meet on neutral territory first, next to a fish and chip stall by the entrance to the pier. When he had asked how he would identify her as her face didn't always appear clearly on the photos she had sent him, she had joked he would have no difficulty in doing so. This of course provided her with the opportunity not to make contact if her initial sight of him in the flesh did not please her.

He arrived a few minutes early and was thinking of treating himself to a portion of chips when a chirpy voice greeted him.

'Hello, Dominik.'

'Liana, I presume?'

'Were you expecting anyone else?' She sounded amused.

'Do you have a real name?' he asked.

'Liana.'

'Good.'

She was slight in stature, almost spindly at first appearance, but stood resolutely straight, the weight of an oversize rucksack strapped to her shoulders maintaining her equilibrium, an untidy mop of auburn hair, almost boyish, crowning her delicate features. She wore a thin silk choker around her neck. On others it would have looked like an affectation or a misplaced attempt at being fashionable; on her it hinted at so much more. Just a hint. Now he knew what she had meant. However, she was not dressed, contrary to his expectation, in fierce black leather or torn jeans to compound some punk ethos, but in a surprisingly demure beige cotton blouse and a pleated skirt in darker brown which reached down to just below her knees. Around each wrist she wore identical thin silver bracelets. And clearly secure in her lack of height, she wore flat ballet shoes.

Her features were impish, making her look much younger than she probably was, small, turned-up nose, a weakish chin but full scarlet lips, eyes dark-green pits and a natural Snow White circle of crimson highlighting her prominent cheekbones. He thought she had a good figure, though the looseness of her blouse obscured her curves.

Liana looked up at him.

'Do you like what you see? So far?' she asked him.

'I do.'

In his mind over the past few days, Dominik had long rehearsed the situation, imagining some of the games they could play, indulge in, how he could get the best out of Liana's undeniable nature, make her properly his. He'd always been ignorant or confused about the etiquette of such situations. Should he offer her a drink, a coffee, something stronger, and engage in innocuous conversation to delay the inevitable moment when they would cross into intimacy? Walk along the promenade like a real couple? Or should they proceed straight to the hotel, barely half a mile down the seafront in the direction of Hove? Maybe someone should one day write a book about the dos and don'ts of BDSM encounters.

The room.

In the narrow lift taking them to the top floor, Liana was

pressed tight against him, the rucksack on her back restricting her movements.

'Kiss me,' Dominik ordered.

She got up on tiptoe and he lowered his lips to meet her. She tasted of mint chewing gum.

'I didn't choose the room; it was the only one left. I know it's a bit ridiculous,' he apologised as he unlocked the door and ushered Liana in and she was exposed to the garish decor.

'Wow,' she said, looking at the parade of framed brassieres and thongs circling the walls of the small room like a line of exhibits in a museum. 'Nifty. Although most of them don't appear to be my size, I fear . . .'

She slid the straps of the rucksack from her shoulders and it dropped to the floor.

'What have you got in there, all your mortal belongings?' Dominik queried.

'Nah,' Liana said. 'Stuff, you know. Some toys . . .'

'A bit presumptuous of you, no? Did I say you should bring things along?'

'I just assumed from our chats that you were unlikely to have your own . . .'

'We might not need them.'

'Oh . . .' She smiled.

Dominic dropped his room keys on the bedside table and turned to face her. 'Let me see you, then. Undress.'

'Now?'

'Now.'

She gave him a look of uncertainty, realising they had reached a point of no return.

'As we agreed,' she said firmly, strengthening her resolve. 'No permanent marks?'

'Understood. And you remember your safe word?'

'Of course.'

Liana undressed until all she was wearing was the thin strip of silk around her neck, and the matching bracelets on her wrists.

She was thin and fragile, but beautifully proportioned. The valley leading to her small breasts was peppered by freckles, as were her forearms, her nipples a subtle reddish hue, her thighs milky and, since the photo she had sent him, she had shaved below so that he could now make out a series of intimate piercings. There was a minuscule ring emerging from the actual bud of her clitoris and, below, two larger steel rings seemingly holding her labia apart.

Dominik held his breath.

He knew he could have stood there gazing at the intricate geometry of her cunt and its cyberpunk private landscape of flesh and steel for hours on end out of sheer fascination.

'Turn round,' he ordered her.

She swivelled on one foot like a ballerina rehearsing her stage movements.

Her narrow buttocks were now clean of past bruises.

'Bend.'

Liana followed his instructions, her feet shuffling on the room's thin carpet as she leaned over at a ninety-degree angle, her chest parallel to the floor, her arse prominently on display, the dark line bisecting her cheeks like a frontier carved by a knife, straight and inviolable.

'Legs apart.'

She obeyed.

Dominik approached her, passed his hand between her legs, feeling the heat, extending a finger to gauge her wetness, slipped it inside to get a taste of her heat, brushing against the rings, pulled gently on one of the labia adornments. He heard and felt Liana holding her breath as he did so.

He felt a compulsion to spank her arse cheeks with terrible strength but resisted the craving. He had all the time in the world. There was no hurry. She had submitted already. A part of him wondered why; he was still a stranger to her. As she was to him. He yearned to hear her story, every small step that had brought her to this place and time. The tale of every man who had touched her, made her who she was. Each degree of further submission on a road of unknown destination.

'Hold yourself open,' he barked hoarsely.

Still bent over, Liana brought her hands back and held her arse cheeks apart, providing him with an unimpeded view of the pucker of her arsehole, and the concentric lines and folds of flesh surrounding it like a target and the coral pinkness of her cunt.

It was a spectacle he knew he would never tire of.

'Who owns you now?' he asked the young woman as she stood with her back to him, fully displayed.

'You own me.'

'And what do you want now?' he asked.

'I want you to use me, to fuck me.'

'Why?'

For a brief moment, she was taken aback, as if she hadn't come prepared for the question.

'Because it makes me feel alive,' she finally said.

'Alive?' he queried.

'Yes,' she replied. 'I can't explain it. It's just the way I feel when a man wants me this way. I know it doesn't make sense. It's just the way I am, I suppose . . .' Her voice trailed off.

'Get up.'

She stood up, abandoning the humiliating position she had been holding. Turned to face him, legs still wide apart.

Dominik looked into her eyes. It was the same curious combination of shame, craving, pride and arousal he had seen so often in Kathryn's eyes. And in Summer's.

'Come.'

She stepped up to him. Her nipples were hard, they grazed against his shirt. He lowered his hands and kneaded her arse. Her softness was exquisite for such a slender woman. He again passed his hands between her legs, took hold of the small ring threaded through her clit and pressed hard against the nub of flesh it highlighted. Liana shuddered.

'How long have you had the rings?' he asked her.

'Just under a year.'

'Your decision?'

'Not strictly speaking . . .' She hesitated, as if reluctant to confirm his suspicions.

'Who?'

'I was with a dom for some months. Met him at a fetish club in London.'

'And?'

'He had me pierced. First my labia, and finally my clit.'

'Did it hurt?'

'The clit one hurt like hell. I was told the guy at the tattoo salon who did it was only going to pass the needle through the clit's hood, just a harmless flap of skin, and it came as a shock. I almost passed out in pain.'

'Hmm . . .'

'My dom wanted to go further. Wanted me to get a piercing along my perineum, which he would then put a small metal tag through, you know, like a soldier's dog tag, where his name would be carved, or at any rate something that would indicate I was his property. But we fell apart before that.'

'But you kept the other piercings?'

'Yes. I am what I am,' Liana said, with a strong hint of pride.

Pensive, Dominik looked down at the top of her head.

Right now, he wanted her badly, although he knew that she was at his service and he would only have to say a single word and the sex would be just another transaction between consenting adults. But a nagging thought at the back of his mind also told him he wanted more than sex. Liana was the type of submissive woman whom he wanted not so much to own or use sexually, but that he wanted to possess fully – both her body and her mind. To understand what made her tick. Why the essence of her submissiveness was also the very thing of beauty that attracted him. Damn!

Why did he make things so complicated for himself?

At least there was the sex. He sighed.

'On your knees,' he instructed her.

She kneeled down, understanding his instructions, and raised a hand to his belt and began to unbutton his trousers. Dominik closed his eyes as he felt her pull his cock out from his underpants and take it into the ardent heat of her mouth.

She was talented and he came quickly. Without waiting for any further instruction, she greedily swallowed his come.

Her head bobbed away from his crotch and there was a tumultuous moment of silence as the two of them pondered what was about to happen next. The hotel room's window was half open and the sound of the herring gulls flying wildly across the line of the seafront erupted into a deafening row.

'Get on the bed. On all fours,' Dominik demanded.

Liana rose from the floor. Her knees were pink from the position she had been holding. She moved to the bed and positioned herself, her back to him as he expected, presenting her arse.

Dominik undressed, untidily shedding his clothes on the floor.

His eyes were fixed on the rosebud of her anus.

Briefly wondering whether he might be too thick for her, too big, considering the slightness of her frame, the way her pelvic bones poked out in the posture she was impudently holding.

He slipped on a condom and stepped onto the bed which creaked under his additional weight. Crouching just above Liana, his semi-hard cock brushing against the small of her back, in a stand-up parody of spooning. He hadn't brought lubricant and reluctantly forced himself to puncture the tense nature of the moment by asking her if she had any in her rucksack of unknown delights. She had. He squeezed some on his fingers and over her tight opening and brought them down to spread the dampness around her sphincter.

All of a sudden he felt an irresistible compulsion to kiss the young woman again, to feel the taste of her breath in his mouth. He leaned closer but positioned as he was, ready to breach her, his mouth was too far from her lips. Instead he allowed his tongue to slip across the lobe of her left ear and was about to affectionately nibble it with his teeth when the fragrance of her hair reached his nostril. It was like a dagger to his heart.

It wasn't a specific perfume, more the background of the shampoo she had used to wash her short auburn hair with before travelling to this assignment. The faded perfume was laced with her own natural scent, a subtle blend of spices, musk and green flower notes, the tang of a woman.

A smell that he could recognise anywhere.

The same as Summer's.

A million memories came flooding back like a torrent, draining emotion, highs and lows in their wake.

If he closed his eyes now, he could pretend he was fucking Summer.

But he didn't want to pretend.

And realised he'd gone limp and the condom was hanging by a thread from his shrivelled cock.

Below him, he felt Liana tense, as if her own body had become aware of the change in their circumstances.

'What is it?' she asked.

'Nothing,' he said, but he knew he would be unable to perform further. 'It's just not going to work,' he apologised and moved away from her and the bed.

'Please . . .' Liana began to plead as she watched Dominik hastily dress, oblivious to her nudity and her state of arousal.

'I'm sorry, so sorry,' was all he could say. How could he explain it to her without making things worse?

Later, having pacified the uncomprehending Liana and paid for a cab to get her home by way of apology, Dominik felt a need for fresh air, if only to clear the heavy cloud of confusion orbiting his brain, and took to the sea front. It was still mid-afternoon. Time had passed so slowly today.

The sea was sullen, spread out all the way to a grey horizon, lines of white dotting its surface, the ruins of the old West Pier emerging from the dormant waves like the skeleton of some rusty prehistoric animal.

Holidaymakers and idle conventioneers shared the promenade with children and joggers, dodging the cyclists who rushed about in their badly marked allocated lane as if they owned it. Dominik felt hollow and as his stomach rumbled he remembered that he hadn't eaten anything today, having rushed to catch the train at Waterloo without helping himself to any breakfast. He remembered the fish and chip stand at the entrance of the main Palace Pier and he turned in its direction, walking briskly by the parade of hotels, past the Metropole, the concrete mass of the Brighton Conference Centre, and the Old Ship, before crossing towards the pier.

The comfort of the chips warmed him both physically and psychologically, unsophisticated but necessary comfort food for the soul. He quickly gulped them down to the very last crumb and was tempted to take a walk up West Street in search of a small second-hand bookshop he had once visited ten years earlier. By now, he'd decided he would stay the night as the hotel room at the Pelirocco had already been paid for and he was in no rush to return to London.

About to turn the corner, his attention was caught by the multitude of posters displayed outside the Brighton Centre. As well as hosting conferences and conventions, the warren-like building was also a major venue for music concerts and even featured ice-skating in the summer.

He had once seen Arcade Fire here when he had been unable to get tickets for their sold-out London gig. Maybe some music tonight would clear his mind. None of the posters displayed outside the centre appeared to be for tonight though. He walked in to the venue and located the box office.

Yes, there was a concert scheduled for the evening, but it wasn't heavily advertised, although tickets were on sale, he was told. They were quite cheap, it was pointed out to him, as the band playing saw this as something of a warm-up, a rehearsal for a possible tour away from the prying eyes of the press and fans.

'Do they have a name, at least?' Dominik asked the cashier.

'Oh yes, of course,' the frumpy middle-aged woman remarked, and pulled out a small flyer which she handed over to him. She read from it. 'They're called Groucho Nights. Can't say I've heard of them before. They've got some classical violin girl playing with them.' She peered at the small print. 'Some foreign name . . .'

Dominik took hold of the flimsy flyer.

'Featuring Summer Zahova.'

He just stood there for a while, silent, stunned.

'Groucho Nights, featuring Summer Zahova – One

Night Only, first UK performance before their European Tour

'Their First Complete Public Performance Together.'

'So do you want a ticket?' The cashier's voice brought him back to reality.

'Yes, yes, of course.'

He handed over some cash.

The gig was not until 8.30. Almost five hours to go.

He was about to make his way back onto the street when a thought occurred to him.

He doubled back and asked the cashier, who was by now reading a celebrity magazine.

'Do you know if tonight's band are already here? Maybe doing a soundcheck?'

'How would I know?' was her desultory response. 'There's a duty manager on the first floor. He might be able to help you.'

Dominik rushed upstairs, searching for the office where he might get his question answered.

After being bounced from one jobsworth to another, he finally found a guy who seemed to know what he was talking about but was warned that rehearsals were essentially private and that no members of the public were allowed to watch.

'But are the musicians already here?' he asked.

And just as he did so, the muffled sound of an electrically amplified violin, or maybe it was merely a guitar, reached his ears, wafting upwards on invisible wings of song from the distant depths of the building.

'Is that them? The rehearsal is already under way, isn't it?'

The other man nodded.

'I need to see one of the musicians, the violin player, she's called Summer Zahova,' Dominik insisted.

'They can't be disturbed,' he was told.

'She knows me. She will come, you'll see. I promise you.'

'Listen, mate, it just ain't possible.'

Feeling like a walking cliché, Dominik pulled a twenty-pound note from his wallet and offered it to the centre staffer. 'Tell her it's Dominik, and that I need to talk to her. If she comes back, I'll give you another note.'

The young guy looked dubious, but pocketed the money.

'Stay there,' he said. 'I'm not making any promises. I just hope they're not going to complain if I intrude on their rehearsal. But I'll see what I can do.' He skipped his way to the stairs.

Dominik stood there, rooted to the spot, the sounds of the music reaching him, loud, muffled, broken, dominated by the thump of drums and bass drowning out any sense of melody.

It felt like an eternity to wait.

The distant music came to an end, or maybe it had just faded away, echoing its way into silence.

He had his eyes fixed on the stairs that led to the centre's foyer and underground performance spaces but no one came up.

Dominik had his back to the lift and heard a rush of air as the car reached the floor he was on. He turned round. The door opened.

'There you are.'

The staffer walked out with a smile on his face. Followed by Summer.

She wore tight skinny jeans and a simple white silk blouse, her hair its customary jungle of fiery curls. She hadn't changed one bit. She looked at him in silence.

The centre staffer also gazed at Dominik, with an air of expectancy. Dominik snapped out of his reverie, remembering his promise, and dug a hand into the inside pocket of his jacket, pulling out a further banknote which he handed to the guy.

'Thanks, mate.'

He walked away, leaving Dominik and Summer alone.

Neither of them had yet spoken a word.

Looking at each other in silence, hesitant, tentative, as if locked in a contest as to who would utter the first words. Thoughts crashing in their minds like a nuclear reactor stampeding and veering wildly out of control.

Dominik was the one who finally realised he had to take the initiative.

'Hello.'

'Hi.' Her voice was quiet, enquiring.

'I happened to be in Brighton and found out by total coincidence you were playing here tonight . . .'

'Yes, it's not heavily advertised. It's the way we wanted it to be. Away from prying eyes. To see how we would gel as a group.'

'So, it's goodbye to classical music, is it?'

'No, no, not at all,' she protested, anxious he not get the wrong impression and somehow disapprove of her actions. 'Just a sabbatical, you know. I was getting a little stale and thought going on the road with Chris's group might do me good.'

'Groucho Nights is Chris?'

'Yes. They changed the name. Felt Brother & Cousin was a bit too folkish and they needed a change of direction . . .' Her words tailed off as she realised this was not the way she wanted the conversation to go.

'You look great,' Dominik said. 'How are you?'

'I'm fine. You?'

'I just hope I'm not interrupting your rehearsals?'

'It's OK. We were just about to complete the sound-check. It was time for a break. But I have to go back in soon. The technicians need me for the lighting run-through.'

'Oh . . . Time for a coffee, at least?'

'I can spare half an hour, I suppose. I'm not doing a whole set with the band. Just the second half. A lot of the songs are a bit too loud for the violin. They already had them down pat long before I came along. As they say, I'm just a featured guest. Whatever that means.'

'Sounds fun.'

'I think there's a bar area somewhere in the building. We should find it.'

They went in search of caffeine.

Again a wall of silence rose between them as they slowly sipped their insipid dispensing machine coffees in the deserted cafeteria.

This time it was Summer who rebooted the conversation.

'New York . . . I'm sorry about New York.'

'So am I,' Dominik reluctantly replied.

'I shouldn't have agreed to go; I know it now. But it happened. I don't want to justify myself, Dominik.'

'Yes, shit happens. I shouldn't have been there too.'

'But you were.'

'I was.'

'I was in shock for a few days. But by the time I came to the loft on Spring Street, you were gone. Back to London . . .'

'I waited a bit, then thought that was the best thing to do.'

'I understand.'

'So, how is New York?' he asked. 'I read an article in a magazine that you were now with Simón. Makes sense. So much in common. Musically . . .'

'I've left New York,' Summer remarked, looking him straight in the eyes. 'I came back to London just a few weeks ago.'

'I didn't know that.'

'I needed a change of scenery. Met up with Chris and his guys again and we decided we'd play together for a while. Today's gig is just an unofficial warm-up for a short European tour. New cities, new music. A bit of an experiment.'

'What did Simón have to say about it?' Dominik enquired.

'He's not involved. We split.'

There was a moment's silence, as Dominik registered the news.

Noting his impassive response, Summer felt obliged to keep the conversation going. 'I recently got involved with someone else, though. Another of those things. I wasn't looking for anything, for anyone, we just met and things clicked, so to speak. Viggo Franck. The singer and guitarist. You've probably heard of him?'

He nodded.

'And you,' Summer continued. 'Are you with anyone right now?'

He knew he shouldn't have said so, but he said it anyway. He was still processing the implications of Viggo Franck, and the devil inside seemed to be in control of his tongue.

'Lauralynn lives with me. You remember her, don't you?'

'She's lovely,' Summer remarked, forcing a smile. 'I really like her.'

'Good,' he said. Then added sarcastically, 'I'm glad you approve.'

She ignored his barb.

They were both now holding empty plastic coffee cups. Neither of them wanted to make another trip to the dispensing machine.

'So where does this European tour begin?' he finally asked.

'Paris. In two weeks.'

'Are you looking forward to it?'

'Yes, but Chris and I are still not fully satisfied with the sound we're achieving. There's something missing. We can't quite put a finger on it. Viggo says we need more oomph.'

'He's now your musical adviser?'

'He's taken Chris and the group under his wing. Got them signed to his record label, too. Oh, you know Fran?'

'Your sister, yes. You often mentioned her.'

'She's also come to London. We now live together. We're staying at Chris's place in Camden Town while I look for something more permanent of my own. It's working out quite well, so far.'

'Amazing,' he conceded with a visible lack of enthusiasm, uninterested by the gossipy way the meeting was unfolding.

'Still playing the Bailly?' he asked.

A shadow passed across her face.

'No.'

'Why?'

'It's been stolen.'

'Fuck! When, where?'

'Since I've been back in London. Just disappeared from a heavily guarded changing room at another gig. I was gutted. I'm so sorry. I know it meant a lot to you too . . .'

Dominik sighed. It wasn't just the news of the instrument's disappearance but hearing her make a concession to their previous life.

This time, he couldn't control what he said on the spur of the moment, but it came from the heart.

'You meant a lot to me, too, Summer . . .'

Their eyes locked.

Unable to sustain his gaze, she was the one to blink first.

'I know . . .' No louder than a whisper.

'It's good to see you, though. So often I've wanted to get in touch, but could never summon the mental strength to do so.'

'Me too.'

'But I'm pleased everything is going so well for you. Apart from the Bailly, of course. It must have come as a terrible shock.'

'It was awful.'

'I can imagine. I since found out a lot of curious stories about the Bailly. Did you know it's also called the Angelique?'

'No. How come?'

'A lot of superstition and urban legends, no doubt. I

came across the information researching another book . . .'
As he said this, Dominik realised the Paris novel had not
yet been mentioned in their halting conversation.

'I liked your novel, Dominik. I really did.' Summer said.

'You didn't mind . . .'

'You using me as a model for the character? Not at all. It
was a lovely thought. Not that I would have done all the
things Elena does in your story, though.'

Dominik smiled, a wave of relief racing through him.

Ella, the drummer for Groucho Nights, walked in to the
cafeteria, interrupting them.

'Ah, there you are, Sum. I've been looking all over for
you. You're needed downstairs – the techies say they can't
finalise the lighting prompts without you being in position.'

'In the spotlight, eh?' Dominik remarked.

Summer rose from the rickety table.

'We must stay in touch,' she said. 'I know we both now
have different lives. New partners, lovers. But surely we can
be friends. Again?'

'I'd like that,' Dominik said.

She was already walking away when she turned round
and said, 'And maybe you can help me find the violin.
What was its name?'

'The Angelique.'

'You say there are all these stories about it. Maybe they'd
give us a clue to its whereabouts?'

'If I can help, I will. In any way I can.'

'I have some suspicions. But it's rather delicate, you see. I
can't really explain now. Listen – phone me, my number is
still the same. We can talk about it.'

Her red hair faded as she stepped down the stairs, her

round, denim-clad arse swaying in perfect harmony, her scent still lingering in the air. Dominik took a deep breath and tried to calm his beating heart.

'*Ciao*,' he whispered under his breath, although he knew she could no longer hear him. And it wasn't a goodbye; it felt like a hello all over again.

7

Of Violins and Cameras

Losing the Bailly was like parting with half of my soul.

For a few days I felt as if I would never be able to play the same music again.

It wasn't just the unique sound I had been able to coax out of its strings with so much ease but all the associations the instrument had with my immediate past in London and New York.

Viggo said he was furious about its loss, blaming himself for not having arranged heavier security at the Academy – where we assumed the instrument had been stolen, sometime between our arrival when I had stupidly left the violin in the Green Room along with the rest of the band's gear and when we left the venue for Viggo's party.

I felt terribly guilty for leaving it, and blamed myself for my carelessness.

But in the dark stretches of the night, in the hours when shadows haunted my mind as well as my bedroom, I couldn't help but wonder what Viggo kept behind that one locked door in the basement, the only secured room in the house.

It seemed like a crazy proposition. The man had enough money to buy a hundred Baillys. He could have wallpapered the house with them if he had wanted to. I couldn't imagine why he would want my violin above all others, even if it had an unusual history, as Dominik had suggested.

Nonetheless, the thought lurked in the far reaches of my mind and it may have been one of the reasons why I fell into a semi-relationship of sorts with the rock star, and Luba, his seductive and ethereal companion.

It wasn't as strange as you might think, having a relationship with two people at once. We spent most of our time in, rather than out, because I was terrified of being photographed with the three of us together and appearing in the tabloids as part of a *ménage à trois*.

Viggo had a bit of a break between working in the studio with his band on their next album and going on the road again, and Luba didn't appear to have any regular employment of sorts, aside from working as an improvised PA to Viggo. She was like a less prim version of Pepper Potts in the Iron Man films, always on hand to fulfil his whims. They had a relationship that I could never quite put my finger on.

She was remarkably self-assured and appeared to have no sign of jealousy, and surprisingly, neither did I. Viggo's bed was enormous, so that solved the first problem that would usually arise, of fitting more people in comfortably. The house was huge, so we each had plenty of space if we grew tired of one of the others, or if any two particularly wanted privacy.

The set-up suited Viggo's temperament particularly well. Where I thought many men might baulk at the prospect of keeping two women entertained, he seemed to have an almost endless desire to make the two of us orgasm repeatedly, and a peculiar stamina for both fucking and wielding sex toys. Luba was more like a child at a candy store; she treated me like a new toy to be explored and discovered, possibly to be discarded at some future time when the next shiny thing would appear. And I was just enjoying being almost constantly physically sated.

Almost constantly, because there was still a small part of me that longed for Dominik. He'd arrived out of the blue before our show in Brighton. I'd played it cool, but after he left, I'd had to take a break for fifteen minutes before I could rejoin the rehearsal because my hands had been shaking too much to pick up my bow. He was seeing someone else, Lauralynn, the tall blonde who I had once double-dommed with at her flat in West London. Lauralynn and I had both worn strap-on dildos, and had sex with a submissive man on her bed. Both of us fully dressed, and him naked. I had found the experience educational, though not exactly arousing.

I'd told Dominik about Viggo without thinking, even though I didn't think of the three of us as anything more than passing fun, really. If he could move on, then so could I.

But that didn't stop me from thinking about him. That peculiar smell he had, just plain soap, without any cologne. His sometimes infuriatingly polite and old-fashioned turns of phrase. His accent, at times hard to place – hints of a childhood abroad that he never really talked about – other times, utterly British, just on the right side of posh. His straight-backed posture and broad shoulders from years of athletics training which had given him a firmness he hadn't lost, despite never appearing to make efforts to maintain his fitness. The strong line of his jaw and sensuous mouth. The softness of his skin. His cock, which I had always thought to be perfect. So straight, evenly coloured and large.

Most of all, I missed his wicked imagination and that way he had of always keeping me guessing, so that I never knew what he had up his sleeve next. It had made our relationship, for all its flaws, seem so alive. Dominik challenged me. He made me do things that I didn't think I could, or would. He made me feel present, somehow managed to meld my mind to my body in a way that only playing music had before, so that with him I was aware of his every word and every touch.

He seemed to understand me also, in a way that other men I had dated hadn't. Simón wanted to, I knew that, and perhaps he did, but we had different paths and plans for the future that could never mix successfully. Viggo probably came closest, but although he was good-natured, he lacked empathy. He sometimes stared at me in the way that you might look at a goldfish in a bowl, and I wondered whether he really thought of me as a person, or just the way that Luba did, as a new toy, a new pretty thing to add to his collection, to play with for a time.

That morning, I'd made a date to see Fran. With her working nights, and me now spending most of my time at Viggo's, we hadn't seen much of each other.

We met at Verde & Co., a tiny cafe in Spitalfields market that made the best coffee in the area, and certainly on a par with the few others that I thought were the best in London, though those titles were fiercely debated by the other Kiwis and Aussies I knew, who seemed to forget that

Italians came up with espresso long before we invented flat whites.

She was already there when I arrived, perched on one of the cafe's wooden stools, admiring the glass jars of marmalade stacked up with the light shining through from behind so the mixture inside glowed in warm shades of red, orange and yellow, depending on the particular variety of fruit within.

All sorts of products lined every surface of the tiny shop, speciality Italian pastas, dried into shapes that seemed unusual to eyes accustomed to the more ordinary supermarket varieties, wicker baskets filled with cherries, peaches, or whatever happened to be in season, a silver dish with sugar cubes and a pair of tongs to pick them up with, and of course the glass case filled with the most beautiful-looking sweets, Pierre Marcolini chocolates of every shape and flavour laid out in a way that promised each mouthful would be more luscious than the last.

It had been one of my favourite hang-outs when I last lived in London, and I'd always taken pleasure from looking at the chocolates through the glass, but never actually buying one; enjoying the thrill from a pleasure imagined and denied but always at arm's length. I liked the feeling of desire, even if it was never realised.

'Nice place,' Fran said. She'd seen me coming and already ordered and paid for the coffees at the counter.

'Thanks for the drink,' I said, 'but stop buying things for me, you're on a tenner an hour and I'm loaded.'

'I knew you would say that,' she said, plucking up one cube of sugar after another and dropping it into the small cup, reminding me of Dominik's habit of sweetening his drinks to the extreme. Every tiny thing reminded me of him these days.

'Since when did you take sugar?'

'Since I saw it in these pretty cubes. This is posh sugar. It doesn't come like this in Te Aroha.'

'But it still tastes the same. How are you, anyway?'

'Same as I was last fortnight. The bar is good fun. Hard work but it's a good way to meet people.'

'Are you still looking for a place to live?'

'Not really. I quite like staying with Chris . . . and he'd only have to replace me, if you're not coming back. Are you coming back? How's life with the rock star? Chris tells me you're dating the dancer as well? How the fuck does that work?'

'Dating is probably too strong a word for it. I'm hardly going to bring them both back home for Christmas.'

'Can you imagine that? The parents would be so proud.' She giggled.

'People do it . . . triads aren't that uncommon.'

'They are where we're from.'

'I wouldn't bet on it. People in small towns just try harder to hide things.'

The waitress returned with a large slice of lemon cake which Fran had ordered earlier and slipped it between us.

'That looks tasty,' I said, distracted from my train of thought by the cake's arrival. 'You're not worried about the Heathrow injection then?' Weight gain was a common problem for travellers arriving in the UK, tempted by the colder weather to abandon their previously held hobbies of outdoor exercise in favour of pints and pub meals.

Fran scoffed at me.

'Eat the damn cake,' she said, pushing the teaspoon over to my side, 'and tell me more about the rock life. I want to hear everything. Haven't you ever noticed I live my life vicariously through you? Throw me a bone here.'

'Vicariously through me? Aren't you sleeping with Dagur, the drummer?'

'Sadly, no. We did end up in bed together but we were both comatose by then after all the cocktails. Woke up next to him with all my clothes on.'

'And you didn't ask for his number?'

'He asked for mine. But I'm not into rock musicians.'

'Oh, really? Not even Chris?' I teased her.

'Well, I'm not into most of them.'

She was blushing.

I ignored the sound of my phone as it began to buzz loudly, and Fran seized the opportunity for a change of subject by taking it out of my pocket and handing it to me.

'It's an international call, they're always important. Answer it.'

It was a New York number, which meant either Simón or Susan, most likely the latter as Simón was still in Venezuela last time I heard, and Susan would be on the warpath now as I still hadn't replied to her emails to explain my whereabouts.

I slipped off the stool and hurried outside, catching the call just before it went to voicemail.

'Hello?'

'Summer, where the hell are you and what are you doing there?'

It was Susan.

'I'm still in London. Just taking a break.'

'So I thought, until I heard on the grapevine that your impromptu rock performances in London and Brighton have been attracting rave reviews. The press have got wind of it and there's a piece coming up in a tabloid about your supposed rock rebellion. Classical darling goes wild and all that . . .'

'I was just playing with a friend.'

'Well, I need to spin these things, unless you want to be labelled a classical musician who is having a career melt-down.'

'My violin was stolen,' I said, in a small voice, close to tears.

'I'm sorry to hear that. But surely you have enough in royalties to buy a new one? I can probably arrange a sponsor if you've spent all your money on shoes.'

'It's not the same for classical music. I just can't face going back on stage without the Bailly.'

'Well, I suppose it doesn't need to be a classical stage. What about this band you're playing with?'

'Groucho Nights. They opened for Viggo Franck and The Holy Criminals . . . You've probably heard of him? He's helping them to organise a European tour soon.'

'Of course I know him. According to the tabloids he's sleeping with half the world's celebrities. Fine. You can play with them. Just for God's sake don't get your picture taken falling out of a bar with Viggo Franck, at least before I get started promoting your move to rock stardom. In fact . . . are you still in touch with that photographer who did your photo for the New York show?'

It was more than two years since Simón had run the poster of me naked from the neck down, my modesty covered by my violin, which had made my first concert a sell-out. Susan had a good memory.

'No . . . he moved back to Australia, I think.' I remembered the photographer who had taken my picture at Torture Garden with Fran and Chris a few weeks earlier. He would at least be discreet. 'I might know someone else though.'

'Good. That's settled then. I'm ringing Franck's manager now. Leave all the arrangements to me. If you want to be a rock star too, it has to be done right.'

She had hung up before I'd had a chance to protest.

I sat back down again next to Fran, feeling slightly dazed. Maybe it was lucky I hadn't found a flat of my own after all, as it looked like I'd be going back on the road.

'Well then? What's the story?' Fran asked, looking at me quizzically.

'My agent – she wants me to go on tour with Chris and the band.'

'Well that's a great idea! Chris would love you to play with him. He talks about it all the time. He gets on with Ted and Ella, of course, but you're his best friend, Sum . . . you should definitely think about it.'

'Think about it? I don't think it's really up to me. My agent is already calling his people, and Susan could badger just about anyone into anything. But it might be too late, they're leaving in a few days. They'd have to do last-minute announcements, arrange the gear for me and the promo . . . all kinds of things.'

'It's not like they're the Rolling Stones. It's a few venues in Europe, sure, but not the end of the world. I'm sure they can shuffle something around, and if Viggo tells them to, they won't have a choice.'

'I guess so.'

'I'll be at a bit of a loose end though, without the two of you here. I wonder what Chris will do with the flat.'

'You could always come. I'll need a road manager, and so do Groucho Nights, as far as I know. We could get you on the payroll. And you could see a bit of Europe. And keep me company. You're trained in this sort of stuff, you've worked in banking. You could do it.'

Fran's face lit up as if I'd handed her a winning lottery ticket, and she yelped loud enough to make the waitress jump.

'Oh my God I'd love to!'

'Calm down . . . sometimes I'd swear that you're twenty-one. And none of this is confirmed yet. For a start, I don't even have an instrument.'

'Oh God, that's right. It hasn't turned up yet then? And what's this business about not telling the police?'

'Viggo is worried about having his road crew investigated. He doesn't want to lose his people, if they get the hump for being accused of theft. And it would badly affect his insurance premiums. He'd rather pay me the violin's full value instead.'

'Too bad, someone stole it. If someone doesn't like being investigated, maybe that's your guy.'

'But I don't care about the money. Just the violin. It was a gift.'

'Oh yeah. Chris told me about that guy.'

Fran cocked an eyebrow suspiciously.

'You two talk a lot. I'm not sure if I approve.'

'Does he know that it's been stolen?'

'Dominik? Yeah. Oddly, I ran into him in Brighton. He

was there, noticed the flyers for our concert, came in to say hello. He's seeing someone else now. But he did mention something about the violin. Said it had a strange history. He's doing some research on it for a novel. I asked him to let me know if he heard anything, but it's a bit of a long shot.'

'Call him.'

'What? Now?'

'Now. Find out if he knows anything. I know you and telephones, you'll never do it if I don't make you. And don't try to pretend you deleted his number.'

'Fine.'

I picked up the phone again, this time in a bit of a huff, and, hoping the conversation would be short, I didn't bother to leave my chair.

His number rang out.

'Voicemail,' I said, with a hint of triumph.

'Well, leave him a message then.'

'Hi . . . it's me. Summer.' I kicked myself for first assuming he would immediately know the sound of my voice, and then for assuming that he wouldn't, and leaving my name. There was an uncomfortable pause as I gathered my wits again and continued. 'Just wanted to check in, about the violin. Call me.' I hit the end call button.

'Wow, that was smooth.'

'Shut it.'

By the time that we got back to the flat, Chris had already heard the news, and he was jubilant. It seemed neither Susan nor Viggo had wasted any time pulling strings to make it happen. By early afternoon, they'd updated most of the venues and started working on new promo material. I was officially going on the road with Groucho Nights as a featured guest star.

We spent the next few days in a flurry of rehearsals, going through all the old numbers that we used to play together and rejigging some of their other songs where the violin suited. It took a bit of fiddling around, to give me enough time on stage without drowning out the sound, and the dynamics on stage were slightly odd with four musicians rather than three. Previously, Chris had been the focus with Ted alongside, and Ella of course at the back with drums. I was a bit like the third wheel, most of the time, and the sound didn't always blend properly.

After our fourth successive night of rehearsals, we were back in Chris's flat, feeling inexplicably morose.

Fran was in the kitchen, cooking pizza. She'd been at it for hours, making the dough and the tomato paste base from scratch. The flat was full of the smell of yeast from the bread dough and garlic from the marinara. Chris was sitting opposite me on the round wooden table next to the open-plan kitchen, with his shoulders hunched, flipping a screw-top beer cap repeatedly through his thumb and forefinger. I was watching him and waiting patiently, leaning my elbows on the table and resting my chin in my hands.

'There's something missing,' he said, softly, almost to himself.

I waited for him to continue.

'The sound is . . . not quite right. Unbalanced.'

'If it's not right, it's OK, Chris. It's not too late to bow out, just go with the three of you. I won't be offended, truly.'

There was a part of me that slightly resented being swept along by Viggo and Susan. A rock phase had seemed like a rebellion, a grand idea for a change and a rest when it was my idea. Now that it had become someone else's, I was feeling a little forlorn about being uprooted and sent off travelling again, as much as I was looking forward to the prospect of spending more time with Chris.

'No, it's not you. The violin is great. I just have the feeling that we need something more.'

'More cowbell?' Fran piped up from the kitchen.

He laughed and glanced over at her fondly.

'That's not a bad idea, you know,' he mused, balancing the beer cap on one finger, deep in thought. 'All this time, we've been thinking we need less, but maybe we need more.'

'More? More what? Where would we get the musicians from?'

'We need another layer of sound. But at this short notice it would have to be people who already play together.'

He was still talking to himself, staring deep into space, not even bothering to flick the stubborn curls away from his forehead.

A nugget of an idea began to take root in my brain.

Before I could nurture the idea into thought and speech, Fran appeared in front of us bearing a steaming platter of doughballs, each with a smattering of crispy parmesan on top and a slightly charred basil leaf. She had arranged them into a pyramid.

'Wow,' Chris said, 'that's the most amazing thing I've ever seen.'

I held back a snicker. Fran still seemed unaware of the effect she had on him. I'd known Chris for a few years, and never seen him behave like this over anyone. He'd started ironing his T-shirts, even for a night in, despite the fact that Fran was one of the scruffiest dressers I knew, her clothes rarely making it onto a hanger, let alone an ironing board.

'What you need,' she replied, ignoring his compliment, 'is a trumpet or three.'

'I might be able to help with that,' I added. I still kept in touch with Marija and her husband Baldo, the flatmates I had lived with in New York before moving in with Dominik. Marija played flute in the orchestra, but she had trained on the trumpet, and was almost as good as Baldo on his; certainly good enough for our needs. They might not be able to get the time off, or get over here quick enough, but I knew they'd been bored since Simón left and had been replaced by an apparently much duller conductor, so a stint in a rock band might appeal.

Viggo agreed to the addition of a brass section, and Susan pulled some strings to extract Marija and Baldo from their commitments in New York.

'You need one more,' she said to me the next day, 'so I'm sending Alex as well.'

Alex was the sax player who Marija had once tried to set me up with, on a date which had ended with me going home with an insurance broker who lived on the Upper East side in a posh apartment that smelled of salmon. Dominik had found the whole thing amusing, and Alex had been, fortunately, not too offended, as he'd managed to pick up another girl at the bar whilst I was on the balcony flirting with Derek.

The three of them would fly straight into Paris. They'd have just enough time to recover from jetlag, and we'd have a day or so to cram in rehearsals before the opening show, booked at La Cigale on the Boulevard Rochechouart. I'd been to Paris once, about four years earlier, but had little time for sightseeing – even so, I had fond but vague memories of the place. We were staying in a part of town that I hadn't visited. Fran, in her new role as road manager had arranged all the accommodation.

All I had to do was pack, and attend the photo shoot that Susan was so keen on. It was too late to get any extra posters out, but she planned to send some of the pics to the reviewers and music mags, to at least keep any rumours at bay that I had lost the plot or gone off the rails, and instead push my career change as a temporary new direction. She thought the rock persona might add a bit of sex appeal that could help my classical records sell. Susan had always been enthusiastic on promoting my sex appeal, and she was very happy with my suggestion of photographer, Jack Grayson, who it turned out had a background in fashion and was behind a few risqué celebrity shoots. He had also had a fine art nude exhibit at a gallery in London, which had become notorious when the police had appeared, following complaints from some puritanical member of the public.

Out of curiosity, I'd looked the images up. They were all tasteful, I thought, though didn't doubt that more conservative folk might find them shocking. One which particularly caught my eye featured a woman bending over alongside a pile of books, with a perfect strawberry peeking out from her arsehole. Another woman sat behind her, presumably responsible for the insertion of the strawberry. I was dying to ask Jack, or Grayson, as it seemed he was more commonly called, how he got the strawberry to stay there, but that seemed a conversation more appropriate for another time, perhaps over a beer.

Grayson lived and worked in an old school conversion, not far from the bedsit in Whitechapel, where I'd lived when I first met Dominik. He offered me a coffee when I arrived, and I drank it overlooking his balcony, a view of a graveyard and an seventeenth-century church. The presence of death and religion lent a sombre tone to his otherwise girly decor. The interior was fitted out in shades of cream, with a variety of ornate chairs dotted around and tall vases filled with flowers.

The room he used as his main studio was filled with lights, backdrops, and bits of equipment that I couldn't identify, with large dishes and flat silver plates for catching the light.

Jack looked almost like a different person out of his latex. He was dressed in a pair of jeans and a white and black Religion T-shirt with a picture of a nude woman on the front, resting in a shopping trolley. His assistant, Jess, was laying out her make-up and hair products on the kitchen table, just about enough to fill a pharmacy I reckoned, and certainly enough to fill up her suitcase, which I'd seen her struggling up the stairs with as I came in.

I had never actually had a photo shoot before, at least, not officially. A few men who I had dated had taken pictures of me in the buff. Fortunately, either they hadn't tried to send them to the papers once I'd found fame as a solo artist, or the papers hadn't been interested. The picture that I'd showed to Simón, which had then been made into flyers for my first New York concert, had been one of those. I'd had a brief fling with an Australian photographer who had taken a couple of shots of me naked, playing my violin or holding it in front of me, over my breasts. But I'd never tried to pose under studio lighting in formal circumstances like this.

Grayson had sent me an email to confirm everything beforehand. It was clearly one that he sent to all of his clients, advising the address, directions and what to bring with me. He'd also asked me to specify what level of photography that I was comfortable with. Clothed, lingerie, or nude. His email said that he preferred to be clear up front, rather than risk making a model feel uncomfortable by asking on the day, or have someone do something on the spur of the moment that they might regret later.

I wouldn't be able to bring a friend to the shoot with me, as this might be distracting and affect my posing, but his female make-up artist would be on site at all times, so that I would feel comfortable. He clearly wasn't a creep then, or one of the 'guys with cameras' I'd heard about who apparently invited girls over for spurious photo shoots when they really just wanted to watch them undress. I was paying for the shoot for personal use, and Susan had told me in no uncertain terms that I shouldn't sign a model release form if asked, so the photographer wouldn't be able to sell the pictures on without my express consent.

I replied with an outline of the sorts of shots we were

looking for, and added that I was entirely comfortable with nudity. Susan had suggested it should all be kept within the bounds of good taste, and only the more innocuous images would be used as part of the promotion.

'Did you bring any outfits with you?' he asked, taking my empty coffee cup out of my hands and placing it into the sink.

'A few,' I replied, digging around in the oversized bag I'd brought along with everything packed into it. I had a mixture of my clothes and Fran's, most of which were a size too small but would do the job in a pinch. A pair of wet-look leggings, a leather jacket, a couple of dresses, Fran's thigh-high boots and the shoes that I had splashed out on as a reward after my first tour had been a success: a pair of black Louboutins covered in silver studs. None of it was really my style. I looked at the laid out clothes and thought 'dominatrix' not 'rock chick', but Grayson seemed happy enough with my haul.

'And you wanted to do some semi-nude shots too, just with the violin?'

'Yes,' I replied. I'd already started thinking about the prospect of stripping off, and my voice came out in an excited squeak. Nerves, I told myself, though there was a hint of exhibitionism, which had long been buried, rising to the surface. There had been times when I had stripped off in public, and enjoyed the process, but each occasion had been the result of an instruction, either from Dominik or from Victor, the dominant man that I'd fallen in with in New York.

'We'll start with the clothed shots first, to get you warmed up.'

His manner was friendly, but so professional it verged on cold, as if he'd spent his working life making a very deliberate effort to not be flirtatious, even by accident. I felt odd taking my bag of clothes into the bathroom to change, since the mirror was in the living room near where the make-up artist had set up, and they were both going to see me naked later anyway.

So I changed in front of them, first pulling my blouse over my head and then slipping my skirt off and kicking them both away as if I did this sort of thing every day, producing a stream of small talk as I did so to try to appear relaxed. Neither of them were paying any attention to me at all, but I still felt awkward.

I put on the wet-look leggings, studded Louboutins and leather jacket over a black bra to start. Fran and I had had a sort of dress rehearsal with the outfits and decided that this was the most rock star in style.

The make-up and hair took about an hour, and by the end of it, I barely recognised myself. My eyes were smouldering, coated in thick black eyeliner, grey shadow and fake eyelashes so long that when I opened my eyes the lashes tickled my eyebrows. Jess had slicked my hair into a high quiff, and had highlighted the contours of my face with various pots of powder so that my cheekbones stood out like a cat's. Combined with the leggings and the jacket, I looked like a bit of a tough bitch really, a femme fatale. Not the kind of girl that you would introduce to your mother.

'Arch your back a little more. That's it.'

I'd been slow to catch on to the posing at first, and Grayson, at first endlessly patient, had eventually given up and arranged my limbs for me. As he did so, I felt that familiar slow burn, just an inkling of a thought, recognition of the way that he was taking control of my body which fanned the flame of a flickering idea until it became a fully blown fantasy. Before I knew it, I was responding to his instructions in the same way that I had responded to Dominik's. Old habits die hard.

He paused for a moment, flicking back through the shots onscreen to check his work, as I struggled to keep my legs still and my back arched at exactly the same angle so he wouldn't need to readjust the lighting.

'Try it with the bra off,' he said. 'The bra breaks up the line of your skin, I think.'

'Oh, sure,' I replied casually, struggling to unclip the hook at the back without moving too far out of the position that he'd spent so long manoeuvring me into.

I did my best to hide my reaction, not wanting to make the photographer feel uncomfortable, but by the time that we got to the nude shots, my nipples were erect, and my panties were wet.

'No,' he said, as I started to kick off my Louboutins, 'leave the shoes on.'

Dominik had said exactly the same thing to me once, when I had performed for him nude in the crypt, with Lauralynn playing the cello, blindfolded behind me. The memory sent another sharp pang of desire throbbing through me, though it wasn't directed at Grayson. He just happened to be here, caught in the shadow of my peculiar sexual quirks and the memory of a failed previous relationship.

I swallowed hard, tried to concentrate on the task at hand, or at least to will my nipples into submission. I couldn't even pretend that I was cold, as he had the heating up high and his flat was toasty. It didn't help that he was really quite attractive, both in and out of his fetish gear. He was tall and lean, with friendly, grey-blue eyes that smiled when he talked, and he had a way of holding the camera that made it seem as though it was an extension of his body, in the same way that I felt when I held a violin. His posture, the way that he moved, seemed so much in control of each detail of the shoot.

He'd set up a dark backdrop, and put a black sheet down on the floor. I was surrounded by lights which he was adjusting so that half of my body would be in shadow, to produce a mysterious, artful rather than pornographic effect. Each time the flash went off, a bright white light glared, not enough to blind me, but enough to concentrate the feeling that I was being watched, on display, the object of a voyeur; even if that voyeur's purpose was professional rather than sexual, it still had the same effect on me. I was glad that Grayson's focus was fixed entirely on getting the picture and that in the scheme of things, I was as much an object to be posed and lit in the right way as the violin. I just hoped he didn't notice that my thighs were beginning to get slippery when he enlarged the pictures for retouching.

Every now and again, Jess would pop into the room to offer us another cup of tea, brush some more powder on my face or fix a stray lock of hair into place. Her touch was feather light, and she'd clearly seen enough naked women in her life to not give my body a second glance. I'd always concentrated on seeing the good in myself, and did my utmost to avoid reading diet magazines or mulling on any

Vina Jackson

perceived flaws, but I still wondered what the other women were like that he usually photographed. I felt a little like I had when Dominik had commanded me to dance after Luba's incredible performance in New Orleans. Very much like an amateur, playing at something that wasn't really me. I was a musician, not a model.

But the idea of being stuck in a situation that I was not in control of, out of my depth, watched, at the mercy of another's commands – all of these things just intensified my arousal.

We did a few shots standing, with me delicately positioning the violin and my hands and arms in ways that would cover all of the bits that couldn't be printed in a mainstream magazine, and then a couple of me sitting, with my legs spread and the body of the violin sitting between my thighs, and my head either resting on the neck of the instrument looking soulfully into the distance or staring provocatively at the camera. I remembered, at last, what the Australian photographer that I had dated briefly had said to me about posing – that I should try to imagine feeling whatever emotion I was trying to portray, and ideally make the camera part of it. So, he'd said, to look sexy, imagine the camera lens is a phallus, or whatever else it is that works for you.

I tried this, turning all of my focus and frustration and aiming it directly at Grayson's long lens, as he snapped away.

'Woah,' he said after a few shots. 'That's great but I'm not sure if you're going to be able to use these, depending on what sort of magazine you're planning to send them to, of course . . . maybe you could try closing your legs a little bit?'

'Actually, I wouldn't mind having some more . . . personal shots. Just for me.' I felt my face flush a brilliant scarlet. 'If that's outside your remit for today I don't mind paying extra for them. If you don't mention it to my agent.'

'So they weren't joking about your rock rebellion, then, huh?' he chuckled. 'I'm happy to do whatever you're comfortable with, and don't worry, your secret is safe with me.'

From that point onward, I became more and more daring, and more and more turned on.

'Pose like you're making love to the violin,' he said, 'instead of the camera.'

I switched my focus, so that rather than seeing his lens as the object of my sexual attention I imagined my violin not as a phallus but as a memory holder, the core of all the experiences which had, perhaps, not made me the way that I was but which had formed the stepping stones of the path that I'd chosen to travel down. Memories of Dominik were the first to come rushing back, and the most powerful, and almost all of them were associated with music, with the Bailly. That violin was gone, but the memories still belonged to me. Playing for Dominik on the bandstand on Hampstead Heath, in the crypt, in the apartment in New York, waiting for him to come home to find me nude with my violin in hand. It had been my symbolic message to him that a part of me was his.

'These are amazing,' Grayson said at the end, when he quickly ran through the shots he'd downloaded onto his big computer screen. 'I'll make the colours punchier, get rid of the noise, cut out the odd distraction in the background, all that kind of thing, but other than that there's very little retouching. I like them raw, like this.'

'Yes. They're beautiful. Thank you.' I felt a strange sense of gratitude to the photographer for managing to catch something so personal in an image. The expressions on my face were the thing that got me, that made me gasp, when the shots appeared onscreen. The look in my eyes was pure sex, but not in a tawdry, porn-star way. I looked like a siren, as if my whole being had been cast in pheromones instead of atoms. And I really did look as though I was making love to my violin.

He promised to email me all of the files, so that I could select the ones that I liked best for retouching, and I thanked him again and managed to get dressed, with fumbling fingers and my heart racing. I'd forgotten my embarrassment over being the only naked person in the room in front of the photographer and the make-up artist. I just wanted to hurry home, to find some space alone to ponder the thoughts and memories that seemed to have taken permanent root in my head.

Knowing that if I headed either to Chris and Fran's or to Viggo's I would have company, I took a detour into the park outside Grayson's house, by the cemetery. I sat down on one of the park benches and stared at the old stones that formed the foundations of the church which towered into the sky. Churches usually give me the creeps, but this one didn't. The stones were a pale grey, almost white, and not crumbling or covered in moss. On closer inspection, the building had a lightness about it, a grandeur that was uplifting rather than eerie.

I found the entrance and went inside. The main door was locked but I was able to get into a large, circular room, made from the same pale stones that reached into the sky, several storeys over my head. I leaned against one wall, enjoying the coolness of its touch, and gradually slipped down to a crouch.

I wanted Dominik desperately. Not just to fuck, for once in my life. I wanted to talk to him, to feel him fold me into his arms, to lay my head on his shoulder and run my hand over his chest. I just wanted to be with him.

He was with Lauralynn though, and it was too late for regrets. I had made my bed, and now I was sleeping in it.

But I could at least hear the sound of his voice, and maybe find a way to get my Bailly back, the instrument that still somehow connected me to him.

I pulled my phone out of my bag.

8

Parisian Melodies

The phone rang. It was Summer.

Dominik had been waiting for days now, since they'd shared a coffee in Brighton. Arguing with himself whether he should phone her or not. Yearning to hear the sound of her voice, to feel her close again.

But every time it just didn't feel like the right moment. Coming across her in Brighton had been a genuine co-incidence but phoning her first now would feel stalkerish, he feared.

Time and time again, he'd dialled her number but not called, riven by doubts and hesitation. He'd since contacted LaValle and had told him about the theft of the Bailly. He had wanted to gather information on the likely market for stolen musical instruments. LaValle had given him the name of a go-between who happened to live in the Paris suburbs and sometimes facilitated matters when it came to the less legal sides of the business. The dealer had sounded amused to hear that the notorious Bailly was still creating waves, as if its theft lent further credence to the Angelique legend.

Dominik wanted to discuss the development with Summer. Twice today already he'd tentatively reached for the phone on the desk as if it were a lump of hot coal. He'd gone for a walk on the Heath to clear his mind, only to find a message from Summer on his return. After all this, he had missed her! How quickly should he now return the call?

The vibration of the phone as it stuttered across his desk snapped him out of his reverie.

'Dominik?' It sounded as though she was right there next to him.

'Yes.'

'It's me, Summer.'

'I was hoping you'd call.'

'Were you?' She couldn't hide her pleasure on hearing his words.

'Of course. Still no news of the Bailly?'

'No.' The disappointment in that one word was heart-breaking.

'I've been given the name of someone who might be able to help. It would mean having to go to Paris, though . . .'

'Paris?' Summer exclaimed. 'We're going there next week. Performing. Opening our tour at La Cigale.'

'That's wonderful,' Dominik said.

'If you arranged to go at the same time, you could come to the concert, it would be great. I'd have you put on the guest list, of course. Would you? Please?'

'I'd love to,' Dominik said.

'After the gig, maybe we could meet up for a coffee. Have a longer chat. I'd really like that, Dominik . . .'

'I always wanted to take you to Paris.'

'I know, but we never got round to it, did we?'

'Isn't it a bit late now?' said Dominik, brushing away an emerging wave of depression. 'Will Viggo Franck be there also?'

'Maybe,' she said. 'But we have a . . . loose arrangement, you know.'

'Loose?'

'Anyway, just a chat for old times' sake. I'm sure Laura-lynn won't mind, will she? You can bring her along if you feel you need a chaperone,' she joked.

'Lauralynn's in the States right now. Family stuff.'

'Oh.'

There was a heavy silence, as both considered the situation.

He thought he heard Summer take a deep breath on the other end of the line, as if she was summoning her determination.

'Come to Paris,' she said calmly.

Dominik smiled. 'Now who's giving orders,' he said with an amused tone in his voice.

He heard her gently giggling.

'Maybe I should take the initiative again,' Dominik suggested.

'The initiative?'

'Giving you orders . . .'

For a brief moment, he felt he had gone too far, become overfamiliar. Time had passed, things had changed. That particular game was over.

'Maybe you should?' Summer's voice was curiously muted. Her bedroom voice. Her intimate voice, the one that went with the darker lipstick she would wear at night.

'Hmm . . .' Dominik considered. 'I don't quite think asking you to appear naked on a Paris stage is advisable at this stage,' he pointed out. 'Too many Frenchmen in the audience to begin with.'

Summer laughed.

'Maybe I've reached the stage where I don't have to take orders or suggestions any more,' she said.

'Meaning?'

'Come to Paris, Dominik. I'll have your name put on the list. The gig is at La Cigale, on Boulevard Rochechouart. On the nineteenth. The promoters tell us it's a good venue to play, has a great vibe.'

'I will,' he said.

'I'll think of something,' she added.

'I'm sure you will,' Dominik said, relief flooding through his veins.

The Eurostar train arrived late at the Gare du Nord, following unexplained technical delays on the line. The colours of sunset were spreading across the Paris sky as Dominik disembarked and made his way to the cab rank.

He dropped his overnight bag at his usual hotel on the Rue Monsieur-le-Prince, close to the Odéon, and went in search of a meal. The whole area had been colonised over the past years by new-style Japanese restaurants so he didn't have to step more than a few minutes away from the hotel doorstep.

He knew Summer and Groucho Nights had been put up by the gig's promoters on the other side of the Seine, but old habits died hard and he felt more comfortable staying in the Latin Quarter, an area where he had spent much of his youth. His room was small and sparse, but all he required was a bed and a roof above his head; anything else would have proved a distraction.

Dominik planned to contact the go-between, the man LaValle had put him on to, early the following morning.

At first the man, who called himself Cavalier, sounded suspicious. But when Dominik explained that the questions were all tied in to the research for a new novel and provided details of his identity, his interlocutor suddenly seemed to warm to him.

'Ah, a writer. I like writers!'

He hadn't read Dominik's novel but had actually heard about it. Ironically, France was one of the countries where, in translation, his Paris novel had not sold particularly well, as if local readers were offended by the presumption of a foreigner writing about their own country.

Cavalier had an appointment in town that same afternoon, and agreed to meet to avoid Dominik having to take a train all the way to his *pavillon* in Nogent-sur-Marne. He suggested a cafe off the Boulevard Saint Germain, Les Editeurs, a literary sort of place, he indicated, 'where they even have shelves full of books all around the walls of the cafe. Amusing, no? Maybe they have yours?' This was just a few minutes' walk from Dominik's hotel so pretty convenient.

It was an odd feeling, knowing he was right now in the same city as Summer. That she was on the other side of the river going about her life. The fact that she had, unknown to him, only been a stone's throw away in Camden Town in London for several weeks already somehow didn't have the same emotional immediacy. Paris made it feel both real and unreal, a bittersweet pull on his heartstrings.

'Collectors they come in all colours, you know,' Cavalier said. He was younger than Dominik had expected. A slight, pencil-thin man, with his jet-black hair brushed back and culminating in a ponytail that peered out from the back of a rakish fedora. He wore a checked jacket and dark, perfectly ironed trousers with a razor-sharp front crease.

'I've come to that conclusion too,' Dominik said, bluffing his way into the conversation.

'It's not the money, you see, that's not the reason they get involved in theft and all sorts of illegal activities. Once they own something, they have no mind to sell it again, let alone for a profit.'

'I know.'

'They do it for beauty. Pure and simple. I even know certain book collectors who hoard rare editions for the sake of it. They never even read actual books, let alone those they own.'

'I was more interested in the underground market for musical instruments.'

'Instruments, books, artwork, jewellery, carpets, it's all the same to them,' Cavalier continued. 'Greed, pure greed, if you ask me. The wealthier collectors even arrange to have items stolen to order . . .'

'Is that where you come in?' Dominik asked him.

'I couldn't say,' Cavalier answered with a broad smile colouring his lips. 'I'm merely in the information business. Assisting all parties to the best of my ability.'

He took a sip of his pastis. It smelled revolting to Dominik who was adding water and sugar to his *citron pressé*.

'So is there anyone notorious for seeking out rare violins?'

'Ah, you come to the point! Let me guess, is this about Monsieur LaValle's famous Bailly, the Angelique?'

'It is.'

'How interesting. An instrument with a most fascinating

183

history. Isn't it strange how sometimes stories have a way of becoming self-fulfilling?'

'Yes. It's the material of novels. Or life . . .'

'Exactly.'

'From your own experience, might there have been anyone actively seeking the instrument out? Mr LaValle did give me that impression.'

'Well, there are always collectors out there seduced by an intriguing story,' he mused. 'But you know I can't give you any specific names. I am bound by confidentiality, you understand.'

'Of course, I realise that, but—'

'I can say one thing, though . . .'

'Yes?'

'There is a particular gentleman, a noted collector, not just of instruments but who also dabbles in artworks, who recently had the item you are investigating taken off his list. Maybe he happened to come across it, and felt it best to eliminate any evidence of his past interest.'

'Really?'

'Well, it would be unwise to retain a specific item on a want list once it has finally come, by hook or by crook, into one's hands. Wouldn't want some enterprising freelancer to come and steal it from you and confuse matters, would you?'

'I suppose not,' Dominik agreed. He knew Cavalier would not release any names; he hadn't expected him to. But there was a streak of vanity in the man, a pride in the treasure chest of knowledge he stored which made his ego vulnerable, if stroked smoothly enough, he reckoned.

'Would Viggo Franck, the musician, mean anything to you?'

There was a glint of recognition in Cavalier's eyes. Though he quickly reined himself in and continued, 'I certainly have read about him in the newspapers. Something of a ladies' man, no?'

'And an eminent collector?'

'So I understand.'

'A man of means?'

'Undeniably.'

Dominik stirred the sugar that had settled at the bottom of his tall glass of lemon juice and watched it dissolve.

The two men looked silently at each other, both lost in thoughts.

'If I didn't know you wrote books,' the Frenchman said, 'I would have said you had the potential to make a good private investigator, Mr Dominik.'

'You compliment me.'

Dominik was aware he would get no more pointers from Cavalier, but his gut feeling told him he was on the right trail.

Even though Summer had suggested he pursue that line of enquiry, he also knew she would not be pleased when he reported back to her that her intuition was being confirmed by other parties and that she was possibly sleeping with a man who had been directly involved in the theft of her precious violin.

'Their' violin, Dominik felt.

The auditorium lights at La Cigale dimmed and you could make out the dark shapes of mountainous towers of amplifiers on the instrument-laden stage and musicians shuffling to their places. Small red lights flickered from various control panels as the audience held its collective breath in anticipation.

A couple of spotlights picked out the tall, thin silhouettes of Chris and his cousin as they positioned themselves behind the two main microphones at the front of the stage.

'A one, a two, a three, a four . . .' Ella's voice, counting down.

The opening song of the Groucho Nights set was an acappella ballad sung by the two front men. It was a loose adaptation of an old English folk melody given a more rhythmic twist, and it always caught the audience's immediate attention with its stark melody and simplicity. The essential quietness of this initial part of the concert, combined with the bare nature of the lighting picking the two men out like an island in the midst of darkness, made this a striking introduction to the group's music, setting the mood for the rest of the evening.

As the voices began to fade and with no pause for the audience to applaud, the bass guitar began plucking the rhythm of their second song. The whole stage lit up, the drums joined in and Groucho Nights went electric. Chris's guitar spelled out a sinuous melody while his cousin's bass underpinned it, and the music took full flight, as the front rows of the audience, no doubt already familiar with some of the band's songs, began to clap along.

Seated on the balcony, Dominik watched as heads nodded and bodies began to sway to the rhythm of the music. The club was full to the rafters with people even standing in the aisles on the ground floor. All ages and classes were represented: the democracy of rock 'n' roll. He wondered which were here for Groucho Nights and which had been attracted by Summer's appearance, out of curiosity for the uncommon blend of rock and classical that was about to unfold. Following the initial four opening songs, Chris stepped towards the mike, milking the cheers from the crowd as he unplugged his Gibson and picked up a different guitar, a sleeker silver Gretsch that drew further applause from some of the connoisseurs in the audience.

'And now for our first special guests . . .'

The crowd roared.

But, to Dominik's surprise, it wasn't Summer's turn to make an appearance.

Trooping out from the wing were three brass players, holding their instruments aloft. Two men and a woman. They installed themselves at the back of the stage, to the right of Ella's drums. On her signal on the hi-hat, they brought their shiny instruments to their mouths and in unison with the rest of the group launched into a funky blues riff. With the addition of the newly arrived brass section, the group sounded ten times as powerful, loud, swinging infectiously, the music wrapping itself like a cloud around the high-ceilinged auditorium of the Paris club, notching up a measured sense of frenzy with every note. The effect of the transformation was mesmerising, Dominik had to admit. How would Summer cope with such a barrage of noise and emotion with just a fragile violin? By now Chris was literally screaming into his mike to make his voice heard above the roaring sound of the augmented band, his lyrics stretched to abstraction.

Back on her drum stand, Ella was sweating madly, her backing vocals almost inaudible, arms beating a wild, frantic tattoo, while Ted stood motionless to the right, a fixed point of steadfast calm, anchoring the din, his thumb attacking the strings of his bass with metronomic repetition.

The whole hall shook.

As the song climaxed with a final flourish, the brass players sustaining their ultimate notes until they almost ran out of breath, Dominik noticed a large smile of satisfaction spread across Chris's face as he realised he had the audience eating out of his hand.

From his vantage point up on the balcony and his sideways view of the stage, Dominik could see a gathering of onlookers standing in the wings, clapping along and watching the group; road crew, friends, guests. There was no sign of Summer, but he thought he caught a glimpse of Viggo Franck in his customary tight trousers and studied bohemian state of vestimentary disarray.

There was a brief lull between songs as both the crowd and the musicians onstage caught their breath, Chris and Ella taking a sip of water and towelling themselves while Ted remained his steadfast immobile self.

Chris then switched back to his original Gibson and launched into a delicate riff as the lights dimmed.

Then Summer walked on to the stage from the opposite wing.

She was all in white, picked out by a single spotlight, a flowing dress that reached to her ankles, her violin a delicate shade of reddish orange that almost rhymed with the thousand curls in her hair. She wore shiny, heavy black boots, a deliberately coarse contrast with the frailty of her dress.

There was a hush in the audience as she plugged her lead

into one of the massive Marshall amplifiers dotted around the stage. Her bow rose in her hand and slowly alighted on the violin and the first, heartbreakingly pure note rose, echoing the sound of Chris's guitar.

It was a while until the rest of the band joined in, the mellifluous melody unfolding on just violin and guitar, although Chris was still hidden in the penumbra as the sole spotlight remained on Summer, her small figure dominating the immensity of the dark stage.

Dominik felt his heart jump. It was as if, once again, she was playing just for him.

Beneath the white dress he could guess the unforgettable shape of her body. An image long carved into the deepest level of his brain.

His eyes fixed on Summer, he abandoned himself to her music and the spectacle of her movements on stage as she played, caressed and tamed the new electric violin, her sound soaring above the rest of the band then blending in with uncanny precision before taking off again as she dived into one of her fiery solos. All too soon the song came to an end in a flurry of feedback and the stage was bathed in lights of all colours.

Chris nodded at her and they began a new song, echoes of which Dominik now recalled having heard filter its way towards him from the bowels of the Brighton Centre when they had rehearsed. As the tune grew faster and faster, Summer was sketching little dance steps while she played. Her white dress floated around her with every successive movement. Dominik remembered her dancing on that New Orleans stage after the New Year, back when they were together. It now felt like a century ago. He closed his eyes, forcibly dragging images from that time to the surface of his mind.

There was a tap on his shoulder.

'Hello.' A strong foreign accent. A woman.

Dominik turned round to see who was sitting in the row behind him and attempting to catch his attention.

He identified her the moment he looked back.

The dancer from New Orleans.

Serendipity or what?

'I know who you are,' she said over the increasing sound of 'Roadhouse Blues', the new song Groucho Nights were now attacking with much gusto down on stage.

He smiled back at the enigmatic beauty.

'And I know you.'

The volume became deafening, and she made a sign that she could no longer hear him, shrugged her shoulders and began watching the stage again.

Intrigued by the brief encounter, Dominik also turned his attention back to the music.

Ella was now dictating the beat with frenzied authority, her arms flailing away in wild abandon, her drums carrying the band onwards and upwards to new heights as Chris sang, Ted harmonised in counterpoint and Summer undulated on the spot to the fearsome beat generated by her Groucho Nights bandmates. The brass trio was swinging from side to side, punctuating the rhythm like a Soul Revue section in overdrive.

The sound rose to a roaring crescendo as the number reached its climax, the final note sustained by Chris's guitar and Summer's plugged-in violin, then it suddenly fell, and the applause burst out. Triumphant, Baldo, Marija and

Alex all raised their instruments to the sky while the core members of the band took a bow.

Dominik had to admit to himself that the way they had integrated Summer's violin and the newly acquired brass section propelled the music into another, altogether more exhilarating, dimension.

Basking in the crowd's adoration, the musicians set their instruments down and, with Ted and Ella waving their hands at the crowd in acknowledgment, began to walk in single file back to the wings. The steady applause continued even after they disappeared. Dominik, like most of the spectators, was standing and still clapping. He glanced across his shoulders but Luba was gone.

The whole club vibrated with the sustained waves of continuous cheering. The roar rose in volume when Ella made her way back onto the stage. She had swapped her previously sweat-drenched top for a torn Holy Criminals-logoed shirt. The others followed with Summer coming last.

Dominik's heart tightened.

She was still wearing the flowing white dress she had performed in earlier, but had now put on a corset over it. The combination was remarkably effective. The tightness of the new garment as it imprisoned her slim waist and emphasised her shape, and the deep contrast between light and dark, was like a shot across his bow, dredging back so many memories that only belonged to the two of them. He immediately recognised the corset he had once bought her and which she had modelled for him in the most private of circumstances.

Dominik now knew what she had meant on the phone.

It was like a signal. Just for him. So much more than a wink.

The musicians all plugged in again and the crowd's applause subsided now that it had been granted its obligatory encore.

Ella gave the signal and the sound of Summer's violin pierced the buzzing silence with a distinctive melody soon punctuated by the rhythm of the bass.

Vivaldi.

The lead melody from one of the movements of *The Four Seasons*.

It was as if she was talking directly to him.

The rest of the band quickly joined in and the collective improvisation soon drowned Summer's pure line of sound, the piece fracturing into a mass of showcasing solos before Summer, with a sharp movement of her wrist, re-established the main melody and her authority and, stamping her booted left foot in the most unclassical manner, brought the first encore to an end. Chris segued immediately into 'Sugarcane', but Dominik's mind was already drifting.

The first people Dominik came across backstage as he was guided by a stagehand to the dressing room area were Edward and Clarissa.

Before he could wonder if this was all some sort of bizarre BDSM reunion, and speculate as to whether his old foe, Victor, was also in Paris on some nefarious business too, he was effusively greeted by the American couple as if he was a long-lost relative. As they noted the puzzlement on his face at finding them here, they quickly explained that their son, Alex, was in the brass section and they had taken advantage of the occasion to drop in as they happened to be holidaying in Europe.

'Nothing sinister, sweetheart,' Clarissa had said, noting his wariness. 'We're just here on a civilian mission. Supporting the family, so to speak.'

'We leave for Italy in the morning. We've always wanted to see Capri. Paris is just a pit stop,' Edward declared with a benevolent smile.

The band's dressing room was swamped with guests and freeloaders. Dominik noticed Viggo Franck in one corner, nursing a can of beer, in deep conversation with Chris. Hanging on his arm was Luba. Next to them was, he assumed, Fran, Summer's sister. There was a distinct likeness, although to him she looked like a preliminary sketch rather than the real article, but they had the same nose and chin and her laughter had the same deep growl. But her shorter hair was an identikit shade of bottle blond and lacked the fire and shine of Summer's.

He couldn't see Summer. Maybe she was still somewhere else in the backstage area, changing or showering after her exertions?

Waiting for her to make an appearance, Dominik fell into a desultory conversation with Edward and Clarissa and they were soon joined by Chris and Fran. Noticing Dominik's presence, there was a look of disapproval in Chris's eyes, but this soon passed as the adrenalin from the recent show, alcohol and Fran's roving hands and closeness quickly saw him relax and become mellower.

Although they were at least a generation older than anyone else in the crowded room and in no way rock 'n' roll in either appearance or attitude, Edward and Clarissa looked as if they owned the joint, effortlessly gliding along the flow of half-snatched conversations, introducing people to each other, kindly social overseers intent on ensuring everyone present remained in the best of moods.

Fending off the questions of a couple of leather-jacketed youthful French rock journalists who'd just been informed by Edward that he was a bona fide novelist, Dominik noticed, out of the corner of his eye, Fran whispering something in Chris's ear, with a mischievous gleam lighting up her eyes. Shortly after, the two excused themselves from the improvised party and left the room together.

Summer entered the room shortly after. She'd changed into a simple choice of white T-shirt and carefully distressed jeans. Her hair was still wet from the shower and more full of curls than ever. She noticed Dominik's presence and acknowledged him but was called over by Viggo who handed her a drink and then planted himself between her and the majestically tall Luba. He was like a monarch proudly displaying his twin consorts.

Dominik winced.

Regardless of the suspicions raised by the disappearance of Summer's violin, he had already taken a violent dislike to the rock star.

He excused himself from Edward and Clarissa, the group of people congregating around them and the members of the brass section they seemed to have taken under their wing, and moved to the bar – which had been set up at one end of the room on a trestle table – in search of something non-alcoholic.

Perusing the varied bottles, cans and plastic cups scattered randomly across the table, he took hold of a half-full bottle of San Pellegrino and brought it directly to his mouth in the absence of any clean glass.

'Wouldn't you rather have something stronger?' a voice suggested in his ear. That familiar accent. Luba, who had detached herself from the Viggo triptych.

'No, this is good enough for me,' Dominik replied. She wore a thin silk tunic which glittered with every movement of her body, and barely reached her knees. It clung to her form as if it had been painted on.

'How disciplined,' she remarked. 'My friend Viggo, he never says no to a drink . . . or a drug.' She nodded in Viggo Franck's direction. The singer had his arm around Summer's waist as he gesticulated for his audience of attentive fans.

'It's a long way from New Orleans,' Dominik said.

'I was only there on a short engagement,' Luba replied. 'Yesterday New Orleans, then Seattle. Have you been there? It's very rainy but quite vibrant. Then I go to London. Who knows where tomorrow?'

'You like to travel?'

'There is always something new, someone new. Life would be very boring if you stuck to just one thing, one person. Don't you agree?' Her breath smelled of vodka. No doubt authentic Russian vodka, as she didn't seem like the sort of girl who sampled anything but the best things in life.

'Are you with Viggo Franck?'

'With? Yes and no – he's convenient, just the right man at the right time. That's how it plays,' she said, as if bored by the prospect of further questions of a personal nature. 'And you? Still friendly with our pretty fiddle player?'

'Maybe.'

'That does not sound like a yes . . .'

'And what do you do when you're not dancing?' he asked, trying to steer the conversation in a different direction.

'I live.'

'Where?'

'At Viggo's place in London right now. In Belsize Park.'

'I live close by,' Dominik said.

'And you write books,' she remarked.

'How did you know that?' He was surprised.

'I have your book. There's no photo of you on the dust jacket, but I was curious, once I liked it, so I checked you out online. Just because I am a dancer does not mean I do not read,' she pointed out. 'I recognise you from that night in New Orleans. I always remember faces.'

Just then there was a roar of communal laughter from the group where Edward and Clarissa stood, where they had been joined by Viggo and Summer. Summer appeared to be in deep conversation with the Croatian couple who'd formed part of tonight's brass section, while Viggo was guffawing loudly at something Edward had just said. From the corner of his eye as he faced the statuesque Luba, Dominik noticed Summer giving him a sideways glance.

'Party!' shouted Viggo.

A few others echoed his cry.

Dominik felt Luba's hand brush against his and a small folded piece of paper being handed over. He looked up at her questioningly.

She boldly held his gaze, and as she walked away to join the main group, said, 'You are interesting. I like interesting men,' and stepped away from him.

Dominik discreetly unfolded the piece of paper and peered at it. A telephone number.

Seeing Luba return to his side, Viggo beamed and embraced her, his other hand still wandering close to Summer's midriff.

'These lovely people here,' he proclaimed, pointing at the elegantly attired Edward and Clarissa, 'have suggested we all go out and have a party. What was the name of the club you were proposing we visit?'

'It's called Les Chandelles,' Edward said, with an impeccable French enunciation. 'Not far by cab. Off the Champs Elysées. We are members of long standing; there should be no problem getting you all in.'

'The more the merrier, eh?' Viggo said.

Dominik had heard of the place. It was quite notorious, a highly upmarket *club échangiste*, a swing club where anything went. No doubt to the sound of popping champagne corks and much wealth on initial display before the clothes came off.

Viggo asked around, 'So, who's with me?'

A few further people checked out of the proceedings at this stage, including Alex, Edward and Clarissa's somewhat conservative son, as well as Ted and the Croatian couple who evidently had their hands full with each other. The survivors from the dressing room party began trooping down the corridor that led to La Cigale's main entrance. A handful of fans were standing there in the cold hoping for autographs, which Viggo happily dispensed. Ironically, none of them paid any attention to the members of Groucho Nights or Summer.

The Paris night was streaked with dark clouds.

A stretch limo was waiting by the kerb. Not all the revellers could fit in and half a dozen or so were left behind, including Dominik who was unenthusiastically following the pack. Clarissa shouted out the address of the club so the others could order a couple of taxis and join them there. As the limo took off, Dominik noticed that Summer was not on board and had remained behind on some pretext or another and was standing by his side. She hadn't brought a jacket or a coat along and was shivering.

She looked up at him, and seeing her eyes again so close made Dominik feel almost drunk.

'Do you really want to go there? Meet up and play with the others?' she asked him as some of the other stragglers began hailing passing cabs.

'Not really,' he said.

'Good.'

They barged their way to the front and appropriated the first taxi.

As the cab crossed the Seine by the Musée d'Orsay, Summer pressed her body against Dominik's.

The car took a sharp turn left to take the one-way street that would return them to the Boulevard Saint Germain and, following its movement, Summer leaned her head on Dominik's shoulder.

The elevator was the most exiguous he had ever experienced and Summer and Dominik had to twist and turn to both fit in.

The room was small.

And the bed was narrow.

'I spoke to someone about the Bailly,' he'd said, as they crossed the road from the taxi which had dropped them off and buzzed for the hotel nightwatchman to let them in.

'Anything about its possible whereabouts?' Summer asked.

'No, but—'

'Don't tell me then,' she interrupted him. 'It can wait for the morning. I don't want to know right now.'

She moved closer to him. Her eyes hesitant, his drawing her to him; both unsure what to say or do next. As if they were both being moved by a power they had no control over. Like magnets coming together. He could feel the heat radiating from her. He could hear the sound of her shallow breath as if through an amplifier, every beat of her heart. He stepped towards her in turn. There was an inevitability about it all.

They kissed.

It felt like coming home again. Not one day since New York had Dominik not thought of holding Summer in his arms again, and at first the moment felt almost unreal.

The top floor room was still shielded in darkness, the closed window looking out on the rickety roofs of the nearby buildings; not a room with a view.

As Dominik settled into the familiar and easy groove of the intoxicating softness of Summer's lips and the reassuring sensation of holding her close again, he began to revel in the relaxed way they fitted together. His hands dropped from her chin to her sides and beneath the thin material of the T-shirt, he felt the ridges and resistance of the corset she had briefly worn on stage.

She had kept it on.

'Arms up,' he instructed.

She raised them and Dominik pulled the T-shirt over her head.

'Jeans,' he insisted.

Summer unzipped herself and, with a shake and shimmy, shook off the jeans, which fell down to her ankles. She stood there with the corset her only remaining item of clothing. Whoever had tightened its grip when she had put it on between the main set and the encores in the backstage changing room – Ella, maybe – had cinched it particularly tight and it cut into her waist with ferocious efficiency, highlighting her slim figure and framing her breasts, nipples pointing upwards, at attention, hard and dark.

Dominik lowered his lips towards the uncovered top half of her breasts and took one of the nipples into his mouth, reading its pliant texture with his roving tongue, wetting it, lubricating it, then delicately took it between his teeth, testing its consistency, finally biting it gently and then harder.

Summer gasped, her whole body speared by a wave of arousal and pain.

She rode the crest of the sensation, teeth clenched, until the endorphins in her system kicked in and the discomfort began turning into pleasure as Dominik's sharp teeth continued digging into the cratered, rougher skin of her nipples, although never hard enough to draw blood. He held her there for what felt like an eternity, balanced between pain and pleasure and her whole body switching on, one area at a time, beginning in the pit of her stomach, the depths of her cunt, until the tidal wave reached her brain and she felt herself willingly drowning in a muddy sea of warmth, navigating the unstable sea floor with primal instinct.

Just as she was about to abandon herself fully to the intoxicating sensations Dominik was coaxing out of her unconscious memories, his teeth withdrew suddenly and his lips moved to her ear, cruelly toying with the even more delicate flesh of her lobe and the see-saw of pain and pleasure began all over again.

She flinched, shuddered uncontrollably as the sensations piled up inside her, her spine briefly losing its will to stand straight and firm, and she felt Dominik hold her under her arms, steadying her position, preventing her fall.

She could now feel the fierce hardness of his cock pressing against her through the rough material of his black slacks, rubbing against her curling bush. Her anticipation rose as she felt the wetness spread between her thighs, the well of lust filling her one drop at a time, readying her, transforming her very nature.

He finally moved his teeth away and a deep feeling of dread and abandon assaulted her like a slap to the face, the sudden realisation that this might be the end of the stop-go-stop circular nature of his assault, just as she had comfortably settled into the fire of its repetition. They held each other in silence for a second or two, then his lips returned to her ear, this time teasing its hollow, wetting it, licking this most intimate of her domains, journeying into its small pit and the sensation was overwhelming as wave upon wave of miniature seismic shifts percolated inside her across the minefield of her senses.

She realised that, once again, the point of no return was about to be reached, a territory only Dominik knew how to breach and dominate like the lord of all he could survey. So far it had just been a few bites, and affectionate ones at that, but her soul screamed out for more, inviting her on a mad race towards genuine pain. And it scared her that this so often out-of-reach place felt like home, where she truly belonged.

Right now, all Summer wanted was to feel Dominik inside her, but she knew he would deliberately take his time, play her body and her mind like an instrument before she would be granted that sweet release.

A refrain in her mind, *Damn you, damn you, I want you, I hate you, I love you*, going round in endless circles. *Dominik. Dominik. Do bad things to me.* She wanted to say it out loud, but she knew that silence was his thing, it gave him power, and all she wanted to do was melt inside his arms. Summer bit her lip. Hard. She felt a thin drop of blood squeeze its way through the thin incision he had just made and saw Dominik avidly swoop on it like a welcoming vampire out of the darkness and lick it away, with the kindest of smiles illuminating his face.

With a gentle pressure against her shoulders, Dominik guided her to the bed.

She sank into its soft embrace, looked up at him and spread her legs in delightful anticipation.

Time stood still for a minute or so as the two of them gazed at each other, a million lines of unspoken dialogue unfolding. Dominik then undressed as Summer watched. His body still as white as she remembered, the English skin so unfamiliar with the sun.

The pleasurable thought of spending time on a hot,

Mediterranean beach with him flashed through Summer's mind.

Now naked, he picked up his black trousers from the floor where he had shed them and unthreaded their thick leather belt and climbed onto the bed, squatting above her, his strong cock tantalisingly close to her half-open mouth, and took hold of her hands, pinning them behind her head and tying them with the belt to the bars of the bed.

Summer's heart skipped a beat and she closed her eyes.

Towering over her, he guided his penis down to her mouth and let it graze her lips. Instinctively, she opened her mouth, but, teasingly, he refused to lower himself inside her and she was forced to bring her head upward and meet his cock as it hovered, hard and hot, just an inch away. The moment her tongue stretched far enough to travel across the smooth surface of his glans, she felt an electric shock course through her soul and her body.

Even though she was the violin player, Dominik knew just how to play her, each touch, each feint orchestrating her journey towards total submission. Finally, she allowed her head to drop again, collapse into the cushion that supported it, and this time his wonderful cock followed her down, barely breaching her, denying her appetite for a while, until she could bear it no longer and her tongue darted across it, wetting it, smoothing its path, lubricating its animal ardour.

'Yes,' Dominik said.

Summer groaned.

'Swallow me whole,' he whispered.

'Hmmm . . .' Summer gasped as he suddenly thrust forward.

And he began to fuck her mouth. Tenderly, ragefully, deep, thick, lovingly, roughly. The way she always wanted him to be.

By abdicating all control, she became whole.

The night was sex. Paris was sex.

And all was right with the world. At least for tonight, she belonged to Dominik.

When they woke in the morning, bruised and spent, both emotionally and physically, Summer frantically realised she barely had enough time to get back to her own hotel and pack up for the next leg of the European tour with the band. She couldn't keep the others waiting. By now, all the equipment would have been loaded onto the specially hired coach. There was still the matter of the missing violin to discuss, they realised.

'Another time,' they agreed, both dressing hastily. As she ran out of the door, blowing him a perfunctory kiss, Dominik felt gutted they hadn't found the occasion to speak properly this morning.

About what had just happened. And then he glanced at his watch and noted that he barely had an hour left before his own train at the Gare du Nord and the journey back to London.

9

Girls Together

I made it to the tour bus in the nick of time.

'Christ, Sum, you like to cut it fine,' Chris said, as I leaped onboard.

Fran shot me a worried look, and I shook my head slightly in return, a silent gesture to indicate that I was OK, and please could she not mention it.

She and Chris were sitting next to each other. She was curled up with her head on his shoulder, and they both dozed off minutes after we got on the road. Ella and Ted were both already asleep and so was Marija. Baldo and Alex smiled at me and waved a friendly greeting but they both looked as rough as I felt. It must have been a long night for all of us.

I wondered what they'd got up to. I didn't want to think about my sister's interests, and couldn't imagine Chris being the swinging sort. He was a one woman kind of guy. Ella and Ted were friendly enough but they didn't gossip about their personal lives and I didn't even know whether they were straight, gay, bi, dating each other or asexual. Marija and Baldo were certainly both creatures of passion. When we had lived together, rarely had a night or a morning gone by when I hadn't fallen asleep or woken up to the sounds of their noisy lovemaking. Whether or not they would feel comfortable making their affection for each other as public as it might be at Les Chandelles, the famous French swinging joint, I had no idea. As for Alex, I could only imagine that he had gone home feeling ill at the thought of his parents partying in that manner, but maybe he was more open-minded than I gave him credit for. It was something I'd be interested in talking about maybe with Marija, or Edward and Clarissa. But not right now.

I was still wearing yesterday's clothes. I hadn't even had time for a shower, never mind doing my hair and make-up. I'd slept late, soothed and wrapped up in the contentment of lying alongside Dominik.

We'd barely talked. Just hadn't had the time. We'd spent the night in bed together and that had been wonderful, as it always was. We had fitted into each other as if we'd never been apart, slipped into our own, very personal brand of lovemaking without a word.

But I hadn't had a chance to tell him how I felt. Or even to work out how I felt. I'd had to dress, kiss him goodbye and race for the coach as though my life depended on it, and now that I was settled in for the long ride to Brussels with little to distract me besides the occasional chatter from my bandmates whenever they roused, new scenes rushing by the windows as we passed through towns and cities, all I could think about was Dominik.

My lips were still tender from the viciousness of his kisses, not to mention my nipples which were both swollen and sore, and which bore some slight bruising where his teeth had grazed my skin. I was still wet, as I'd begun thinking about going back to his bed as soon as I'd left it, and along with the physical aches and sadness I was filled with a desire to be with him that I doubted would never be sated, at least while we were apart.

I wanted to push the feelings out of my head somehow, to get into a swimming pool and thrash out lap after lap, or to put on my running shoes and tear along footpaths until the pain in my body cancelled out the pain in my heart. But it was no good, I was stuck on a comfortable seat for the next five hours. Not long enough to sleep, and too long to sit quietly without any distraction. I wished I'd thought to strap myself into the corset tightly under my T-shirt again. The discomfort in that would have blunted the terrible longing that tore me like a constant scream.

I hadn't even asked him about the Bailly. Truth be told, I wanted Dominik more than I wanted the violin back. I'd have lost the Bailly a thousand times over to have another chance with him. If I could have made a pact with the devil at that moment, I'd have sold my soul to him and destroyed the violin with my own hands, if it would bring Dominik back.

But it was no good. He was on his way to London, and to Lauralynn. Knowing them both as I did, they must have an open relationship. I couldn't see Lauralynn settling down, and though Dominik never seemed able to quite release his jealousy, he had a fiercely independent streak. I doubted that he would agree to a monogamous relationship with anyone. Nonetheless, I wished I knew what our night together had meant to him. Lauralynn didn't have a submissive streak in her body, so perhaps it had been a chance for him to top someone who appreciated it. A fling with an old playmate, and nothing more. I wondered if he'd tell Lauralynn, if they'd laugh at me together and reminisce fondly about the silly fiddler they both once knew who liked her sex hard and rough and didn't appear to have a romantic bone in her body. Well, I did, but only for the right person, and that right person was Dominik. Without him, I might be reduced to relationships like the kind that I had with Simón for the rest of my life. Friendship, and nothing more. I didn't want to hurt anyone again the way that I had hurt Simón, so had no plans to try my hand on the dating scene.

Luba had seemed rather interested in Dominik, and I'd been so enormously thankful that he hadn't wanted to pursue her, or to go to the swingers' club. Sharing him with another was the last thing I wanted to do right now, while whatever connection we had left still felt so uncertain, so fragile. Even if he hadn't wanted to spend time with me, seeing him with someone else would have broken my heart.

We were playing again that night; another gig, another city. I pulled my running shoes on as soon as we stepped into the hotel, caught the Métro to the city centre and took a spin around the Parc de Bruxelles, past the palace and the embassies, drumming all the tension that had gathered during the journey into the pavement.

When Dominik rang, I almost didn't answer. It wasn't that I didn't want to speak to him. Quite the opposite. I wished I could capture the sound of his voice and replay it in my mind over and over, but I was afraid of what he might say, and what I might say in return. We had so much to talk about and I've never been good on the phone – something about the lack of his physical presence made my thoughts scatter like leaves in the wind and my feelings so difficult to articulate.

Between the two of us, we barely managed a couple of minutes of conversation, and nothing which settled anything, or hinted at how we might continue our relationship, or if there was a relationship left to continue. He was on his way to Spain to promote his book about Elena. He had some news about the violin which suggested that Viggo might be behind the theft. In a way I wasn't surprised. I had always had a nagging suspicion. But I was so morose about Dominik that the loss of the violin had just combined with my loss of Dominik, and my longing for them both formed one angry ball inside me, a depression that I couldn't shake.

I didn't know where to begin with Viggo. Any way I looked at it, I was in a hole that I wouldn't be able to dig myself out of in a hurry. If I upset him, he might pull the plug on his support of Groucho Nights, and then I'd be responsible for Chris's dreams going down the toilet. If I didn't do anything, I might lose the Bailly for ever. And if I continued to ask Dominik for his help, he'd be stuck with the knowledge that I was sleeping with the guy who had stolen his gift to me.

I didn't sleep a wink that night. Just lay awake, staring at the bland walls of the hotel room and hoping that an idea would come to me that might solve all my problems, but it didn't. For perhaps one of the first times in my life, I was up early with my running shoes on again, wearing my frustrations out through my feet, slowing to a walk when my shins began to throb. I didn't mind the pain, it kept my mind off Dominik, but fear of getting shin splints and having to rest for a month or more reduced my exertions to a more sensible pace.

This time I remembered to lace the corset on for the journey. Another eight hours by coach to Berlin.

It was early evening by the time we pulled into Berlin. We were staying in Neukölln, near the Festsaal Kreuzberg where our first gig was taking place the following night. Berlin was the first city that we'd been booked two nights running to play. Susan had somehow managed to get one of Grayson's pictures of me into a couple of popular German music mags, a shot that was just on the right side of risqué, with me holding a violin seductively whilst clad in Fran's wet-look leggings and leather jacket and my studded Louboutins. My solo music had already been popular here, and Groucho Nights' promised mix of classical, sex and rock 'n' roll had proved a winning combination, and a sell-out.

Consequently, the band was in a good mood and we'd booked a short break and a few extra nights in the city, the first time on the tour any of us would really have a chance to look around like proper tourists, rather than just play and then ship out to the next destination.

Fran, frugal as ever, had booked us into a budget hotel with a secure storage facility for the gear we couldn't leave in the van overnight. The hotel was down a fairly quiet, mainly residential street, opposite a winding canal where swans floated by peacefully and pairs of lovers walked hand in hand under the trees. The smell of pastry, meat and spices wafted like a cloud from the Turkish restaurant next door.

I fell into bed as soon as we checked in and slept properly that night for the first time in as long as I could remember. Perhaps it was the memory of Dominik's voice, or the thought that I might see him again, and that we might at least manage to be friends that lulled me into relaxation.

The place that we were playing was on a road beneath a railway bridge, opposite a car dealership. From the outside it was nondescript, just a small sign advertised the name. But by the time we were due on, the whole joint was heaving. It was standing-room only, and so many people had managed to pile into the upstairs balcony that I worried the whole thing was going to fall down on our heads. We'd had some problems with the soundcheck, and were a little late starting. By the time we walked out onto the stage, the audience were stamping their feet and screaming their heads off.

It was the first night that we'd run out of our planned encores and had to pull an extra number out of the bag before they'd let us off stage again.

We'd packed up all the gear and were making plans to head out on the town when I heard a familiar voice calling out across the front courtyard.

'Hello, stranger.'

I swung around at the sound of the sultry New York accent.

It was Lauralynn, standing dressed in her trademark skin-tight jeans, a plain white T-shirt and stiletto heels. She was obviously bra-less. She must have been the only woman I knew to go out in public without one, but it appeared that where I went to the other extreme, enjoying the restriction of a corset, Lauralynn liked the freedom of absence from constraints, and also the reaction she drew from passers-by who had a clear view of her pierced nipples. She had the sort of breasts that look good even without the support of a bra, and I was a little envious.

Initially I was elated that a familiar face had travelled this far to see us in action, but my elation turned to confusion and fear when I remembered that she was dating Dominik, who I'd spent the night with in a hotel in Paris a few nights earlier.

The expression on Lauralynn's face certainly didn't suggest that she was here in anger to accuse me of stealing her man. If anything, she looked delighted to see me. I didn't know what to say, or do, so I just stood there, mouth agape, staring at her.

'Jeez,' she said, 'I always thought you were a cold fish, but are you going to just stand there?'

'Sorry,' I said, 'you took me by surprise. Thanks for coming to see the show.'

She wrapped her arms around me and held me against her, so that I could feel her breasts pushing up against mine.

'You were amazing,' she said. 'Who would have thought Dominik's classical gal would turn into a rock chick, huh?'

'Dominik's girl?'

'Yeah, where is the man in question? I thought he'd be in the front row cheering you on. I've been keeping my eyes peeled for him all night.'

'You thought he was here with me? I'd assumed he was in London with you,' I added, confused.

'No. I've been away. Got home and found the house empty so I came looking. Never been a fan of my own company,' she said, giving my arm another squeeze as if to check that I was real. 'Don't tell me he went all the way to Paris and still didn't tell you that he's madly in love with you?'

'What are you talking about? I thought he was dating you?'

'Christ, no. We're just old friends . . . well, friends with benefits might be a better description. I don't mind the male creatures, you know, they can be charming, and Dominik has certain very useful talents.' She winked flirtatiously at me when she said this. 'But they're not really my type long term. Unless they're under my stilettos. They can make good pets if you train them properly, but I wouldn't keep one for ever.'

This news nearly made my knees buckle beneath me. I sank down onto one of the outdoor picnic tables, and Lauralynn crouched down to meet my eyes, her long legs folding under her like a grasshopper's.

'You really thought we were dating?' she asked, more kindly this time, stroking a lock of my hair away from my face so she could look me in the eyes.

'Yes, Dominik told me you were.'

'And I suppose you told him that you're dating that rock star I hear you've been hanging about with?'

'Yes, I did.'

'You two drive me crazy, you know that. Both as proud as punch and blind as bats. When I heard that he was going to Paris to watch your opening night I thought he'd finally seen sense, but I guess I should have known better.'

Lauralynn not dating Dominik. That changed every-thing. But why on earth did he tell me he was? Because I'd told him that I was spending my nights with Viggo Franck, if he hadn't already read it in the gossip columns. I cursed myself again for that wilful stubborn streak that was always getting me into trouble, and my total inability to make people realise how much I cared about them. Why couldn't I have just told him how I felt?

I sank over further, holding my head in my hands as if I could somehow rewind time if I concentrated hard enough.

'Right,' said Lauralynn. I recognised the narrowing of her eyes, and the tone of her voice. She had switched into her domme mode. I envied that part of her too, she'd always been secure in herself and her desires. She didn't seem to lose a minute's sleep over the type of person she had become and why. She just enjoyed herself.

'You're going to have to pull yourself together, or I'm going to do it for you, and we can't stay here all night. Where's the rest of your band gone?'

'Party in the dressing rooms most likely, or back at the hotel. They won't miss me though.'

'Don't act so sorry for yourself. Tell them you've bumped into an old friend so they don't think you've been kidnapped by a crazed fan, and let's go and have a drink, and you can tell me all your woes.'

She took my arm in hers and steered me out of the bar onto the streets of Kreuzberg. It was still reasonably early for northern Europe. Unlike Londoners, Berliners didn't have last tubes to race for at midnight or pubs that closed at eleven, so most of the parties wouldn't get started until midnight at the earliest, and they wouldn't really get going until 2 a.m. All I wanted to do was go home and sleep, curl into a ball and indulge in my misery.

'First,' she said, 'food. It's much harder to feel miserable on a full stomach.'

We walked up to the late-night takeaway bar on the

corner by the canal, and Lauralynn ordered pizza, two currywursts, and a serving of curly frites.

'Don't screw up your nose,' she said, as I questioned the wisdom of pouring curry sauce over a hot dog sausage, 'these are delicious.'

She was right. The food was good, warming, and put me in a much better mood.

'So,' I said. 'Tell me everything. Why are you here in Berlin? Did you come all this way to see me?'

'I had to take off home in a hurry. My brother hasn't been well, so I went back to New York for a few weeks.'

'Oh. Sorry to hear that.'

Lauralynn shrugged. She was picking her frites up three at a time and using them as a scoop to scrape the remaining curry sauce from her plate. I was too upset to eat much, but managed most of my sausage. The sauce was a strange mixture of curry flavouring and sweetness, more sugar than spice, but it worked, somehow.

'Family stuff. All sorted now though. I got a couple of emails from Dominik while I was away. You two are remarkably alike, you know, both miserable sods if left to your own devices, so I keep an eye on him.' She was staring at me with her piercing blue eyes, trying to read my response. I was hanging on her every word, wishing she'd get to the point and tell me more about Dominik.

She took a long sip of her cola, leaving the end of her straw reddened with lipstick, and continued. 'He mentioned some stuff about your violin, and the novel that he's been working on. He's had terrible trouble with that too, you know. The first one was a breeze, when he was writing about you. Now that he's been writing about your violin, he seems to be flying again. Doesn't that tell you something?'

I stared at her, uncomprehending. 'I guessed he just needed a female character to make it work, and I was the first one that came to mind.'

'Exactly. You were the first one who came to mind. He's spent two years thinking about you every day. And he still can't get you out of his head.'

'I haven't stopped thinking about him, either,' I replied morosely, stuffing in a handful of frites, although I'd stopped feeling hungry after the first couple of mouthfuls. They looked a little like onion rings, only redder, as if they were coated in paprika.

'Tell me something then,' she said, wiping her fingers thoroughly on a napkin. She had painted her nails blood red, to match her lipstick.

'Yes?'

'Why don't you just tell him? Tell him that you're in love with him?'

'I don't know . . . I . . . I know how he likes to be in control. I didn't want to be the one to say it.'

'Bullshit. This isn't about control. And you've got to be the least submissive sub I've ever met. More of a bottom, really.'

'A bottom?'

'Yes. You just get your thrills out of being topped, being dominated, with or without the emotional connection. It's just how you like your sex.'

'I suppose so. But it doesn't feel the same with anyone other than Dominik. With other people it's just . . . sex. With Dominik, it's something more.'

'That's just what it's like to fuck someone that you're in love with. Haven't you ever been in love?'

I thought about it. Viggo, Simón, Darren. Will, a boyfriend I'd had in New Zealand, before moving overseas. The most I could say was that I'd been very fond of them. Simón, I thought I had really loved. But sexually we didn't have the same connection, so at times he felt more like a brother than a lover.

'No, I don't think I have.'

She shook her head from side to side in disbelief.

'No wonder that you're a bit emotionally stunted then, I suppose,' she sighed.

She stared down at her empty plate regretfully, and then over at my leftovers. 'Waste not, want not,' she added, skewering the remains of my sausage on her fork.

'How long are you staying in Berlin?' I asked her, hoping to get the subject off me and my love life.

'I don't know,' she said. 'I haven't booked a hotel yet. I took the first flight I could find when I found the house in Hampstead vacant. Couldn't face being at home alone. I presumed Dominik had followed you here. Thought I could bunk in with your band or just party the night away, save on accommodation. I spent last night with a girl I picked up at Roses, that was fun, but I didn't get her number.'

She glanced up and winked at me over the last mouthful of currywurst. 'Now that I've seen the state you're in, I can hardly leave you here all alone, can I?'

'I can look after myself,' I replied, beginning to bristle.

'That's exactly the problem with you, Summer, you're too proud, and too ready to look after yourself. You need to learn to let people into that hard shell of yours. I'm sure there's a softie hiding under the bristly exterior.'

'Well, you can stay with me, I've got a double bed, in a hotel just round the corner.'

'That'll do me fine,' she said, grinning wickedly. 'But I don't think there's any need to turn in just yet. Berlin is party central. I've done all the bars on this side of town but there's another place I want to try, just a cab ride away.'

'I'm really not in the mood to party.'

'You're as bad as Dominik. Never wants to go out either, and when he does it's for a soft drink. Humour me. Nothing serious. Just a dance and a drink, it'll take your mind off your woes.'

Lauralynn was like a train headed full speed down a track once she got started, and I didn't have the energy to talk her out of it, so agreed to tag along, though it was already close to one in the morning.

'You can sleep when you're dead,' she replied when I reminded her of the time. Lauralynn didn't wheedle, she ordered, and I could feel my defences beginning to drop under the weight of her commands.

'I have nothing to wear,' I protested pitifully.

She narrowed her eyes as though she had X-ray vision and assessed me from head to toe.

'Do you have a corset on under that dress?'

'Yes, but not one I want to wear in public.'

She ignored my response.

'And those are thigh-length boots?'

I nodded miserably.

'That'll be just perfect.'

She led me across the street and flagged down a taxi.

I didn't catch the address that she gave to the driver, just the name of the bar: Insomnia.

'You speak German?'

'Not very well. But well enough to get around. I did a student exchange for a few months in Berlin when I was in high school . . . I wasn't old enough to get into the best clubs then, but I was tall enough to fool some of the bouncers.'

Twenty minutes later, we pulled up into a side street, dark and quiet aside from the red sign advertising the club and the two security guys standing out front, eyeing up the couples arriving one after the other.

We were greeted warmly by the blonde girl on the door, who took the cover charge. She looked us up and down, examining our state of dress, and Lauralynn said a few words to her in German. The girl waved us on.

The entryway was decorated entirely in red, seemingly the universal colour of sex. There was a glass case on the right, displaying a couple of porno DVDs and a purple latex bolero with a white frill for sale. A poster advertised a special night coming up, 'Fuck party'.

Lauralynn was sitting down on a red, velvet-covered bench that lined one wall, pulling off her high heels and then shimmying down her skinny jeans.

'Lauralynn,' I hissed at her.

'It's OK,' she replied. 'It's meant to be fetish wear but they're pretty casual about the dress code. They'll let us through in our underwear. You can get changed here.'

She had pulled off her T-shirt, and was slipping back into her high heels, wearing nothing else besides a black thong.

'I really don't feel like this sort of party.'

The last thing I wanted to do was have sex, or watch people having sex. Or dance, for that matter, and dance naked least of all. If Lauralynn had wanted to purposefully engineer a way to make me feel more depressed, she couldn't have done much better than this. Maybe she would let me lie down in the cloakroom and curl up in the foetal position while she partied on without me.

'Trust me,' she said, 'and take off your clothes.'

She had an authoritative way of speaking that brooked no argument, even if I had been in the sort of mood to put up a fight. The domme in her talking, I suppose, and dommes, in my experience, are even harder to say no to than their male equivalents.

I slipped out of my dress, a muted leopard-print shift, revealing a pair of long boots, black underwear and my black underbust corset, the one that Dominik had bought me, which had followed me halfway around the world and held more memories, both painful and pleasant, than I cared to remember.

Lauralynn took my hand and led me up the red carpeted steps to the bar. She handed me a shot of tequila, without asking me what I wanted to drink.

'Get this down you,' she said. 'It'll take the edge off.'

I didn't bother with the lemon and salt, just threw the shot back in one and pushed the glass back onto the counter. I stared around the room to see what she was planning on getting me into tonight, all in the name of cheering me up.

Alongside the bar was a dance floor, which was still fairly quiet although it was quite late.

'The girl on the door said it doesn't really get going until two, when they open the upstairs area,' Lauralynn said. She had finished her shot, and was licking the remaining salt and sugar off her fingers. A couple of guys were staring at us hungrily, the usual handful of single men, most of them in uniforms of black shirt and trousers, that occupied these sorts of places, apparently in every country in the world. At least so far they were looking at us from a safe distance.

Lauralynn followed my gaze and nervous expression as I automatically shuffled in closer to her, feeling very aware of my naked breasts and fighting the desire to wrap my arms around my chest and hide them, which would only draw more attention.

'Ignore them,' she said glancing at the lone men disdainfully, as if they weren't worth more attention than something unpleasant she had discovered on the soles of her shoes. 'Let's look around.'

We entered a room on the right. It was dark, so dark that I could barely make out a couple of bodies curled up on a bed in the corner of the room. The people sitting on top appeared to be just cuddling, but I couldn't be sure, and averted my eyes hurriedly. I was in no mood for voyeurism tonight. It took me a minute to work out that the glowing artwork on the walls represented genitalia, both the male and female variety. Near the entrance was a large glow-in-the-dark vagina sculpture which stuck out of the wall in brightly coloured 3D. A large green ring was attached to the sculpture's clitoris. On other walls, similar sculptures showed a large phallus and animated men and women in various stages of copulation.

There was a small St Andrew's cross, and a spanking bench, both pushed out of the way. In the next room, a sex swing, and another couple of beds. These ones contained more couples, but my eyes still hadn't quite adjusted and I just caught glimpses, a breast here, a red high-heeled shoe there, a woman moaning with pleasure surrounded by a ring of single men watching her.

Lauralynn was looking around with an interested gaze, drinking it all in.

I couldn't stand to watch.

'I have to get out of here,' I said to her, pushing my way through to the exit, back onto the dance floor. A porno film was playing on a loop. The first thing I noticed was that all the women had pubic hair, and none of them were blond. The cultural language of sex.

The DJ was playing dance music, and bright lights drifted through the room. The people on the dance floor were lost in the music, and seemed immune to the sex around them. A woman dressed like Lauralynn, in just a thong, was dancing with her partner who was similarly clad in just his underwear. Other than their states of mutual undress, they could have been any middle-aged couple dancing at a wedding. At least, thank heaven for small mercies, I hadn't seen any flaccid cocks bouncing, or men stroking themselves yet.

Lauralynn took my hand again, and swept me along, past the bar, to a pair of velvet curtains that signalled the entrance to another room at the back.

I grumbled in protest again, but she didn't even turn, never mind stop and listen.

'Here we are,' she said, as we stepped through and turned to the right. 'This is what I brought you for. Nothing like a bath to improve one's state of mind.'

We were standing alongside a jacuzzi, as yet unoccupied. Fresh, fluffy white towels were piled alongside, and a sign pointed to a large shower room around the corner, requesting that patrons rinse off first before taking a turn in the pool. Lauralynn had already shimmied out of her thong, taken a towel, and turned the water on. I hurried after her, to avoid standing next to the hot tub for more than a few moments alone, in case one of the stray single men took my solitary presence as an invitation.

I tried not to stare at the rivulets of water that raced over the curves of Lauralynn's body.

I'd previously seen her in her orchestral black and whites, signature skinny jeans and then a latex catsuit so tight it could have been painted on. Naked, she was all that the catsuit had promised, tall and curvaceous with legs that went on for miles. It was her manner that truly turned her into a bona fide sex bomb, the message in her eyes that invited attention but assured the onlooker that they would never be in with a chance. It was no wonder that men wanted to worship her. It wasn't just that she wouldn't give them a second look under any other circumstances, but also something in her nature that made me want to throw myself at her feet in return for half a smile. There was something queenly about her.

I joined her in the stream of the shower, washing away the sorrows of the last day and night under the flow of hot water.

We stepped into the jacuzzi together, and sat still, soaking, for another hour, barely exchanging a word. If anyone endeavoured to join us, then Lauralynn sent them on their way again with one cold look.

I was utterly relaxed, and close to sound asleep by the time she began to unfurl herself from her position in the tub and dried off.

Sounds emanating from neighbouring alcoves and rooms near the shower room suggested that the party was now in full swing. I hadn't become any more interested in joining the fray, but was no longer disturbed by the soft moans of pleasure and occasional grunt.

It was 3 a.m. by the time we flagged a taxi to get home again. The bars down Oranienstraße were still open and filled with people. Even IchOrya, the coffee shop that I'd spent most of the day in yesterday, still had its lights on, and a couple of people sitting out front smoking cigarettes. Berlin was truly the city that never slept.

I buzzed us into the hotel. We were all on the same floor, our rooms joined by the empty corridor. The others were either still out or sound asleep, probably the former, as we had all become virtually nocturnal, resting during the day, performing and partying at night.

Lauralynn stripped straight off again, and I did the same. We'd already spent half the evening with our clothes off in each other's company and I was too tired to think about finding the pyjamas that I carried in my suitcase in case of platonic company.

It was lunchtime by the time either of us stirred. I woke up to find myself curled into Lauralynn's arms, my cheek resting on her breasts and the sweet smell of her shampoo filling my nostrils. It was a distinctly comfortable place to be, and for a moment I thought I might understand how it might feel to be a man, waking up alongside a woman. She was taller than me, and in the position of the person giving comfort, so in that respect it was not so different, but she was much softer and the scent of her body had a different sort of musk to it.

She ran her fingers through my hair when she woke, as though we were lovers, and held me closer to her. I wondered for a moment what it would be like to kiss her, but even if I had had the confidence, it didn't seem like the right thing to do. I couldn't hit on one of Dominik's friends, or lovers, or whatever she was to him, even if he and I were still technically free from any formal commitment to each other.

'I think I might die without caffeine,' she said.

A girl after my own heart.

We dressed quickly, eager to find fresh air and food. I hadn't eaten much of the takeaway food and Lauralynn had an appetite like a furnace that constantly needed stoking.

I stopped en route to listen to a busker playing Bruce Springsteen's 'I'm on Fire', batting away Lauralynn's protests that she would pass out any minute if she didn't get breakfast in a hurry. I was always sentimental about buskers, remembering when I had been one of them, and dropped a five-euro note in his case in exchange for a CD in a sleeve with a cover that looked halfway between home-made and professional. It read: 'Kaurna Cronin, Feathers'. I smiled at the artist, who doffed his trilby to me as Laura-lynn hopped impatiently from one foot to another.

'Can't you flirt after I've been fed?' she asked grumpily, as I tucked the CD into my bag.

We had coffee, and a plate of bread, sliced meat and cheese at Matilda's. Chris and Fran were already there, but just finishing off their meal, with plans to root around in the record store next door. We were booked again that evening in the same venue, so just had the afternoon and early evening to kill.

Fran sized up Lauralynn, and stared at me with a raised eyebrow. 'Sleep well?'

I introduced her, as an old friend of a friend. Soon Fran and Chris were off again, with promises to see us later in the day.

'Your sister?' Lauralynn asked.

'Yes.'

'You look alike. Different, but still the same underneath. She has the same spark in her eye.'

'Don't you start. Chris is obviously after her and one friend messing with my sister is about all I can stand.'

We ordered another round of coffees and sat outside the cafe for a while on the pink blankets that lined the wooden bench seats, looking out at the street and watching the people go by.

Lauralynn was easy company. She didn't seem to require any input from me, and was content to just sit still by my side. Being alongside her was soothing, and gave me a sense of hope. She wasn't the sort to be anything other than deadpan honest, no matter how much it might hurt me, so if she thought that Dominik and I stood a chance, then we did.

Eventually, she broke the silence.

'Let's go exploring.'

'Sure,' I shrugged. We were leaving Berlin in a couple of days, and despite my best intentions, I'd spent more time sleeping than looking around. The rest of the tour was just single nights here and there, and no further breaks until we got back to London.

We rented bicycles and cycled over to the Flohmarkt in Mauerpark. It was packed with people. Half the population of Berlin seemed to be there, rooting around the stalls for knick-knacks, vintage clothing and second-hand furniture. I spotted a pair of zebra-print ankle boots in a size too small for me, and acquired them for Fran.

We bought two plastic cups of fresh orange juice and picked our way through the crowds to the park opposite the market. It was a fairly barren place compared with some of the other green places that I had seen in the city, just straggly grass and few trees, but it was also full of people, stretched out on the grass or sitting and watching a group of musicians at one end, who were singing into a karaoke machine.

My phone rang again. I answered it hurriedly, realising just as I pressed the answer button that I didn't recognise the number. This time, it wasn't Dominik.

'Hi, Summer. It's Grayson. I have something to ask you about your photographs . . .'

10

Private Dancer

The one night in Paris with Summer had been too short. They hadn't even found the time to really speak about the loss of the violin, about the true reasons they had come apart in New York. He knew that neither of them had any wish to start apportioning blame; it was clear to him now that they had both been equally at fault. Because of what they were, the dark things that made them tick. If that underground river on which their lives floated had not existed and carried them along with its flow, they would probably not even have met, so there was no point debating the minutiae. They were what they were: supremely imperfect and unlikely to change. It was just a question now of living with the past and hoping they could find some sort of compromise with the cravings, appetites and emotional demands of their respective characters.

There was a message from Lauralynn on the answer machine, informing him that she was hoping to be back in London by the end of the week. Her reunion with her brother had been a qualified success, some bonds had been re-established, and his wounds were not serious enough to have a lasting effect. She was looking forward to being back. As much as he enjoyed her conviviality, Dominik was now somewhat unsure, in view of the reunion with Summer, whether it would be advisable for them to keep on living under the same roof. He was aware that Summer and Lauralynn had once spent some time together but didn't know how close they might have become. It was just another added layer of complication.

His mind was still reeling with images of Summer in the Paris hotel room, and the sounds and smells of the French capital which he would now always associate with her. The heady fragrance of newly baked pâtisserie greeting him in the street as he passed the hotel door for his walk to the Métro and the brief journey to the train station. The topographical wilderness of wall graffiti on the often dilapidated and crumbling walls and tunnels through which the Eurostar moved as it bridged the no man's land between Paris and its suburbs.

The gleam in her eyes as she came, his cock deep inside her, bathing in her heat.

The muted sounds escaping from her throat with every successive thrust.

The way she held her breath silently, expecting the worst, hoping for the worst, whenever he slowed his motions down and paused, anticipating another improvisation in his assault, his dominance, her levels of arousal zigzagging back and forth, one step back, a dreadful torrent, and two steps forward, a wonderful, uncontrollable storm, as Dominik forced her body into new positions, a finger here, the flat of his hand there, Summer like a beautiful animal being guided through its dressage, full of pride, lust and the steady invasion of Dominik's hard cock.

Her face in repose as she slept afterwards, a thin film of sweat slowly drying across the surface of her pale skin, an involuntary shudder racing through her, skimming at the speed of light below the surface of her skin, like the aftershock of a localised earthquake. The peace. The beauty of her closeness. The serene acceptance of her trust in him.

Dominik felt alive again, as if he was emerging from a long sleep, a regrettable hiatus in his life. And all it had taken was another night with Summer. Unplanned, spontaneous, unforced.

He would phone her in the morning, he decided. Right now, he was weary, but it was a pleasant feeling of lassitude, as if his senses had been overwhelmed, his batteries overcharged, and he needed some time to complete his own transformation. But he also knew he was far from tired and would find this coming night difficult and restless, his mind in gentle tumult, the buzz still in electric control of his whole body.

He walked upstairs to his study. Called up the notes for the new novel on his laptop screen.

He opened a new folder and began to write on automatic pilot about the feelings and impressions the night with Summer in Paris evoked, while it still burned like a fire inside him, fearful the immediacy of the experience might fade all too quickly, leaving him with no mementoes he could cannibalise in his search for emotions to bring his pages alive.

It felt a bit like dreams that pierce your wall of sleep and that you feel you should write down as you know they will be gone in the morning and you will not remember them again. The only problem, Dominik realised from experience, is that whenever you did so, the notes you looked at again the following day were just random words and seldom made any sense whatsoever.

Her skin.

Her eyes.

The clean, curved lines of her body.

The sharp and rounded angles of her privacy.

Dominik sighed. Sometimes words were not enough.

He sighed and realised he hadn't even checked his emails since returning from Paris earlier that afternoon. A sure sign of distraction.

He clicked on the Inbox.

Fortunately, there was little of importance. Yet more proof the world did not revolve around him and his romantic preoccupations. The usual spam, newsletters he subscribed to, speaking invitations.

There was, however, a reminder that he was expected in Barcelona the following weekend for promotional appearances on the occasion of Sant Jordi, on behalf of his local publishers. A commitment he'd almost forgotten in the midst of all the recent turmoil. He wondered whether the Catalan capital was on the Groucho Nights touring itinerary. It would have been too much of a coincidence, surely?

Finally unable to keep his eyes open much longer, he reluctantly made his way to his bedroom.

The following morning, careful not to call too early, all too well aware how much Summer enjoyed her morning lie-ins, he rang her in Brussels, where Groucho Nights were playing before moving on to Berlin.

She was out running.

'You OK?'

'I'm fine.' Slightly out of breath.

'When is the gig?'

'At the end of the week, Saturday and then Sunday. We're doing two shows. The initial one sold out fast so the venue suggested we do another. Then we're staying in town for a few days before we move on.'

'Where next?'

'Amsterdam, and then some cities across Scandinavia, Copenhagen, Oslo, Malmo, Stockholm, and Helsinki, although I'm not sure in what order without consulting the tour sheet first. Then we go down to Austria and the Balkans. We're even doing Sarajevo and Ljubljana.'

'That should be fun.'

'Yes,' she agreed with obvious enthusiasm. 'They're all places I've never been to before.'

'We never did get much of a chance to speak, did we?'

'I know.'

'Listen,' Dominik said, searching for some form of vocal gravitas. 'I had a meeting with that guy I was put in touch with. In Paris. Someone who knows the shady side of the market for musical instruments. You were right. Viggo does have a reputation as a collector in the field and it appears he was definitely aware of the Bailly. Had been for some time. It was on his want list . . .'

'Damn it,' she swore. 'I really didn't want it to be him.'

'It doesn't necessarily mean he's involved,' Dominik tried to reassure her, 'but it is a bit coincidental.'

'I agree. God, I just don't know what I should do. Confront him, maybe?'

'I'm not sure. Is he still touring with you?'

'No, he went back to London today. With Luba. He has

some recording commitments there over the coming weeks. He said he would try and rejoin the tour once we hit Stockholm. Even hinted to Chris he might come onstage for a number there. Give us his seal of approval, so to speak.'

'Is there anything I can do?' Dominik asked.

'Let me think.'

There was a pause. He could hear the sound of cars behind her. She must be running alongside a busy road.

'You're not all going to Barcelona at some stage, by any chance, are you?'

'Not on this leg of the tour,' Summer said. 'Maybe at a later date, though. We'd come back to London in between. Why are you asking?'

'I have to go there myself this week. Some sort of book promotion. I'd agreed to it some time back.'

'That'll be good.'

'I'd sort of wondered whether our dates might have coincided . . .'

'Hmm . . .' He couldn't read the expression in her voice. 'Not this time.'

'Listen, the other night—'

'I know, Dominik . . . maybe we should talk about it all once I'm back in London. I'd like that.'

'I understand.'

'Another thing,' she said.

'Yes.'

'The Russian dancer from New Orleans . . .' Summer's voice tailed off.

'Luba. Yes, she knew who I was. I'd recognised her anyway.'

'She's with Viggo.'

'I noticed. But . . . the two of you . . . and him?'

'It's complicated.'

'Sounds that way. But it doesn't matter. The main thing is that we are on speaking terms again.'

'I would call it more than speaking terms now,' Summer remarked, and there was the hint of a smile in her voice. But there was also a wariness he could detect. She had never been a telephone sort of person. She needed the immediacy of closeness to communicate fully, to express herself.

'I'll let you get on with your run,' Dominik said. 'Can I call you later in the week?'

'Of course.'

Sant Jordi was the Catalonia equivalent of Valentine's Day, even though it was named after St George. It was held annually on a Sunday and the centre of Barcelona was transformed into a huge street market north of Plaza Catalunya all the way to Diagonal, with lavish flower tents and bookstalls, with tables crumbling under the weight of hundreds of new and older volumes. A celebration of nature and reading, with crowds of writers moving from stall to stall to sign their books which were then sold to the public. The stalls were organised by both local bookstores and publishers. The tradition had been for women to buy books for their male companions and men to acquire flowers, preferably roses, for their paramours. So on a sunny day, half the city paraded up and down the Rambla Catalunya laden with books and flowers. A spectacle that brought a smile to Dominik's face as he hopped from stall to stall, urged by his minders.

Had Summer been here, he speculated, what book might

she have bought for him? Although to be fair, as the majority of the titles on offer were in Spanish, it would have made little difference, he realised. But the thought struck him: books are permanent, while flowers wilt and die, and what did that say about the balance of things between men and women?

He was at his final bookstall of the day, sitting idle by now although the local authors sitting at the same table were still busy autographing and chatting amiably with fans and buyers, when a long, thin pale arm handed over a well-travelled copy of an original English edition of his book.

Dominik looked up.

The peripatetic Luba.

As ever, dressed to kill, her long, thin body sheathed in a skin-tight, flame-red woollen Roland Mouret dress.

'You?' Dominik couldn't disguise his surprise.

'You wouldn't begrudge a friend a signature, no?'

'A friend or a stalker?'

Luba's laughter was crystal clear.

'Well, I gave you my number and you didn't call. What is a young woman to do?'

He took hold of the book, opened it to the title page and signed it for her. So she had been telling the truth when she had told him she had read it. *To a private dancer*, he wrote.

A late afternoon breeze was sweeping up the Ramblas and Luba's white-blond hair floated like a silk veil in the cradle of its invisible currents as she stood facing his table reading the inscription.

'Nice,' she remarked.

'My pleasure.'

'I see you've almost finished here,' she said. 'Why don't we go have a drink, or a coffee, or maybe even tapas?'

The publicity assistant from his publishers indicated his duties were over and she didn't mind him leaving. He thanked her and the people manning the stand and stood up.

'So how did you know I was going to be in Barcelona? And don't tell me you just happened to just be passing through, Luba.'

'Elementary, my dear Dominik. I Googled you . . . And then your Spanish publisher had a list of writers who are attending Sant Jordi on their website. It was all rather easy.' Her smile was disarming.

Dominik couldn't quite picture someone as ethereal and sexual as Luba sitting by a computer, but it made sense. There was nowhere to hide these days.

'So you came all the way to Barcelona just to get your book signed?'

'No. I also came to work. Dance.'

'Ah . . .'

'A private hire.'

'Like New Orleans?' he asked.

'Not quite,' she said.

'Does Viggo approve of your . . . freelance work?'

'It's none of his business,' she said simply. 'He does not own me.'

'Good.'

They'd walked up the Passeig de Gràcia and found a small bar situated down a set of stone steps, low-ceilinged, half underground, where the smells of coffee, tobacco and smoked ham lingered in the air and made the mouth water.

Neither of them spoke fluent Spanish so they just pointed at the small circular plates laden with mouthfuls of delicacies and strewn across the top of the bar to indicate which they wanted. The eyes of every man in the bar were on Luba. She stood out here like a sore thumb, lithe and graceful, imperious, almost perfect, the red of her dress like a beacon in the dying light of the day.

'They are sending a car for me at ten tonight,' Luba said.

'Your clients?'

'Yes. I think they are Russian too. Rich ones. So many of those these days. Wasn't like that when I was younger. It will be on a boat. My dancing.'

'You have quite a reputation, I see. In demand internationally.'

'Maybe,' she said with a modest smile.

She bit into one of the tapas, a minuscule square of potato overflowing with sour cream and dotted with paprika.

'It's very nice,' she remarked. 'You must try some.'

Dominik gulped down a few green olives, stuffed with anchovies. The balance of tastes was subtle and addictive. As soon as he had finished one he wanted more. The coffees they had been served were piping hot and sharp. He called the barman over for some mineral water.

'I liked your book,' Luba said. 'Elena, the woman in it in Paris, she feels very real. But very self-destructive, I would say.'

'And that's why you wanted to see me,' Dominik said. 'It's too late in the day to change her, you know. The book is done and dusted.'

'Dusted?'

'Just an expression. Finished, I mean. I'm now working on a new book. Different story, other characters.'

'I've always thought that writers must be complicated men, that's all. Makes me curious.'

'Would that everyone did . . .'

'And what is the new book about? Am I allowed to ask?'

'It's about musical instruments. In particular the story of a particular one, a violin, and the people who owned it – its story over a couple of centuries.'

'Oh, that is a genius idea,' Luba remarked, clapping her hands together. 'I see where you got it, maybe?'

'Summer, you mean?'

'She plays violin. But I was also interested in meeting the man who asked his woman to dance back in New Orleans.'

'I'm pleased to hear you find us entertaining.'

'The lives of other people have always held much fascination for me,' Luba continued.

'So you're not only a nude dancer but also a voyeur, in your own way.'

'Why not? Anything to make life more varied, don't you think?'

'Tell me about your . . . friend, Viggo?'

'What do you want to know?'

'I'm told he collects things. Artwork, instruments too, no?'

Luba smiled enigmatically. 'Ah, I see why you are also interested.'

'Exactly. I'd like to know more. So?'

'Ask me questions,' she said. 'I'll do my best to answer.'

Luba agreed when Dominik expressed interest in seeing her dance again. He was to meet up with her in her hotel lobby shortly before ten that evening when the limo would be picking her up. She was staying in the Condal, away from the noisy hubbub of Barcelona's centre, a plush but discreet hotel off the beaten track. The male receptionists – all clad in identical black outfits, would have fitted effortlessly onto a fashion show boardwalk – gave him a knowing glance when he indicated he would wait downstairs for their stunning blonde guest.

She emerged from the lift, a vision in white, her long silhouette a blur of ivory silk, endless legs prolonged by towering silvery heels, her mad mane of untamed blond curls hanging loose, her bare arms a porcelain vision of pallor. Her eyes were highlighted by smouldering kohl, and the difference between the fierce make-up surrounding them and the rest of her face, just an artful smear of pale red lipstick and blusher across her sharply defined high cheekbones, was like a study in contrasts.

The limousine was waiting for them outside, its impassive chauffeur in grey uniform and cap holding the door open for them.

Dominik had been warned by Luba to wear a suit. Fortunately he had packed one on the off chance before leaving London, although he had no tie and had spent most of the time since their meeting in the cafe hunting down a decent one at the Corte Inglés store on Plaza Catalunya.

As the large car left the kerb, its engine purring delicately, Dominik, isolated from the driver by a thick glass partition, asked Luba where they were being taken.

'I never ask,' she said and made no effort to elaborate.

The limo soon left the city and followed the highway leading south. They drove for half an hour, a full moon shimmering over the night sea on their left, rushing through a succession of tunnels cut into the hillsides along the way, and then the sight of small fishing villages or resorts dotting the coastline.

Throughout the short journey Luba had remained silent, calmly retreating into a meditative state, deep in concentration, as if already rehearsing her performance, getting into the zone.

Following a road sign indicating Sitges, the car drove off the main road and made its way into and through the small town, steering clear of the narrow alleys of the Gothic quarters and navigating through further hills dotted with large luxury hotels, then crossed the railway line and descended towards a brightly lit marina.

There was a security gate on the approach to the entrance to the restricted area. The driver entered a code on a panel on the dashboard and the gate rose.

The yacht, a monstrous construction of decks stacked over each other, embedded in a tangle of wood and steel like a *matriochka*, was moored at the very end of the large marina, isolated from the other boats, its lights dimmed, its opulent elegance cleverly understated.

A burly security guard checked Luba's name against a list he held, and waved the couple up onto the lower deck where a crowd of well-dressed people milled around drinking and chatting. He could hear English, French, Spanish, Russian, probably, and a variety of other languages being spoken.

A middle-aged woman wearing a dark evening gown noticed Luba's arrival and signalled to her. Luba suggested Dominik now mingle with the crowd and enjoy himself as she walked away, accompanied by the woman, to a dressing room in preparation for her act.

Dominik headed for the bar, hoping against hope he would not stand out, wearing his inexpensive off-the-peg black suit, in this garden of unabashed wealth. The bald barman handed him a flute of champagne, which Dominik declined, requesting a Perrier or a San Pellegrino instead. Unsurprisingly, the barman had both mineral water varieties. And almost every other beverage under the sun.

He tried to mingle as best he could, although he knew no one there, flitting between groups, nodding, catching the tail end of conversations, often in languages he did not understand. None of the guests seemed to query his presence there, although he felt quite out of place. At least the yacht was moored and not navigating the high seas; Dominik had a propensity for seasickness and would have cut a poor figure had the boat sailed, he knew.

The same woman who had escorted Luba away earlier returned to the deck and began to corral the guests down towards a lower level of the ship. Dominik obediently followed the crowd. They were led to a luxurious salon in which a small stage had been erected, facing rows of fold-up camp chairs and, towards the back of the room, by the wide glass bays that looked out on the waters of the marina on one side and the open sea on the other, a collection of shiny leather divans. On these sat a set of expensively clad spectators, who he assumed were the owners of the boat, the hosts for tonight; Russian oligarchs and their molls from the Slavic look of their features. Male waiters in identical attire circulated between the seats handing out more glasses

of champagne to the guests. Dominik found a chair in the
furthest corner of the room.

Once everyone was sitting comfortably, the fleeting conversations died down and a visible rush of anticipation raced
through the room. The already dim lights of the salon were
turned even lower.

Two attendants standing by the stairs carried in a couple
of heavy light-boxes which they attached to tripods and
switched on. The improvised stage was bathed in harsh
light and Dominik, through the buzz of a pair of loud-
speakers, recognised the voice, the tape she seemingly
always used as part of her number. 'My Name is Luba . . .'
and then the gentle strains of the Debussy music as Luba,
in her white cotton robe, indolently made her way to the
stage and stood, still like a statue, her perfect shape mercilessly counterpointed in the savage glare of the studio-issue
spotlights.

He'd already seen her perform that time in New Orleans,
but once again could not help but marvel at the grace
and solemnity of her movements, slower than slow, teasing,
elegant, sensual, every inch of her skin eventually bared and
nuder than nude while her face remained so totally impassive, as if lost in thoughts, inhabiting another world
altogether, far away from the yacht and the Sitges Aguadolc
marina.

Her breasts stood high and firm, undisturbed by the
swaying rhythm of her body. As she turned, her smooth
mound now in full view of the whole, silent, audience, he
saw the small blue-inked tattoo of the gun just a nail's
length away from her opening. Intriguing, provocative, like
a final way of expressing her allure, dotting the i's of her

left-of-field persona. He realised he should have asked her about the significance, the reason for the tattoo, when he'd had the opportunity. He could feel the men – and women – in the audience holding their breath as Luba continued to contort herself, sinuous, adhering reptile-like to the shimmering, impressionistic flow of the music, every refuge of her intimacy mercilessly displayed, flaunted even.

The final notes of the music dripped note by note through the speakers and Luba slowly reverted to her position as a living statue. But, this time, the lights remained on and a new piece of music began. A tango.

A hot, lascivious, drawn-out melody, piercing the quietness that had settled on the room in the wake of Luba's dance.

A man stepped onto the dance floor, confronting Luba. He was naked too, and young, probably in his early to mid-twenties. His skin was a burnished gold, almost the colour of a new penny. In another environment it might have looked too much, as if he had spent days lounging on a sunbed, but here the glow gave him a look like a South Seas god, athletic, with strong legs and defined abdominal muscles, his chest rippling with each in and outward breath. His hair was slicked back, highlighting the fierceness and masculine line of his jaw.

His cock, its softness lost amongst the hardness of the rest of his body, began to grow the longer he stood in Luba's presence, taking in the richness of her nudity as he waited for the next movement in her dance.

Luba opened her eyes. Theatrically fluttered her lashes as if his apparition had been a surprise and not an integral part of the evening's act. With a sharp turn, the male dancer took hold of her hand and pulled her against him, their naked bodies making contact. With his other hand, he took her chin, his fingers lingering with intent across the soft skin of her neck, and the newly formed statue stood there for an instant, eye to eye, skin to skin, until the tango's principal melody unfurled and they began dancing together, legs interlaced, bodies coiled together.

Dominik watched the couple slide languorously across the restricted dance floor, wondering how much of this routine had been rehearsed, and where.

Her partner led Luba to the relentless echoes of the music, as she surrendered to gravity and his authoritative embrace, legs and body in perfect extension before her shape was broken time and time again on the altar of his demands. Heat rose inexorably from the room in response to the closeness of the dancers' bodies and the obscene way Luba was stretched, exposed, moved from side to side by the tanned, muscled, god-like creature whose facial expression never changed, severe, dominant.

Her legs briefly parted at an extreme angle, revealing her, and then he pulled her against him, his cock now as hard as the rest of his body and pressed between their torsos in a tight embrace. It was shocking, but beautiful, Dominik had to admit.

A dance of pure desire, of danger, as Luba appeared to simply relax into her partner and allow him to move her here, there and everywhere according to his will, as if she had abdicated her own. It was impossible to keep one's eyes away from the glistening sheen now covering the bodies of both Luba and the man, the pornographic vision of the man's arousal in such close contact with the Russian dancer's exquisite body. Dominik watched the way his cock brushed against her midriff, the long bridge of her legs impeccably straight, her feet extended like a trained ballerina's, her head thrown back, rigid, impervious.

The music was raised a notch, the male dancer threw Luba to the floor where she unfurled, spreadeagled in a perfect geometric position, and then he leaned over towards her, took hold of her hand and pulled her back to him, every alignment of their naked bodies a ritual, a ceremony of lust.

Vertical again, she raised her leg until she achieved the perfect angle, and to gasps from the audience the man impaled her in one swift movement, his hard cock plunging straight inside the lips of her offered cunt.

He disappeared inside her to the hilt, leaving the couple now locked together and shuddering to the music. Their dancing movements continued, his embedded cock now leading her as well as his arms as they continued their tango. Not once did he move out of her, Dominik noticed, or did the figures of the dance lose their elegant flow.

In the chairs ahead of him he saw the hands of a woman grip her neighbour's thigh.

Somehow it didn't feel as if they were fucking, it was still a dance, a primal dance, a thing of terrible beauty taken to another level, where the inherent grace of their bodies transcended the obscenity of the moment.

Dominik caught his breath. His eyes were drawn to the shimmering surface tension of Luba's buttocks as she swirled around on the male dancer, his penis now an extension of her spine as if, were he to suddenly withdraw, she would collapse like a rag doll with no means of physical support.

The music began to fade and in parallel the dance slowed to a halt until Luba and the handsome male dancer just stood there, still connected, like statues of flesh, their perfect immobility barely betrayed by the way his chest moved up and down as he regained his composure and the pink flush of arousal spreading between her neck and the valley of her breasts.

You could have heard a pin drop.

On a signal from the older woman who had earlier been orchestrating the event, the sailors on either side now switched off the strong lights.

Dominik took a long, deep gulp of mineral water; he knew that some of tonight's images would remain carved into the screen at the back of his brain for ever. His mind was prompted by the fiery spectacle of Luba and the dancers' interlocked genitals to evoke the ardent warmth he always experienced whenever he was inside Summer, the way her body responded to him, the perfection in the way that their desires coincided, their inner darknesses meeting at some invisible crossroads of the soul. He was man enough to realise what a tissue of imperfections they both were, unlike Luba whose serene felicity had something of the uncanny. But they complemented each other. Felt whole together.

The limousine drove them back to their respective hotels in Barcelona. The full Mediterranean moon shone high above the sea as the car raced up the empty coastal highway.

'That was beautiful,' Dominik told Luba.

'It was well paid,' she replied.

'I can imagine. Was he your normal . . . dance partner?'

'There are several. It depends on the engagements. It's a somewhat . . . specialist field of expertise,' she said.

'He looked South American but maybe I got that impression because it was a tango. What's his name?'

'I don't know. It never bothers me.' She turned away, her eyes fixed on the darkness outside.

'Really?'

'What's the point? I make myself available, the male dancer directs, I follow. That's all.' She turned back to him. 'But tell me, Dominik?'

'What?'

'You must promise to never put me in one of your books. Yes?'

Dominik hesitated. All through the drive he'd been thinking how to translate the exquisite if transgressive spectacle into words. It was such a temptation.

Luba noted his visible reluctance.

'Promise me,' she repeated.

'OK.' Dominik acceded to her demand.

An uneasy silence took over as the limo reached the city suburbs and leapfrogged through traffic lights.

'It's how I met Viggo,' Luba said, out of the blue. 'I was involved in another live sex show. With a different partner. A Ukrainian too, like me. It was in Amsterdam.'

'And you became . . . friends?'

'Yes, Viggo asked me to be with him afterwards. Said he collected beautiful things and I would be the crown in his empire. It's a silly way to seduce a woman, but he was rich, charismatic, funny and I needed a change from the dancing life.'

'So you followed him to London?'

'Yes, he even hired a private jet for the journey back. He likes to spoil me, and of course himself. But he is a good man deep down. And an interesting lover.'

'Is that how you rate men – by level of interest?'

'Why not?' She smiled, playfulness now overtaking the tiredness caused by her recent performance.

'But you decided to go back to your dancing?'

'I was getting bored,' she said. 'Anyway, who needs a reason? I can do what I want. With Viggo it's not a marriage, just a friendship of equals. He's not a jealous man.'

'I see,' Dominik noted. 'Tell me more about his collections, then?'

Viggo Franck's pride and joy was the collection of musical instruments he had gathered. He owned two electric guitars that Jimi Hendrix had used, an acoustic Spanish guitar allegedly played by John Lennon, a battered Satchmo trumpet, an actual Paganini violin and an assortment of other rare instruments associated with famous musicians, whether from the classical or the rock field. Not content with such a treasure trove, he also hoarded various Picasso sketches, an original early Warhol, a Hirst, and sundry high-value limited-edition prints. In addition, he also had a full set of F. Scott Fitzgerald, William Faulkner and Hemingway first editions, all with dust jackets, some actually signed.

The collection was liberally spread throughout several temperature-regulated rooms in his Belsize Park mansion.

'Sounds fascinating,' Dominik remarked. 'Doesn't he keep some of the more valuable pieces somewhere else?'

It seemed there was a locked room in the basement which Luba had never visited and that Viggo was also a touch secretive about when it came to its contents. Stated that he only kept his rare vinyl records there, which made little sense. Anyway, neither Luba nor Viggo's ever-changing entourage were interested in that particular portion of his collection.

'Maybe it's because the items he keeps there are more fragile?' Luba speculated.

'It could be,' Dominik agreed, not wishing to pursue the subject further for now. They were driving up Diagonal and soon reached the hotel which the oligarchs had booked Luba into. He offered to walk back to his own hotel, which was barely ten minutes away on foot, but Luba insisted on asking the mute chauffeur to drop him off after her. They agreed to chat again in London one day.

Dominik returned to the UK two days later. The first thing he noticed on arriving at his house in Hampstead was Lauralynn's large Samsonite suitcase parked by the door, alongside a large plastic duty-free bag.

Dominik called out for her but there was no response.

He walked up the stairs to the room she was using and gently rapped on the door in case she was still sleeping this late in the morning.

The room was empty and the bed had visibly not been slept in. There was a mess of clothes scattered across the room and shoes in disarray across the carpeted floor, as if she had been in a rush – not so much to unpack but to gather things up again.

He suddenly remembered that he had forgotten to leave

her a note telling her he was going to Barcelona for a short time. Maybe, finding the house empty, she had decided to spend a few days elsewhere, with another friend.

Dominik felt emotionally exhausted. He decided to leave his overnight bag in the hall, sitting fraternally next to Lauralynn's luggage, and made a beeline for his bedroom, firmly intent on sleeping all his worries away. He'd had to check in at Barcelona airport at six that morning.

Dropping his clothes along the floor in his wake, Dominik wearily collapsed onto the bed, too lazy to pull the covers on to his body, and was soon sound asleep.

He awoke late in the afternoon to the caress of warm breath against the bare skin of his uncovered arse.

'Hello, stranger . . .'

He half opened his eyes, wiping the sleep away, turned his head and saw Lauralynn overlooking him, her face a portrait of amusement. Realising he was naked and aroused, he attempted to pull a sheet over himself, which only made her laugh.

'Oh, Dominik, I've seen it all before,' she said. 'Why this sudden coyness?'

'I suppose so,' he mumbled.

She wore a black promotional T-shirt for a band he'd never heard of, white jeans and laced leather boots that reached to mid-calf. From his perspective lying on the bed, she seemed even taller than he had ever known her.

'Welcome back,' Dominik said, pulling her down so they were sitting companionably side by side on the bed.

'The same to you. You didn't say you were going to be away.'

'I know. I'm sorry.'

'I thought you were in Berlin. So, I went over there, hoping to surprise you.'

'Berlin?'

'Yes. I assumed you'd found out Summer was playing there with Chris and his band. It was the final bookmark on your computer history. But you weren't there. I'd sure make a bad Sherlock, eh?'

'I was in Barcelona. A promo gig for my publishers there.'

'Barcelona!' Lauralynn burst out laughing. 'And there I go following you to the wrong end of Europe.'

'How was Berlin?' Dominik asked.

'How was Barcelona?'

'It was interesting,' he mused.

'Is that all you're going to say about it?'

'Yes.' A thin smile was spreading across Dominik's lips as he recalled Luba and the show, the bookstalls along the Ramblas, the roses in full bloom.

'I met up with Summer,' Lauralynn said.

'And?' He tried to sound uninterested.

'It was fun . . .'

'Fun?'

'Listen, I like her. A lot.' She noticed a cloud pass before his eyes. 'Not in that way,' she quickly added. 'Just as a friend, a mate.'

'OK.'

'And you're an idiot, Dominik. A total idiot. Why the hell did you allow her to believe you and me had become an item? You know full well that's not what we have.'

Dominik paled.

'I heard she was now shacked up with Viggo Franck. I could sense she still had some feelings for me. Didn't want her to feel bad about it. I never said we were actually together in that sense,' he said. 'Just mentioned that you were living here.'

'And what did you realistically think she would make of that; the conclusions she would draw? Ah, you're both complete morons.'

'Both?'

'Yes, you two are your own worst enemies. Obstinate, proud, allow me to list the sins . . .'

'You told her how it was, between you and me?'

'Of course I did. Made it very clear to her, something you should have done from the outset when you met up in Brighton. You're like children, the way you play with your emotions, I swear.'

'And Viggo?'

'Come on, don't you see it? He's just a stopgap. Does he look like an exclusive sort of guy? Anyway, he's got that Russian chick, hasn't he?'

'Luba.'

'Is that what she's called? She's just another player, I guess. Not the jealous type.'

'I've come across her.'

'Good for you.'

'She's nice,' he said. 'I think you'd like her, honestly.'

'So make an introduction.'

'I will.'

'The least you can do to make amends.'

'What was Summer's reaction to the news about you and me?'

'Anger, surprise, relief. I don't know. It certainly wasn't what she expected.'

'So what happens now?'

'Call her, you fool. Enough playing games. You were made for each other. But now it's up to you to make it work, find a way.'

Dominik shivered. The bedroom window was half open and outside dusk was falling, the trees on the Heath fluttering in the rising evening breeze.

'And put something on,' she said, looking down at him. 'Or that lovely cock of yours will shrivel down to much less attractive proportions.'

II

Nudes on Walls

Viggo and Luba were curled up together like two ferns, Viggo's arms draped over Luba's back and her long legs overlaying his.

I'd woken up a few feet away from them, hanging off the edge of the bed, and had quietly slipped out from under the covers and padded over to the bathroom, careful not to wake them. Viggo slept like the dead, but Luba had reflexes like a cat's, and I expected to see her long lashes flutter open at any moment.

I didn't want to explain to her why I was up early, or where I was going.

The days of all three of us spooning had disappeared. I now felt suffocated sharing the sheets with a crowd. But ending our relationship might mean the end of Chris's career, and the last that I would see of my Bailly, so for now I was stuck with them, for better or worse.

The tour had been a success, both for me and for Groucho Nights. Chris, Ella and Ted were now busy writing and recording their first studio album. Marija, Baldo and Alex had returned to New York to rejoin the Gramercy Symphonia and the more staid classical world, but might return at a later stage for overdubs. Viggo had agreed to foot the bill when the time came.

And I was getting ready for a date with Dominik.

At least, I hoped it was a date. We had hatched a plan between us, to recover the Bailly which we were both convinced was stored somewhere inside Viggo's mansion, and we were meeting to finalise the details.

I had followed Dominik's instructions to the letter, copying a set of house keys and planning an evening to get Viggo and Luba out of the house. I'd also drawn him a map of all the rooms, including notes showing where the basement was, and the locked room where I thought my violin would most likely be concealed.

The only thing I hadn't been able to work out was the combination to the alarm on the vault door. I'd never seen Viggo open it, or even go down to the basement. He rarely glanced at his art collection, just seemed happy to have things in his possession.

I'd checked everything over and over, scoured the corners of each room for security cameras I might have overlooked, looking at my plans to make sure I hadn't missed anything, but I was still restless, and had spent the whole week nervously pacing the floors in the mansion, torn between the fear that Dominik would get caught and it would all be my fault in the excitement at seeing him again.

We'd talked on the phone a few times since our night in Paris, mainly about the Bailly and his research efforts, never about us. I still wasn't sure whether Lauralynn was right, and he was in love with me. I wasn't even sure if I was in love with him. I felt more like he was the right to my left, the yin to my yang. We were two halves of the one whole, and neither of us operated well without the other. If that was love, then I supposed that we were in love, but I doubted that we'd ever have anything close to the fairy-tale romances promised by popular fiction and Hollywood. I'd get bored, eventually, I reckoned, if my life took a sugary sweet turn as promised in the pages of the pastel-coloured books with their titles embossed in italics that I always avoided like the plague, maybe for fear I might come under their spell.

I liked Dominik for all the reasons that I probably shouldn't. Being with him was like walking a knife's edge. He was everything that I wanted my life to be; unpredictable and just the right side of dangerous. But I still had no idea how he felt about me.

He'd suggested that we meet in the cafe at St Katherine Docks, where we'd had our very first proper encounter just under three years ago now. I wasn't sure whether he'd suggested it out of sentimentality or convenience.

I nearly wore a pair of jeans and a white T-shirt, a combination that I donned so rarely but which he'd always seemed to appreciate, perhaps because he knew that it was a look that I sported without pretence, in situations where I felt truly relaxed and comfortable. But at the last moment I opted for a short skirt, in the hope that he might pull it up and have his wicked way with me in a nearby bathroom, alleyway or the back seat of his car. Even a hand on my thigh would be difficult to encourage with trousers on.

It was raining as I made my way around the dock to the cafe. It had been warm when I had left the house, so I hadn't bothered with an umbrella, and I was wearing open-toed shoes. My blouse was wet and sticking to my skin and water streamed down my legs.

It took me a few moments to open the door to the cafe as

my hands shook so much I couldn't grip the handle. I was filled with a heady mixture of excitement and exhilaration at the thought of seeing him again.

I had hoped to be the first to arrive, so I would have a chance to disappear into the bathroom and dry off a bit, or at least fix my hair which was matted to my shoulders, but Dominik was already waiting for me in the corner under the stairs, in exactly the same place that we had sat on our first date. He'd already ordered. One of the waiters was on his way over with a tray that held an espresso for him, a flat white for me, and a bowl full of sugar.

I slipped into the seat opposite him, my wet thighs slick against the hard wood of the chair.

'Forget your umbrella?' he said with a teasing smile.

'No, I got wet on purpose,' I snapped.

I flushed as soon as I said it, unsure what made me bite at him like that when I had come with the intention of making it clear that I wanted to be with him. I'd meant it as a joke, but the words came out harder than I intended. I was full of nerves, and the desire to stop talking and touch him.

He stared at me, his eyes glittering with something unspoken. Lust, perhaps. I could feel my nipples hardening under the wet fabric of my top and I couldn't blame the cold. It was humid, though perhaps it was Dominik's presence that made me feel hot.

I shivered, in spite of the warmth.

'Go and dry yourself off,' he said. 'You'll catch a cold. We've got a lot to talk about, so you may as well be comfortable.'

I wondered, with a pang, why he hadn't invited me to his

home in Hampstead. I would have gone, gladly, and we could have both stayed warm and dry in his bed. Perhaps inviting me to meet him outside the house was a sign that he didn't want the complication, that after he'd recovered the Bailly for me, we'd just be friends and nothing more.

A part of me hoped that he might not find the violin right away, so that I would have more excuses to see him again. Another part of me wanted my instrument back, desperately, so that the feeling of it in my hands and the sound of it flowing through me would remind me of him, always.

I took my clothes off in the bathroom and held them under the air dryer, standing near the mirror with just my bra and knickers on. I kept hoping that he'd come in, but he didn't. Cubicle sex wasn't Dominik's style. He would have thought it ungentlemanly, perhaps, or proletarian, taken the same view that he did of belly button rings, artless tattoos and love-making in the back seats of taxis.

He'd ordered a second round of coffees by the time that I returned, dry, as the first cup had gone cold while I was in the bathroom.

'Summer—' he started.

'Before I forget,' I interrupted, 'here are the keys. And the notes that you asked for.' He'd been about to say something about us, I was sure, but the pained look on his face made me think that it wasn't good news and I couldn't bear to let him finish his sentence if it was to tell me that he didn't care for me in that way.

'I'm sorry about Viggo,' he said. 'I know you . . . care for him.'

I shrugged, again aware that I wasn't behaving in the way that I had meant to, but unsure how to communicate the way that I felt. I needed the Bailly in my hands so that I could show him, make him hear, make him see all the things that I wanted to say to him. Without it I was mute, the song in my heart locked up in the vice-like grip of my mind.

Then I frowned, screwing up my forehead in an effort to try harder, and not leave this meeting with the sinking sensation that I'd done the wrong thing again.

'I do care for him. But it's not like that. And if he has my violin . . . well . . . I don't owe him anything.'

The expression on Dominik's face was inscrutable. I met his eyes but saw no reaction, followed the curve of his jaw down to his mouth. He was silent, so I continued – anything to avoid an awkward pause between us.

'I love the Bailly. Truly. But it's not worth the risk . . . You don't have to do this.'

My voice broke as I said the last words, and I hung on Dominik's every movement, to see if he had sensed what I meant, if he knew that I wouldn't lose him for anything. I was terrified that he might be caught and arrested, that Viggo might take his revenge, somehow. But Dominik ignored my protests and changed the subject, back to his research. Perhaps that was all I meant to him after all; a way to write novels, something to hang his focus on, because he didn't have any better ideas.

We sat in the cafe for another hour, but I still didn't say any of the things that I had meant to say, or dreamed of saying. Dominik didn't say anything about the two of us at all. Whether he had wanted to and couldn't get the words out, or just didn't have anything to say, I wasn't sure. Maybe he raced home afterwards and wrote it all down, more emotional fuel for his new hero and heroine, whoever they were. Did all writers cannibalise their own lives?

We had confirmed the sequence of events down to each single detail, by the end of it.

I would lure Viggo out of the house at an agreed time and Dominik would break in and somehow work out the code to the vault. This was my sticking point: I was convinced that within seconds he would set the whole mansion screaming and a SWAT team would arrive and carry him away, but he was certain that the code would be something obvious, like Viggo's birthday, or one-two-three-four. He had a low opinion of rock singers' imaginations.

Our plan confirmed, he put the copies of Viggo's house keys into the pocket of his jeans, folded my map up and slipped it inside his jacket, and walked me to the train station at Tower Hill. He kissed me on the forehead good-bye, and I resisted the urge to tangle my hands in his hair, and pull his mouth down to meet mine.

It was just a few days until the planned break-in, and I spent them trying desperately not to think about it. I went out regularly, to remove myself and my odd behaviour from sight so Viggo and Luba wouldn't notice my discomfort. I caught the train from Belsize Park to the East End, my old hunting ground, and watched films at RichMix Cinema. I went to concerts in the bar beneath the theatre to listen to musicians I'd never heard of, sitting at the back with a glass of wine, letting the music fill my mind and wash all my other thoughts away. I regularly asked Fran to join me, but she always dropped out with one pretext or another. I wondered if she was spending time with Chris.

The minutes passed like a tide, unstoppably ticking away, until finally it was the afternoon that we'd planned the break-in to take place. I was tasked with keeping Viggo and Luba occupied, away from the mansion, until Dominik rang me with the all-clear and let me know that he'd departed the house and it was safe to return – whether or not he had found the Bailly and retrieved it.

'You all right, babe?' Viggo asked as we were getting ready to go out. I was struggling to run a comb through my tangled hair, more impatiently than usual. 'Nervous?'

'Petrified.'

'Don't worry, I'm sure it will be fine,' he soothed, taking the comb from me. 'Sit down,' he said, sinking onto the edge of the bed and pointing to the space in front of him. I lowered myself onto the floor, relaxing against his calves and letting him take over the untangling of my knotted locks, as if I was a child. The sensation was pleasant, and at least this way I didn't have to face him. 'I'm sure you'll be amazing.'

He stroked the hair back from my face tenderly and I sank into his caress, utterly torn about the whole thing. I felt like Judas, plotting to betray him, though that notion was ridiculous considering the circumstances. If he did have the Bailly, and I was certain that he did, then I ought to be in a mad, hateful fury with him. He just wasn't the sort of person that it was possible to hate. Viggo was eccentric and wild but there was not a malicious bone in his body. He was like a spoilt child who was so used to getting everything he wanted that he didn't take any care to think about the consequences of grabbing whatever appealed to him. I found it hard to hate someone for their nature, and hypo-critical, as I was all too aware of my own imperfections.

Luba appeared from the shower in a cloud of steam, naked and still dripping wet. It was her habit to drip-dry rather than use a towel. She liked the feeling of wetness, which was why she spent so much time in the basement pool, frolicking in the water like a mermaid.

She crouched down and pressed her lips against mine, running her tongue lightly between my teeth and my top lip. I sighed with pleasure and began to kiss her back.

Dominik had, after all, said that I should take special care to behave as I normally would, and Luba's kisses were intoxicating. Sometimes I wondered if she was even human, or perhaps some sort of witch that Viggo employed to help him steal the stuff he wanted.

Viggo, Luba and I were on our way to the preview of Grayson's photo exhibition. It was the first time that we'd been out in public as a triad, but I had decided to risk Susan's fury, if we were papped together, against the benefit of getting them both out of the house for several hours.

There was a private viewing a few hours prior to the exhibition opening to the public. It would be full of collectors, models and voyeurs. Luba would blend seamlessly into the slew of attractive women that I expected to be present, Viggo was a well-known art collector, and I had been shot by Grayson, so I felt that attending together would not attract undue attention as it would if we had gone out to a restaurant and asked for a table for three.

In fact, the prospect of using it as a way to lure Viggo out of the mansion was the reason why I had agreed to appear in the exhibition in the first place.

When Grayson had phoned me while I was in Berlin, visiting the Flohmarkt in Mauerpark with Lauralynn, it was to ask about the photos.

I'd been initially flattered, when he'd told me that shooting me with the violin had inspired him to do a further series of nudes involving fine-art models posing as musicians with their instruments – an exploration of sexuality and music. But flattery had turned to fear when he'd asked for my permission to include a good number of the more explicit pictures he'd taken of me in his exhibition.

At first, despite Lauralynn's encouragement, I'd said no. He assured me he would crop them in such a way that I would not be recognisable, even excluding my red hair from the final prints, and I knew he'd set the lighting up so that my face only ever appeared in shadow anyway. But I'd felt it risky, considering the sort of audience I played to for my classical gigs. I knew that sex sells, and it had worked for me, but the line between what most people found sexy and what they found offensive was a thin one, and Grayson's photographs would probably cross it.

When I realised that taking Viggo and Luba along to the private view would be the perfect decoy for Dominik's break-in, I changed my mind, called Grayson back and gave him the go-ahead to use some of the photographs.

There was also a part of me that thrilled at the thought of a room full of people staring at full-size pictures of me without any clothes on. It wasn't vanity, but a sort of backwards voyeurism. It gave me the same sense of fearful excitement that I felt when I had played nude for Dominik at his recitals or had stripped naked at private parties.

Grayson was dressed in jeans, a flouncy designer shirt and a soft, sand-coloured suit jacket. His hair was slicked back and to the side in his familiar way. He greeted me with a kiss on each cheek. There was the faintest surge of chemistry between us, but his eyes were friendly and slightly distant in the way of a work colleague or a polite acquaintance.

He caught sight of Luba with particular interest, but was most likely sizing up her potential as a model. She was beautiful, of course, but it was her expressive face and graceful movements, the years as a dancer that had given her the ability to hold poses, and the way that her skin seemed to glow almost unnaturally in the light, that made her a potential photographer's dream.

Viggo was already off, seeking out the pictures, hoping to quickly identify and reserve the prints that he wanted to add to his collection, if any.

I left Luba and Grayson to their introduction, and threaded my way through the crowd to check out the show. We were on the penultimate top floor of an office tower in Southwark, close to the Tate Modern. I'd once been to a sex party in a penthouse hotel suite nearby, in the days when Dominik and I had not long met and he'd encouraged me to continue my sexual explorations. The view through the thick glass that broke up the walls where the photographs hung was not dissimilar to the vision of London that I'd had on that night whilst staring out the hotel room window, soaking up the enthusiastic sounds of coupling behind me.

The lights on the London Eye glimmered to my left,

turning and blinking in their almost imperceptible motion. The water of the Thames shone like onyx, a black arrow dividing the city into binaries, north and south, day and night, vanilla and kinky, sub and dom . . . Summer and Dominik, maybe, if tonight went well. He and the Bailly had become bound together in my mind so that I couldn't imagine having one without the other, and I felt the sort of certainty that belongs to illogical premonitions; if tonight brought my Bailly back, then it would bring Dominik with it.

'Too afraid to look at your pictures, darling?' said a gravelly voice behind me. Viggo had appeared as suddenly as a shadow. The tone of his voice was hypnotic in my ear, and I leaned back against him without even thinking about it, relaxing languidly into his words like a snake responds to its charmer.

I was relieved that I had the pictures as an excuse for my shaky hands, sweaty palms and the steady thrum of my heart. There was still no word from Dominik, and waiting for the message that I was expecting at any moment, to tell me that all had gone as planned, had sent me into a flurry of nerves.

I made a gesture in agreement, halfway between a shrug and an attempt to hide myself away by hunching further into my shoulders like a turtle recedes into its shell, feigning more discomfort than I felt at the surrounding display of my nudity.

'You're beautiful,' he said softly. 'I've bought them all. Come and see.'

*

The photographs were placed in a line around the room, with an arrow indicating where the viewer should begin, so that the images formed a narrative from beginning to end.

Grayson had photographed both men and women, some of them dressed, and some of them nude. Some were allegedly bona fide musicians, or at least appeared to be, judging by the way that they sat and interacted with the instruments in the shot. I didn't recognise any of them, unclothed or clothed.

The first picture showed a handsome blond man wearing a suit, playing saxophone, his tie loosened and shirt buttons partly undone. He looked utterly lost in the music, eyes closed, head back, swinging his instrument high. Another man, nude, kneeled at his feet, apparently engaged in giving the saxophonist a blow job, although neither cock nor mouth was in shot. A flute held the focus of the picture, a sliver of silver lying along the floor, near his knees.

The next was a photograph of two woman embracing, one sitting on a chair and the other straddling her waist, their flesh melded so close together that the curve of their touching breasts was barely visible. One was playing a trumpet and the other was staring into the distance, her hands tangled in her partner's hair.

We passed photograph after photograph, some of them merely beautiful, others shocking. Viggo paused for a long time in front of each of a series of pictures that displayed beautiful women making love to their instruments: flutes, bows and even a clarinet held inside their vaginas. In each case, the model's face and eyes were the focal point of the picture, their expressions varying between lust and an uncommon spirituality. In another, a woman rested on all fours, her full, bare breasts hanging down, her face completely relaxed, as expressionless as a piece of furniture, as a man, fully dressed, beat her back with drumsticks.

The pictures of me were grouped together at the end, and they all had small white tags on the bottom reading 'sold'. Viggo was true to his word, he had bought the lot. They were different from the other photos, as I was the only model who had requested anonymity, so just my body was displayed, without my face. Because of my request that he exclude my recognisable red hair, he hadn't been able to include even a hint of my jaw or lips in shot, so I was completely headless in all of them.

Grayson had still managed to capture a sense of sexuality in the pose of my body, the way that my hands were draped possessively around the neck of the violin, the way that I held the curves of the instrument close to my skin.

In the most striking image, I was sitting down, leaning back slightly with my legs splayed wide apart and the violin held just above my sex, as if I had given birth to my instrument. My arms were dead straight and my fingers tightly entwined in a vice-like grip, as if I was brandishing a weapon, but it was unclear whether I was preparing to bring the violin down to injure myself, or if I was holding it up like a shield. In another, I was lying on my side, spooning the violin like I might caress a lover. My body was completely relaxed, apart from my feet which were pointed like a ballerina's, as if, though reclined, I was ready to take flight at any moment.

I had expected to find viewing the gallery in the presence of others a turn-on. No one knew who I was, didn't realise that I was standing amongst them like any ordinary person as they stared at the most intimate parts of me. But instead I found it alarming. Without a head I was reduced to existing as a body, sex and nothing else, no mind or heart, and I realised why Grayson had selected these pictures to be viewed last in the exhibition. They were the most shocking, although they didn't show any kind of penetration or sexual activity as most of the others did. They were the only pictures without eyes, without expression, without love, affection or human connection.

I began to shiver as a wave of unhappiness surged through me.

Viggo turned me around to face him.

'Hey, what's upset you, sweetheart?'

I couldn't answer him, as I didn't have an answer, and even if I did I doubted that I would be able to articulate it between silent sobs.

'Shhh . . .' he said, wrapping me up in his arms. 'Let's find somewhere to sit and you can tell me all about it.'

12

A Sketch by Degas

The moment he closed the front door behind him, Dominik had approached the alarm panel with shaking hands and, with a tremor of excitement, entered the code for the system, after waiting five whole minutes to see if anyone would respond to his repeatedly ringing the doorbell. He had been assured by Summer that there would be no one in for the rest of the day but, housebreaking not being a regular pastime of his, he was nervous and preferred to verify this information for himself.

The set of keys Summer had made copies of had worked, the locks clicking cleanly into position and the door opening with no resistance. Almost too easy, so far.

3.3.1.3.R.P.M.

With each digit entered on the pad the small LCD moved from red to green in total silence until the whole panel was giving him a blissful go-ahead.

Dominik smiled. Trust Viggo Franck, a musician of the CD and digital downloading age, to have a password inspired by the speed at which most vinyl records revolved. It was a private joke which would have been lost on many, but at least it was more original than a birthday or a famous date in history, which is what most people used.

The large house was bathed in silence. Just the muted

breath of the air-conditioning soft-shoe shuffling across the emptiness of rooms.

He made his way to the spiral staircase Summer had described and cautiously crept down the winding steps to the mansion's underground areas.

He found the airy gallery, its heart full of sculptures and installation pieces, like a room in a museum with its rows of lights recessed into the white ceiling, every spot artfully directed to illuminate a particular painting, print or structure, to present it to its best advantage, regardless of the angle any onlooker would be gazing from. Clear lines of sight between the sculptures of all sizes and colours, the pictures on the surrounding walls all aligned at the same level, a ballet of colours and compositions. Dominik recognised the Warhol industrial-like prints and some erotic sketches of bulls and unclad nymphs straight from Picasso's ebullient pen. There were also more classical images: young ballet dancers in the style of Degas, landscapes of flowers *à la* Van Gogh, abstract geometrical forms whose modernity still lacked art in his eyes, and so much more. It was a gallery of wonders and Dominik could only guess at the value of the works on display.

He knew he could spend ages here, endlessly admiring the beauty of some of the pieces in Viggo's collection, but this was neither the time nor the occasion. He moved out of the room and descended a further level into the mansion's subterranean spaces, finally reaching the low-ceilinged swimming pool area Summer had suggested he investigate.

The emerald-blue shimmer of the water in repose caught his eyes and Dominik, for a moment, couldn't help but imagine Summer's pale, naked beauty vigorously cutting through the narrow, curving pool which wound its way like a stream across the room, her legs closing and opening below the thin surface like the pages of a book, her fiery mane floating in her wake, like a stain of colour melting into the water and bringing it alive.

And, of course, the chiselled perfection of Luba's body, lounging like a mermaid queen by the artificial waterfall and its mound of slick, wet, grey stones. Ah, the stories this room could no doubt tell . . .

Dominik quickly snapped out of his wandering meditation and, peering into the dimmer corner of the room, searched for the glass cabinet where many of Viggo's musical instruments were allegedly displayed. There it was, beyond a gathering of smaller sculptures, artefacts, wood-carved nymphs and grotesques, a large wall-fixed glass-fronted steel edifice that ran halfway across the room's narrowest wall. From where Dominik stood he could see inside it, parallel layers of shelves each laden with various instruments crammed together without breathing space, inert, sorrowful at not having been touched, let alone played, in years.

At one end there was a whole row of electric guitars, some shiny and sleek, attracting the light reflecting from the nearby water, others matt and full-bodied, and yet more standing to attention, lining the cabinet like a parade of soldiers on a stage. Below the assortment of electric guitars, on a lower shelf, were a couple of accordions and next to them various brass instruments, a few trumpets, a trombone and a saxophone, most in poor condition, brass battered and marked in places, like survivors from a shipwreck. Alongside were two shelves with violins.

Dominik approached the tall glass cabinet, skirting the damp edges of the pool.

There were only four violins on display and he quickly glanced at each in succession. None was the Bailly. They were all undeniably beautiful, burnished with the patina of time, delicate, the wood of their bodies morphing into rare combinations of brown and orange, some streaked, others uniform, their elemental shapes sculpted into permanence. Dominik didn't know much about antique violins, beyond the Bailly and the stories that trailed in its wake, but he knew these were evidently rare and works of beauty. There was an undeniable fragility about this set of instruments, as if they were too precious now to even be played, but he knew their sound, in the right hands, would display the utmost warmth and purity.

He noticed the glass case was not even locked, one of its doors yawning slightly off its hinge. He was tempted to take one of the rare violins into his hands but knew it would be pointless as he couldn't even play.

A wave of apprehension raced through his mind. Had he been wrong all along and had Viggo no involvement with the Bailly's disappearance? He then remembered Summer telling him about the glass case: if the Bailly had been here, she would have recognised it. Yes, the vault. The door Luba had mentioned. Where Viggo pretended to keep his vinyl records. Dominik stepped past the display unit and saw the recessed arch and the steel door it sheltered. Maybe the house's initial owners, who'd had these underground floors excavated, had thought of it as some form of panic room.

Dominik half-heartedly gripped the door's handle and

tried to turn it but it wouldn't budge in either direction. He'd not expected it to.

From now on, he was on his own.

There was an electronic number pad on the side of the door.

He had prepared as best he could for this eventuality. Scoured the internet for information about Viggo Franck's life. His birthday, that of his parents, his sister's, the important dates so far reported in his life, his first marriage, the dates his first songs and albums had been released and so on. Dominik typed in Viggo's birth date but there was no reaction. Again no surprise. Normally, these systems required both a series of letters and figures. Desultorily, he tried Viggo's initials followed by a numeric sequence starting with 1. Then 2,3,4,5 but there was no familiar click indicating he had hit on the right password.

He gave the door a hopeless kick but it didn't even flinch.

All this way for nothing.

He then remembered the front door password he had been supplied with by Summer. Again, there was no sign of recognition. Using the same code for two separate doors would indeed have been a bad error of judgment.

A thought occurred to him.

The vinyl vault.

Records.

The front door had been 3.3.1.3. R.P.M.

A thin smile spread across Dominik's lips.

Viggo the joker . . .

He tapped a new code in.

4.5.R.P.M.

There was a loud buzz, and Dominik heard the mechanism inside the heavy door click into place. Holding his breath, he wrapped his fingers around the door's metal handle. There was no resistance this time. The lock was no longer blocking his access.

Dominik felt a surge of pure adrenalin pulsing through his bloodstream.

He applied gentle pressure to the door and it opened silently as if carried on a cushion of air.

It was a small room, shrouded in darkness. Dominik advanced cautiously inside, his hand exploring the wall in vain for a light switch. He couldn't find any within a safe distance of the door but, suddenly, a dull strip of neon light came to life – probably a timing system connected to the door opening – and gradually grew in intensity.

The space was square and windowless, the far wall occupied by shelves, a couple of low-rise display tables situated at its centre while the remainder of the walls displayed a sparse half-dozen paintings and framed prints hung at irregular intervals. For a moment, Dominik wondered why the artwork was in here rather than displayed outside. Was it because it was more valuable? But as his eyes roamed across the room and away from the walls, his attention quickly focused on one of the squat, heavy, glass-topped pieces of furniture on top of which the Bailly was displayed.

A sigh of profound relief left him.

He would have recognised it even if it had been concealed out of sight at the heart of a mountainous pile of similar-looking violins. It was unmistakable.

The sought-after instrument appeared unharmed, its

varnish catching the light and radiating warmth across the small room.

Dominik approached the table, passed his fingers across the violin's strings, finding them taut and responsive, echoes of a thousand melodies played for him by Summer flooding back, and the circumstances under which he had heard each and every one of them.

He sighed.

The Angelique.

A mere instrument, with four strings tuned in perfect fifths. Carved out of wood and strung with gut, glued together, hourglass in shape, just like a woman whose voluptuous curves ceaselessly evoke primal forms of desire.

But an instrument that now held so much significance in his life. It had brought him and Summer together in the first place, had seen them meet, fall apart and drift. It had witnessed their joy and their sadness, their passion and their sorrow.

A violin with its own history. Had Dominik and Summer merely been just another chapter in its unfolding story? Who might follow in their footsteps, be next on the scene?

But Dominik knew this particular chapter had not yet reached a proper ending.

The stolen violin was here. But where was its bow? It hadn't been left with the instrument on the display unit. He didn't even know if the bow actually belonged to the Bailly, if it had been made at the same time, well over a century ago, and had accompanied the violin in its topsy-turvy adventures down the years.

His eyes darted once more across the room.

Some of the paintings and prints hung on the wall closest to the door seemed familiar, as if he had seen them a hundred times in the pages of art books or exhibition catalogues, but he couldn't put a name to any of them. Moving along to the shelves and their bric-a-brac of small stones, vintage toy cars and porcelain dolls, he finally noticed the bow sitting forlornly in one corner. He stepped over to grab it.

Just as he did so, he heard a soft hiss, like air being expelled by a powerful pair of lungs. Dominik turned, trying to locate where the sound was coming from. It was the door to the room. Closing. As he realised what was happening, he rushed forward, dropping the bow, his arms flying forward in an attempt to get hold of the door before the shrinking gap between it and the visibly reinforced frame was bridged.

He missed by a fraction of a second.

'Fuck!'

He frantically tried to turn the handle. It wouldn't budge.

He was locked in.

'Damn, damn, damn.' Swearing under his breath out of sheer anger at his own stupidity. He should have held the door open with something, kept it jammed. How stupid of him.

He was a bloody amateur, that's what he was.

There was no alarm pad on this side of the door in which he could type in the code, or attempt to conjure up another combination that would work in reverse.

His mind was racing, clutching at straws in a rushed attempt at thinking straight, but it was all a mad, desperate jumble and there was just no obvious solution to his predicament. He tried his mobile phone but, as he expected, buried in the depths of the mansion and behind the heavy metal door, there was no signal. Even as he calmed down and became more rational, he realised there was no miracle outcome in sight that he could possibly engineer. He would just have to sit here patiently and wait for the next visitor to the basement of the mansion. Viggo, in all likelihood. It would be embarrassing and he would probably end up getting himself arrested. Dominik could see the headlines already. On a back page, of course, the pettiness of it all would never deserve a single line on a front page. 'Has-been writer caught red-handed robbing rock star's house', 'Prof turns thief'. Whichever way it was worded would be profoundly humiliating.

The only positive thing he could think of was that he might be able to inform Summer where her violin was. As long as he got access to her, he reasoned, but then surely Viggo would have the instrument promptly removed to another, safer location. What an awful mess!

Dominik was still juggling random, fuzzy thoughts when he noticed the room's neon light beginning to dim, its power fading with every passing second. He swore. The timer was connected to the door opening and closing. Very quickly, he would be plunged into darkness.

As this realisation dawned on him, a further seed of fear took hold of him. What about the air in the room, the oxygen? Would that also disappear? He had seen no obvious evidence of ventilation or air-conditioning when the light had still been on.

This was becoming so much more serious than he had initially thought.

How long would the air supply last?

Viggo took off his leather jacket and swung it around my shoulders, and led me out of the gallery room and into the bar that had been set up to supply the VIP exhibition guests with refreshments. It was quiet inside, as most people were picking up their drinks and taking them back into the viewing room. A man in a business suit who looked as though he'd come straight from work was standing alone at the bar, drinking something clear out of a short glass with a small straw, probably a gin and tonic. He gave us a curious glance, perhaps recognising Viggo, or just wondering why I looked so upset, and then went back to his drink. A pair of women wearing cocktail dresses were standing next to a tall table in a corner sneaking glances at the man in the suit, perhaps wondering if he was single, and whether they should approach him to find out. One was in pink and the other in yellow, and they stood out like a pair of brightly coloured birds, shifting their weight from one foot to the other to counter the pain of their high heels.

Viggo swept me onto a booth seat in the darkest corner of the room and headed to the bar, returning a few moments later with two short whisky glasses half full with amber liquid and a cup full of ice.

'Sip this,' he said, 'it'll calm you down.'

I took a mouthful, and nearly spat it out. The liquor burned my throat and the aftertaste was like a mouthful of lighter fluid, but within a couple of seconds my limbs began to feel pleasantly warm, and away from the crowd in the gallery and the presence of the photographs, I relaxed. Viggo leaned forward and ran his thumb gently under one eye and then the other, catching the remainder of my tears.

As he did so, I caught a glimpse of his watch. More than an hour had passed since we arrived, and I still hadn't heard from Dominik. He had promised to send me a text message when he'd completed, or abandoned, the mission so I would know that he was safe, and hadn't set all the alarms off or been arrested. Viggo didn't have any guard dogs, and Dominik was going in through the front door, so he didn't have any dangerous walls to scale or windows to climb through, and I had no cause to be concerned for his safety.

Nonetheless, a pit of fear began to boil inside my stomach, one type of upset turning into another until I began shaking again. I'd turned into a right mess of nerves, so unlike my usual self.

Viggo leaned forward and took my hand. His hands were large and his palms rough, his fingernails bitten down to the quick. He never demonstrated a modicum of stress or nerves besides his habit of chewing his fingernails.

'Tell me what's wrong. I know it's not the pictures. You haven't been yourself since the tour. Is it that man you met?'

'Dominik?' My eyes widened in surprise and fright. 'How did you know about him?' I asked, my own fear of discovery turning my tone of voice into an accusation.

'You don't need to be coy, darling. There's three of us sharing the one bed as it is so you didn't exactly strike me as a one-man kind of girl. I don't imagine that Luba keeps to herself when she goes on tour either. She's out there right now seducing your photographer. If this other guy of yours has hurt you in any way though . . .'

'No, nothing like that. We've had our moments, certainly, but it's never been one-sided. Nobody's perfect, are they, certainly not me.'

Viggo laughed. 'If we spent our lives waiting for the perfect man or woman, we'd be waiting for ever. In fact, that's why I like to have more than one. You get some things from one person, other things from another. It works. For me, at least. And Luba. And you, maybe too.'

'That's a very mature way to look at it. But human emotions don't always add up so easily, do they – love especially so.'

He shrugged. 'Everything is about compromise. And love is the biggest compromise of all.'

'I didn't think rock stars needed to compromise anything,' I replied, morosely.

'I guess I do have an advantage over the average person. There's not much I want that I don't get.'

He was smiling wickedly, and his voice, as ever, held a touch of humour. But his words were like a bucket of cold water over my head. He had my Bailly, the gift that Dominik had given me that I had treasured so much, the instrument that I communicated all of my emotions through. Playing without it hadn't been the same, and I wanted it back.

'You had my violin stolen, didn't you?' I kept my tone even, neutral. It was a statement of fact, not an accusation.

He looked taken aback, but not upset. The total absence of either denial or confusion cemented my certainty that the Bailly was in his possession. Not so much as a flicker of disbelief or surprise crossed his face.

'I'm not sure what you mean,' he replied smoothly, his face now a blank slate, a picture of innocence.

'I mean that you took my Bailly, the violin that you first saw me play with, and added it to your collection. It's in your vault. With the other things that you choose not to display. Your other stolen things. In the basement. Where you said you kept your record collection.'

In for a penny, in for a pound.

Then Viggo did something that I didn't expect, even for a moment.

He began to cry.

At the sight of his upset, all of the anger went out of me, like rising mist. I'd seen very few grown men cry before, and I wasn't quite sure what to do. I leaned forward and gently patted his arm.

He picked up his drink and took a long gulp of his whisky, draining his glass and gritting his teeth as it went down.

'I'm sorry,' he said softly. 'I didn't think you'd mind.'

'You didn't think I'd mind?' I replied in amazement. 'Why on earth didn't you think I'd mind?'

'You had it with you at the rehearsal in that plain case. I figured that you had no idea what it was, and that it can't have been that important to you if you'd take it out to any old practice session. One of your rehearsal violins. Or maybe that some sponsor had lent it to you. You probably had a dozen others waiting in the wings. Besides, they say it's cursed. I might have been doing you a favour, taking it off your hands. And I was only going to look at it some-times, hold it, not damage it. It would be safe, in my vault, looked after, cared for . . .'

He was talking a million miles a minute, like a madman, and his shoulders began to shudder, as if he was about to break down in sobs again. I stole a glance around the bar but no one was paying any attention to us at all; they probably couldn't even see us, tucked away in the corner booth in the dark.

'Viggo,' I said, in the most soothing tone that I could muster, as if I was speaking to a child, 'the violin was a gift. From Dominik. I loved it more than anything in the world. Like I love him,' I added, the last few words as much a revelation to me as they might be to Viggo.

He looked up at me again, brushing a length of his dark hair off his face.

'Well then,' he said, smiling again, despite his red eyes. 'That's easily solved. I'll just give it back to you.'

'That would be wonderful.' The understatement of the century, if there ever was one, but his offer seemed so fragile, I didn't want to make any sudden movements in case he changed his mind.

'But . . .'

'Yes?' he asked eagerly.

'Dominik's already stolen it back. Or at least, he's in the middle of stealing it.'

'What do you mean?' he asked, shock stopping his tears in their tracks.

'I took your keys,' I replied. 'And copied them. I'm sorry, I just wanted it back so badly and I didn't think you'd give it up so easily . . .'

'And you brought me and Luba here to get us out of the house, so he could go in?'

'Yes.'

'But you don't know the alarm code to the vault.'

'He thought it would be your birthday. Or something like that. He must be still down there now, there's no service in your basement. He's meant to be texting me when he's either managed to break in, or given up.'

I'd been sneaking glances at my phone all night, every time Viggo turned his head, just in case I'd somehow missed the beeps that signalled that a text message had arrived.

Viggo knotted his fingers together and leaned forward, resting his chin on his hands, deep in thought, perhaps tracing the steps that Dominik would need to take in order to succeed in his attempted break-in.

'He'll never make it. The rest of the house is easy enough, there's no cameras, no booby traps, nothing like that. The neighbours can't see who's coming in through the front door and even if they could, they'd never suspect anything was wrong if they saw someone they didn't recognise getting in with a key. I'm presuming here that he doesn't look like the breaking and entering type. You haven't shacked up with an art thief, have you? Maybe he's broken in, taken the violin and other stuff, and made a run for it.'

I shook my head vigorously. 'Never. Dominik's a writer . . . he was doing some research on the subject, for a novel. That's his only interest in the Bailly. That and me, I suppose. I hope.'

'Trust me, sweetheart, a man doesn't attempt a felony for a woman that he's not in love with. He must care about you an awful lot to go to all this trouble.'

'I hope so. I guess I'll find out soon enough.' I checked my phone again. The screen was still blank, entirely bereft of any communication.

'We'd better go back and let him in then. He's not carrying a weapon, is he? I don't want him to shoot me on sight, if he thinks he's been caught in the act.'

'Dominik would never—'

'You can't trust a man in love. Does strange things to the brain. Call him and tell him we're on our way, and I'm happy to give up the instrument. I'll even let you pick another, if you like, for compensation. If you won't report me to the police . . .'

'I won't report you. And I don't need another violin. Just the one is enough for me.'

'Maybe something else then.'

I fished my phone out of my bag and dialled Dominik's number hurriedly. His was the only number I knew by heart, the digits burned into my brain.

It went straight to his message box. The familiar tone of his voice, even on the brief recording, filled me with longing.

I left a message, explaining that the gig was up, Viggo had confessed, I had confessed, all was well and we were on our way to access the vault, and not to attempt anything silly.

He probably wouldn't get the message though, unless he abandoned the break-in and headed to one of the upper floors to get a phone signal. Even then it might take a while for the message to come through. The lack of response from him made me panic a little. I wasn't superstitious – I scoffed at horoscopes and smiled when a black cat crossed my path – but I'd feel more comfortable when I could see Dominik with my own eyes and knew that nothing had gone wrong, he was just out of service, or maybe he'd forgotten to charge his battery and his phone was dead.

Luba was in full party mode when we returned to the gallery, with a cocktail glass in each hand, alternating sips from one glass and then the other.

'If you don't mind,' Viggo whispered in my ear, 'I'd rather keep tonight's adventure between us.'

We made our excuses to her and left early, on the pretence of a headache. She was chatting to the woman in the yellow dress that we'd seen at the bar earlier, and seemed entirely happy to be left with her new friend.

Grayson was deep in conversation on the other side of the room. I decided to leave without making my goodbyes. I hadn't quite recovered from the effect that viewing the cropped pictures had on me, and didn't know what to say to him.

'Don't worry,' Viggo said, watching mixed expressions flitting across my face. 'I'll pay him extra to take them out of the exhibition, if you like. And lock them in my vault, safe from prying eyes.'

'That's kind of you,' I replied. 'I'll think about it.'

We waited in the shadow of a building for one of Viggo's cars to come and collect him. I'd suggested that he didn't drive his Buick, to reduce the chances of the three of us being photographed together. He'd thought I was paranoid, but complied.

The cold night air bit into my skin and I shivered, despite the warmth and weight of Viggo's jacket draped over my shoulders.

I pulled my phone out of my bag again, with shaking fingers. Still no response.

Where was Dominik?

*

The more he peered at his watch in the darkness and tried to read the time, the shorter the interval since his last peek was revealed. Time was slowing to a standstill. Dominik knew it was psychological and tried not to panic.

At first the air quality did not alter, but soon the heat in the closed room began to rise and he had to unbutton his shirt, and then when his back began to feel damp with sweat he took it off and set it down across the stone floor.

He tried to remain alert, on the lookout for any sounds coming from the house on the other side of the thick metal door, filtering through to him. But the silence beyond was absolute and all he could hear was the rasping sound of his own breath as he nervously began a mental countdown to some point of no return.

Alone in a dark place with just his memories.

Was that what death would feel like?

Memories of women, of smiles, eyes, torrents of words heard, spoken, written down, all flashing by on the journey to the white light.

Bodies, faces, breasts, scents, the colours, the emotions.

And regrets. Too many to count or list.

Things he had done.

Things he had not done.

Dominik was squatting on the floor, feeling the heat accumulate, the precious Bailly within his reach, orientating himself in the surrounding darkness.

Was the air now growing thinner or was it just him?

He was tempted to close his eyes and fall asleep, but knew it was the one thing he should not do.

How would Summer remember him in years to come, once he was no longer around, Dominik reflected. As a holy fool who'd messed everything up? He knew that if he was to die now, the memories of her would stay him until the very last moment, playing like a loop of film on the screen of his mind. He smiled feebly. The best way to go, he felt, with Summer on his mind, the image of her body in his eyes, there for eternity.

His eyelids fluttering, Dominik thought he heard a sound, far away, faint, indistinct.

He strained to hear but again there was silence. And then again a remote echo. His name. Being called out. He feared briefly this was a hallucination, the sure sign he was on the downward path, but then the sound grew nearer. Summer's voice echoed by another, male one. Viggo. Probably walking down the spiral staircase.

Dominik waited for their voices to reach the lower floor and once the sound of their calls reverberated around the low ceiling of the pool area, he finally cried out.

'I'm here. Inside.'

There was a flurry of steps as they ran to the locked door of the safe room.

Then the door finally opened with a *wooshhh* . . .

The light rushed in from outside, momentarily blinding Dominik, since he'd been plunged into darkness for a few hours, but he could make out the blurry shape of Summer's silhouette and the pencil-thin gangly form of Viggo standing behind her. Their faces were still indistinct.

'Dominik!' cried Summer.

'I'm fine,' he protested.

'Are you sure you're OK?'

'I am. Just a bit hot under the collar.' He realised he was shirtless.

The room's light came back on, triggered by the door's timer.

Summer walked over to him, her eyes full of panic as the realisation of what could have happened struck her.

'I'm so sorry, I really am . . . I never thought . . .'

Stepping up behind her and looking around the room and seeing all his collection undisturbed, Viggo smiled.

'I think you've made a bit of a fool of yourself, haven't you, mate?' He was on the edge of laughter, the tightness of his skinny jeans and knee-high boots giving him the appearance of a scarecrow.

'I most certainly have,' Dominik agreed.

'Right,' Viggo said. 'Look, it's all my fault anyway. I shouldn't have arranged for the Angelique to be stolen from the green room back at the Academy. It's just that I saw it and was left dumbfounded. I regret it now. Never thought it would affect Summer so badly . . . I just didn't think it through . . .'

Slipping his shirt back on again, as Summer stood silently between them, Dominik asked, 'So you don't mind that I broke in to your house?'

'Of course not,' the musician said. 'I brought it on myself. Summer has explained it all to me. Anyway, who says you broke in?' He smiled mischievously. 'You had a key. Consider yourself my guest.'

With a heavy sigh of relief, Dominik stepped past him and began heading towards the pool area. Summer followed in his footsteps.

'Haven't you forgotten something?' Viggo called out.

They both turned their heads.

Viggo was holding the Bailly and its bow in his extended hands.

Summer ran back and took them from him, and gave him a gentle peck on the cheek.

She walked back to where Dominik was now standing, one foot on the edge of the pool, and took his hand in her free one.

'I think the two of you need a shower after all this frantic racing around and the involuntary lock-in, no? And relax a little.' Viggo shouted out at them. 'Be my guests. *Mi casa es su casa . . .*'

'I think that's a really good idea,' Summer said to Dominik as they reached the bottom of the spiral staircase. 'Come,' she said. 'There's a guest suite on the top floor.' And to Viggo she cried out, 'You won't mind, will you, Viggo?'

'Of course not,' Viggo said.

Summer set the Bailly down on a tall chest of drawers as soon as they walked into the guest room and then stood silently watching it with a dreamy look in her eyes. She passed her fingers over the instrument as if caressing it, formally bringing it back to life, back into her life.

Closing the door behind them, Dominik observed her. He felt light-headed, a bit empty. He knew it was the inevitable anticlimax after the few traumatic hours the two of them had just experienced.

She finally abandoned the retrieved instrument and turned to him.

'Thank you, Dominik. For doing all this. I know you

were taking an enormous risk. All for me. I'll always be grateful . . .'

'Thank you for coming to my rescue,' he said. 'I must have looked a bit of a fool, sitting there in the dark, all locked up. At least you'll know next time to employ a professional thief and not a bloody amateur like me.'

Summer smiled.

Her eyes held an undercurrent of sadness, as they always did, but there was a new gleam there. Elation? Relief? Expectation?

Dominik felt his heartstrings tense.

'I suppose it was all my fault,' Summer said. 'I should have been more careful with the violin.'

'I suppose it was,' Dominik replied.

'Maybe I should be punished?' she suggested, the hint of mischief in her tone telling him everything she had in mind.

'Maybe you should. For crass neglect. For reckless acts of a known nature.'

'For being me,' she added.

'For being you.'

There was a moment's silence.

'So, punish me,' Summer said.

'I think we'll have that shower now.' Dominik smiled, pulling her forcibly towards the door.

The showerhead's cascade was pouring down on Summer's head, flattening her red curls, lengthening her hair all the way down her back, spreading it like a damp curtain against her wet skin. Dominik watched as the water drowning her mane emerged from the tangled mass, dividing into thinner streams, pearling across the small of her back and dispersing as it passed the delicate ski-jump of her arse.

'Turn,' he said.

He soaped his hands and passed them across her breasts. Her nipples were already rock hard. He lowered his head and took them between teeth and tongue and nibbled gently away at them. Summer tensed. He straightened and returned to washing her front. Her mouth was half open, lips tantalisingly apart, a tempting glance of the white barrier of her teeth behind them.

He spread the soap suds across her shoulders and the rest of her body, massaging the liquid into her skin, his cock calmly brushing against her in the restricted space of the shower cubicle, water endlessly splashing around them as they twisted and turned. Then, with a thin flannel, he washed the soap away, her skin now glistening as the steam rose around them, idly passing his fingers between her legs, testing her heat, entering her with one finger and then two more, pressing himself inside her. Summer lowered herself ever so slightly to accommodate his long digits, to acknowledge his touch, his investigation of her intimacy, the familiar way he was now taking possession of her again.

'Your turn now,' Dominik urged, passing her the slippery bar of soap he had been using on her.

She took hold of it and in turn began to draw the soap across his body, slowly, sensually, studiously; first his chest, then his back as he swivelled around, then his buttocks and the back of his legs. Finally, he turned round to face her again, and she took his erection in her hands and she rubbed the soap across its hardness, feeling it grow under her ministrations, harder, thicker, more imperious. Summer lingered here, orchestrating the trigger of his full arousal, noting every tremor, listening to the halting sound of Dominik's breath above as she kneeled and massaged him, cleaned him, played with him. Finally, she took the flannel glove and washed the soap away. Dominik's cock was now standing fully to attention. With a brief glance at him, as if seeking his approval, she neared her mouth and took him inside her, cupping his balls with her hand as she did so.

Even though she had carefully cleaned it away, he still smelled of soap, the perfumed dampness washing over her senses like a curtain of rain. Her teeth grazed the swelling mass of him, the dizzying smoothness of his exposed glans and the texture of its ridge, and she rolled her tongue along it in a parody of greed and hunger. Dominik now filled her mouth.

There was a final splash of water rushing down her face as she heard Dominik switch the shower off. His hands moved to her hair and gripped hard, pulling her closer to convert the angle of his penetration so that he could force himself deeper into her throat.

Summer took a deep breath, her knees now feeling the hardness of the cubicle's stone floor.

She did her best to repress her gag reflex.

Watching her as his cock inched its way forward past her lips, Dominik bathed in the glow of Summer's terrible closeness. It was as if the months had melted away. Once he felt she had fully accommodated him, her chest below heaving gently as if animated by the invisible hands of a fluttering breeze, he began a series of progressive thrusts, opening her further, stretching her, still not letting go of the bunch of hair he held tight in his fist and through which he controlled her motions.

The rest of the world faded, their whole universe circumscribed by the narrow shower cubicle, its glass panels still steamed up, shielding them from what lay beyond.

Over and over he struck the back of her throat and she tried to control her spasms, never wanting him to stop, inhaling as much air through her nose as she could manage into her lungs at the counterpoint of every thrust. Treasuring his savage invasion, welcoming him into her body, her soul. Praying it could last for ever. Filled to the brim. His.

Later, after they'd dried in the fluffy white towels liberally distributed throughout Viggo's guest bathroom, Dominik took Summer to bed.

He pulled the dreadful dark-hued chenille bedspread away and threw it to the floor. Summer stepped out of the towel, allowing it to fall to the carpet. Faced Dominik. Presented herself. Remembering his tastes, his quirks, the way he liked her when life was still good.

She climbed sideways onto the uncovered bed, made to get on all fours as she expected Dominik to take her from behind, as was so often his habit. He'd never been much of a missionary man, too much of a slave to his voyeurism, enjoying the spectacle of his cock moving in and out of her.

'No.'

She looked back at him, feeling the harsh, steely gaze of his eyes observing her.

'Tell me what you want,' he asked.

She sought for answers in his stance. He was imperturbable, stone-faced.

What the hell did he want her to say? That she wanted

him, yearned uncontrollably to belong to him against all logic and past experience? Did he want her to abdicate her will, her pride?

'Right now I just want to be fucked by you,' Summer finally said.

His face didn't change.

'I want to be with you . . . Even if it hurts.'

It was at times like this she felt bereft and words were just not enough to express the turmoil raging inside her. She almost wanted to scream, 'Take me, fuck me, hurt me, brand me in my soul, tattoo my heart with indelible ink, make me yours and banish for ever the emptiness inside that plagues me.' In her mind, it made a sort of sense, but spoken out loud, it would just sound ridiculous. Degrading, humiliating even.

Still he didn't respond, standing there impassively, watching her, translating her unspoken words into a language he could understand.

'I want you inside me. Now.'

Was she now reduced to begging?

She almost felt as if she was on the brink of tears. Was he testing her? Playing with her?

'I want you too,' he finally said.

He stepped over to the bed, drew his fingers across her eyes with a tenderness she had never experienced before, like the kindest of undertakers closing a dead woman's eyes, and prompted Summer to lie down. He carefully spread-eagled her and loomed above her, his shadow cast along the room's ceiling as evening fell outside like a blanket of greyness.

He moved between her legs and she took hold of him and guided him in.

'Just accept me for who I am,' she said.

Dominik filled her gloriously.

'Shhh . . .' he whispered.

Summer shivered.

Viggo switched the screen off, a broad smile of satisfaction spreading across his face.

The couple he'd been watching had finally parted, no longer a single entity, a two-backed creature whose every motion combined the grace of birds in flight and the savage cruelty of carnivorous creatures. Both a frenetic and ecstatic dance of bodies with all the wild abandon of tigers fighting to the death.

Now they had come up for air. Become two again. Summer and Dominik.

Of course he was a voyeur, Viggo knew. But then who was perfect?

He was a man who knew beauty when he saw it and often wanted to keep it, save it, put it under glass. Collect it.

If beauty had an essence that could be bottled, he would have been the first in line with cheque book in hand.

True, he had slept with Summer. Alone and with Luba. But watching her fucking with Dominik had been another thing of beauty. He had seen her come alive, observed the radiance spreading through her body, the way all her inborn defiance and anxiety had just melted away as Dominik had taken control, the way she had colluded with her own spirit of surrender, embraced it. Viggo had never been into men, but the sight of Dominik and the way he had fitted into Summer, next to Summer, had been exhilarating.

His mouth was dry.

He picked a bottle of vintage Bourbon from his drinks cabinet and poured himself a generous glass.

'Lovely,' he muttered, addressing himself to both the mellifluous roughness of the liquid tiptoeing down his throat and the memory of the two lovers now absent from his clandestine screen.

Installing a minuscule camera in the guest bedroom had been something of a joke all those years back when he had acquired the mansion and an architect friend had come up with the designs and overseen its conversion. It had felt 'rock 'n' roll', something to uphold his bad-boy reputation. And then he had forgotten about the facility for years. It was actually the unconventional Luba, his international woman of mystery and nude elegance, who had suggested he, one night, watch her at love and play with a young woman she had picked up in a club – a punkette with a thin tattoo of a teardrop below one of her eyes, he remembered. Viggo sighed, evoking the memory, the entrancing vision of women together, their curves, the lasciviousness of their kisses and gestures, the hunger, the perfect geometric alignment of lust and desire.

It wasn't the hydraulics of sex that turned him on, but the slow motion, soundless elegance of bodies joining in ballet, and the vision of two women was so much more powerful than the heterosexual couples he and friends had spied on during wild parties at the mansion, when guests had strayed or been encouraged to venture to the guest room, unaware Viggo and others were watching them with mischievous delight. But none of the duped couples had the savage grace of Summer and Dominik, he reflected. These two had a wild appetite for each other, a passion he felt almost jealous about, a hunger that flirted with danger. More than once he had held his breath as one or the other had ventured into ominous territory, a gesture, a hand, a pulsion that almost went too far, teetering on the edge before reassuringly pulling back. Viggo had never witnessed a man and a woman fuck with such abandon; it had made his flesh crawl at times.

Following the tragicomic incident in the vault, he had suggested they go upstairs, and he knew they would end up in bed, under the gaze of his hidden camera and the temptation to activate the surveillance system had been too strong. He had almost given up, since they had spent an uncommon amount of time in the bathroom, leading him to believe he'd already missed out on all the fun. But eventually they had emerged, draped in white towels, almost circling each other like famished birds of prey, ready to pounce and launch into beautiful madness.

Viggo didn't regret watching them. They wouldn't know. Wouldn't be hurt. The only thing he did fleetingly regret was that he hadn't installed sound in the room in addition to the spy lens.

He thought he would now have the surveillance system disabled. Nothing could follow Summer and Dominik. Others would never match the intensity of what he had witnessed. Best end on a high.

He rose and pulled the sliding bookcase to one side, concealing the small screen.

Dominik and Summer must now be sleeping, he guessed.

Maybe he would do the same, reliving the memories of their embraces, revelling in it. Luba would be back from the gallery soon, he realised. The first time he had seen her dance he had been similarly transfixed. And knew he must have her. She had quickly agreed, although he was aware she would never belong to anyone and he was, for her, just a step along the road, a convenient and a pleasant one, but just a truck stop. Hmmm . . . there was the germ of a song there, Viggo thought.

He headed down to his studio and switched the electric piano on. It was strange the way ideas, words, the sketches of melodies just came about. Out of nowhere, unbidden.

Dominik awoke, rubbed his eyes, wiping away the disorientation of being in an unknown room. They had forgotten to draw the blinds yesterday and the bedroom was now bathed in glorious sunlight.

The softness of Summer's arse nestled, spoon-like, against his stomach. She was still sleeping, the delicate murmur of her breath a faint rumour.

He kissed her neck and she stirred.

He was still wearing his watch and he glanced at the time. It was only mid-morning. It felt later.

Once Summer had opened her eyes and smiled at him, he had asked her, 'Do you keep many of your things here?'

'Not much. Just a few bits and pieces,' she replied. 'Most of my stuff is still at Chris's place.'

'Once we're up I want you to gather everything together. Here. There. We'll go pick them up. You're coming to my place. You're living with me.'

'Am I?'

'You are.' He was completely sincere.

Summer nodded. For now, she would. It hadn't worked first time around, in New York. But she was willing to give it another chance.

She yawned and rolled onto her side. 'Jeez, I'm hungry. But most of all, I need my quota of caffeine.'

'I'm famished too,' Dominik noted. The last thing he had eaten was a small *pain au chocolat* from Patisserie Valerie the previous morning when he had been preparing for his visit to Viggo's house, after which events had overtaken him.

He stretched, detaching himself from the comfortable warmth of Summer's naked body and got off the bed. Looked down at her and the unruly tangle of sheets, the puddle of her red hair spread out against the pillowcase. His cock twitched. She smiled back at him.

He stepped into his black trousers and handed her the white T-shirt she had been wearing the previous day. She slipped it on, sitting on the edge of the bed. Waited for him to hand her something else, underwear or jeans, but he did not, just watched her with a benevolent grin on his face.

Summer rose from the bed. The crumpled T-shirt reached to just below her navel, leaving her arse and cunt fully exposed. It was a particularly intimate form of undress, natural but wanton, the way one would wander in the privacy of one's house without fear of onlookers.

'Come.' Dominik gestured at her. 'Let's find the kitchen.'

'Like this?' Summer queried.

'Yes,' he said.

'Viggo might be there. Others . . .'

'I know,' Dominik said. 'I like you that way. Viggo has

seen it all anyway, hasn't he? I'm happy for others to see you. I don't mind.'

In the knowledge that she was now his, he refrained from saying.

As they left the room, he topless, she bottomless, Summer held back for a moment, a tremor of hesitation assaulting her at the thought of yet again leaving the Bailly behind. Then she realised it was safe. Lightning would not strike twice.

Viggo was sitting at a counter nibbling a slice of toast when they arrived. He gave them a look and wolf-whistled.

'Wow, our love birds! Welcome to another sunny day, kids.'

He was also shirtless, his skinny hairless torso like a white page.

'Coffee?'

'Yes please.'

'Freshly brewed for your pleasure.' He gestured theatrically at the couple, indicating the gleaming NASA-like steel-articulated machine dominating the granite work surface.

As Summer and Dominik helped themselves, Viggo, not without a nostalgic glance at Summer's exposed bottom half, suddenly rose and made his way out of the kitchen.

'Wait for me, kids. I have a surprise for you.'

He returned ten minutes later, holding a small frame in his hands which he reverently handed over to Summer as Dominik watched on.

'By way of apology. A gift. In the hope you'll forgive me.'

Inside the frame was a black and white sketch. Pretty old, by the looks of it.

In the top left-hand corner of the image the drawing of a ballet dancer and her male partner, only their bodies appearing, their heads cut off along the edge of the print's top. Further to the right was the neck of a violin and a bow and the bewigged face of a man with a fancy, ceremonial hat. Lower down, barely sketched, some smoking factory chimneys and some thinly drawn sailing boats.

'What is it?' Summer asked.

'It's by Degas,' Viggo said. 'It's called *Program for an Artistic Soirée*. It's pretty rare. Because of the violin, I thought it would be nice if you had it. It's real, not a copy . . .'

'I don't know what to say,' Summer said.

'Just one thing.' Viggo stopped her.

'Yes?'

'Don't show it around too much. Only to people you can trust.'

'You mean it's stolen?' Dominik queried.

'Yes,' Viggo admitted with a sly smile. 'It's been missing for years. Long story, but at some stage it came into my possession. These things happen, you know. Anyway, after what I've done to you, I felt you deserved it more than me.'

This explained why certain items of his collection were locked away in the panic room, Dominik guessed. They were all stolen.

'Thank you, Viggo. We'll treasure it. Truly,' Summer said.

'Am I forgiven, then?' Viggo asked.

Dominik didn't catch her answer. All he could hear was the fact that she had said 'we'.

Program for an Artistic Soirée
Edgar Degas

13

The Wind Will Carry Us

Moving house took me much longer than it should have.

I had spent the morning with Susan, my agent and de facto manager, at a nondescript Starbucks near Victoria station, discussing my plans for the future. She was based in the US but had turned up out of the blue in London, frustrated with me ignoring one too many of her emails.

I'd arrived late, having rushed from Dominik's side at his Hampstead house. I hadn't wanted to waste a minute of time with him, so we'd spent all morning in much the same way that we'd spent the previous night, and the one before, and the one before that. Entwined in each other's arms, fucking as often as we had the energy for. Some of the time, we'd make love, him full of affection and tenderness, and me brimming with contentment, happy to lie there beneath him, wishing that I could pause time and spend my life in that moment, listening to his deep, throaty laugh, meeting his gaze and waiting for the moment when the look in his eyes would turn from soft and warm to hard and cruel, and he would take hold of the wrist that he'd been gently stroking a moment earlier and pin me to the bed, whispering filthy things in my ear.

Visions of us between the sheets together had played and replayed through my mind as I threw on the nearest clothes

I could find and raced for the tube, aware that Susan was probably already waiting.

She looked just the same as she had when I'd last seen her – perfectly turned out. Whether for a night on the town or coffee with a client, Susan always looked business. Her shift dress was beautifully cut, sea green to offset her reddish brown hair, and accessorised with a chunky gold Chanel necklace. She was engrossed in her BlackBerry, her fingers flying across the keys as quickly as a pianist's.

'Sleep in, did we?' she asked, a little acidly, as I slid onto the barstool alongside her. She'd already ordered me a coffee. It was cold, but I sipped it anyway.

'Sorry,' I replied, blushing. I didn't really have any excuse.

'It's good to see you, Ms Rock Star,' she replied, now giving me a warm smile and a peck on each cheek. 'And I hear you got your violin back.'

'Yes!' I said, enthusiastically.

'So you're ready to play?'

'Never been readier.'

'I am very glad to hear it. At least I'll be able to read a newspaper without worrying about which page you're going to turn up on next.'

Groucho Nights was just Groucho Nights now, without the special guests, and although I might consider a reunion in the future, for now I was eager to get back to my classical repertoire.

I floated the idea of a Kiwi album, and Susan readily agreed. The export market was an important one, she reckoned.

Sounds of home. It felt right. I had spent the past few

years going from pillar to post, bouncing from one situation to another like a prize in a pinball machine. Now I had Dominik, and my violin back, and for the first time in my life I felt settled. It was time to look to my roots, as I had tried to do when I was with Simón, with the Venezuelan numbers. But this time I would look back to my own history, not anyone else's, conjure up the landscape of my home and put it in a song.

The Bailly would be perfect for that. I felt a heady sense of excitement when I thought of it. My initial joy at its return had been fleeting. I'd forgotten the instrument as soon as I had Dominik by my side, had surrendered to the touch of his skin, the firmness of his commands, the sound of his voice. I'd been so happy to have him back, to feel him inside me again, that the violin had lain lonesome for a full day and night as we explored each other again.

When we'd finally worn each other out, I'd pounced on the instrument and begun to play immediately. Dominik had laughed to see my expression, like a child with a Christmas toy, as I pulled the Bailly from the case, ran my hands over the burnished, honey-coloured wood and checked the tuning before launching into all the music that was now ours, the backdrop to our relationship. Vivaldi, of course, and as I ran through the chords of each season I thought of the time that had passed, and the time that we had ahead of us. The way life moved and flowed relentlessly, always changing, but always something new and beautiful around the corner. I ended on the light notes of 'Spring'.

*

My suitcase was only half full, and I hadn't even started on the boxes, when I heard the squeak of the front door. It took me a few moments to pull myself up, because I was curled on the floor, wasting time with nostalgia, handling each last thing before I folded it away, and smiling at all the associated memories I had carried with me from one country to another.

Chris and Fran had arrived home, and not noticed that I had let myself into the house with the key he'd given me when I first moved in. I hadn't returned it, as I still officially lived here, though I had, until recently, spent almost every night at Viggo's.

From my seat on the floor facing into the hallway by the door, I had a perfect view of the pair of them, embracing tightly and kissing as though the world was about to end.

I blinked but when I opened my eyes again, they were still there, only now Chris was running his hand up the leg of my sister's shorts and she had her arms over her head, trying and failing to wrestle her way out of her tight T-shirt.

I coughed loudly, alerting them to my presence before I saw anything more that I really didn't want to see. Chris leaped in fright and swung around, searching for an intruder.

'I'm in here,' I called out.

'Jeezus, Summer, don't you ever knock?'

'Knock? I was here first! Don't you ever check your messages?'

'I've been . . . distracted,' he said with a self-conscious smile.

'I can see that.'

Fran was as red as a beetroot. She was normally totally

dismissive of her passing flings, and I'd never known her to be embarrassed at being caught out. That morning with Dagur, the drummer, she'd shrugged it off unashamedly in front of a much bigger audience.

This must be serious.

'You two are . . . getting along well.'

Fran stepped forward to where Chris was standing, in the doorway of the bedroom that she and I had been sharing together, and took his hand.

'We're dating,' she said. 'I mean, officially.'

Chris grinned from ear to ear. 'Your sister is my girl-friend.'

I threw a sock at him. He caught it easily with his spare hand, and continued to smile smugly.

'So that's why it seemed so tidy in here. I wondered why your stuff wasn't spread all over the place like usual, Fran. You've just moved it all into his room. And here I was thinking that you'd turned over a new leaf.'

'Maybe I have,' she replied. 'Just not in the direction that you were expecting.'

I smiled. I was happy for her. And for Chris. In fact, they made a nice couple, even if I had gritted my teeth at the thought of my best friend dating my sister.

Lauralynn had returned all excited from an overnight session booking at a studio in West London.

'You won't guess who it was for,' she'd said to Dominik, after hanging up her leather jacket, setting down her heavy cello case in her room and rushing into the kitchen that had, by default, become their communal space.

'Let me hazard a guess. The late Herbert Von Karajan is

recording a symphonic suite inspired by the Rolling Stones' drug songs and required a lengthy psychedelic cello solo as its highlight.'

'Actually, that's not far off . . .' Lauralynn said.

'And he's come all the way to Shepherd's Bush from wherever he's been biding his time for over thirty years to do the deed . . .' Dominik continued.

'Stop being facetious. No, the booking was with Viggo Franck and The Holy Criminals. They're recording new songs and needed a cello descant on one of the tracks. Their producer even tells me if the song makes it onto the album, I'll be given a credit.'

Dominik had a wry smile. 'That's just wonderful,' he said. 'I'm happy for you.'

'Mind you, I still haven't met the famous Viggo Franck. He wasn't at the sessions. Just his people. I played to the accompaniment of his backing tapes.'

Lauralynn gave her friend a closer look. He looked different, cheerful but slightly absent.

They hadn't seen much of each other during the previous weeks since she'd returned from America. Either he'd been busy upstairs at his computer, presumably writing, or he'd been furtively slipping out of the house at odd times like a conspirator, avoiding her company and deflecting her questions. Lauralynn had been working nights for several days and she assumed his own nights were busy with Summer. She'd seen Summer's shoes and things hanging about the house in odd places.

'Is there something I should know?' Lauralynn asked. 'You've not been very communicative of late, you know?'

'Well . . .' He hesitated. 'There's been a lot happening.'

'Summer?'

'Yes. To cut a long story short, we've been seeing each other a lot. We're going to give it another go, I think.'

Lauralynn beamed. 'Splendid.'

'We've finally reached a decision. I'm hoping she'll be moving in later. With her stuff. I'm keeping my fingers crossed things will work out this time. We're both nervous, of course, but we managed to find her violin, so I reckon it's a good omen.'

'Fantastic. You deserve each other, I've known it all along. And . . .'

'Yes?'

'I'd been thinking of moving on for some time, Dominik. You and me, we're good mates, but it was never an ideal situation, was it?'

'I suppose not.'

'So all this is timely. As I'm sure you don't want to have me around once Summer moves in, do you?'

'It would be awkward,' he agreed. 'Do you have any-where to go?' he asked, concerned. 'I'd feel awful putting you out on the streets.'

'Hmmm . . .' Lauralynn's eyes sparkled with more mis-chief than usual.

'What is it?'

'I think I have somewhere to go.'

'Perfect.'

'Someone who was at the studio. The session actually ended quite early, we'd got things down after just a couple of takes. A friend of the band, she'd come along thinking Viggo was working at the studio last night, but it turned out he was at meetings with his record company. We got talking. I spent the night with her.'

Lauralynn even blushed slightly. Her overnight stand must have made quite an impression, Dominik thought.

'My turn to be happy for you,' he said.

'Thanks,' she giggled like a teenage girl. 'I know it's just one night but I think she's rather special. You know how it goes, sometimes it takes just one glance.'

'Or more,' Dominik remarked.

'Much, much more,' Lauralynn agreed. 'She's staying at Viggo Franck's big place in Belsize Park, says there are a lot of spare rooms and that he wouldn't mind.'

'You mean the Russian woman?' Dominik said, a curious feeling sweeping over him, as if lots of different pieces of the puzzle were finally clicking into place.

'Yes, Luba. The one you were going to introduce me to, remember?'

'Ah, yes, the one and only Luba.'

'Isn't she wonderful?'

'Oh yes, she is,' he agreed. 'Most definitely.'

Summer had an appointment in town that morning with Susan, who had called a meeting to further discuss Summer's plans to reintegrate herself into the classical world with a return to her sources, and the added possibility of releasing a live album which had been recorded with Groucho Nights on their European tour in Sarajevo. She didn't expect to be free until mid to late afternoon, at which stage she was planning to gather the rest of the belongings she'd kept at Chris's Camden Town flat and come along to Dominik's.

Dominik offered to drive Lauralynn and her stuff down the road to Viggo's.

As he rang the bell at the mansion's door, he couldn't help remembering how just under a week before he had used the clandestinely copied keys to make his way in. He had since returned those keys to Viggo.

It was Luba who opened the door for them.

She rushed ahead to give Lauralynn a lengthy hug and affectionately kissed Dominik on both cheeks and welcomed them in.

Considering all the sexual combinations they had been in or witnessed the other in, Dominik was surprised how damn normal it all felt. Like a story winding down to its natural conclusion. A story possibly dictated from afar by the supposed curse of the Angelique, he smiled to himself.

'Viggo's around somewhere. He will probably come down later,' Luba declared.

Looking at the two women together, Dominik was struck by their similarities. He had not seen it before. Both tall and blonde and built like Amazons. Luba was less voluptuous but, a consequence of her dancer's training no doubt, stood straighter, holding her breasts high and with pride, while Lauralynn's stance was looser and more casual, her strong swimmer's shoulders anchoring her frame and her curves.

They visibly suited each other.

Ah, to be a fly on that bedroom wall, Dominik thought.

He and Lauralynn pulled her two heavy Samsonite cases in, and Dominik returned to the BMW's open boot to carry in a couple of large cardboard boxes, in which Lauralynn had hastily thrown her books and general bric-a-brac.

A surprisingly domesticated Luba offered them both coffee and cupcakes, but Dominik sensed he was fast becoming the third wheel of the carriage and the two women were evidently waiting for him to make his excuses and leave them to their own devices. He was about to bid them farewell when Viggo walked into the room. Skinny trousers as tight as ever, as if he had just spent a fortifying half-hour under the shower or in a steam room in order to tighten them even further across his sylph-like form. His T-shirt had seen better days, and was as full of artful holes as a slice of European cheese.

'Hi, mate,' he greeted Dominik in his customary casual tone.

Then turned his attention to the new arrival.

'This is Lauralynn,' Luba introduced her.

The rock musician stared at the statuesque blonde, his eyes darting busily between her and Luba.

'Welcome, darling. I've heard a lot about you.'

'You mean the cello track I recorded for your new song?' Lauralynn asked.

'Oh yes,' Viggo grinned. 'That too . . .'

Amused by Viggo's early predatory intentions, Luba took Lauralynn by the hand and led her towards the hall-way and in the direction of the house's upper floors.

'I'll show you the room we're giving you, come,' Luba said.

Lauralynn waved at Dominik.

Viggo's eyes followed the two women's silhouettes as they stepped away. His little boy smile was on full display.

'She's a good friend,' Dominik pointed out. 'She's nice. But, one word of warning . . .'

'Yeah?'

'She's not much into men.'

Viggo's smile grew even broader.

'Never say never, mate.'

I began to panic when the furniture arrived.

It was the first time in my life that I'd ever had anything of my own that felt so permanent.

I'd bought a large wardrobe, a set of drawers and a full-length mirror online from a shop in East Sussex that made furniture from recycled timber, all of it solid, nothing flatpack. Neil, the shop's manager who had sold it to me, had taken great pains to stress that it was made to last, all of which increased my panic at being now trapped in Dominik's house with no option to make a quick getaway, suitcase in hand, as I had the last time things hadn't worked out between us.

The wardrobe took four men to lift it up the narrow stairs to the bedroom, and as I watched them straining precariously to heft the thing along all I could think was how I would ever manage to move out again. I calmed myself down by remembering that it was just furniture, and I could always take an axe to it if worst came to worst and carry it back down the stairs again in pieces.

The thought made me immediately guilty, and I was extra nice to Dominik for the rest of the week. I wasn't the only one suffering from the change to our circumstance, and he was coping remarkably well, barely raising an eyebrow as I slipped piles of teenage vampire fiction onto his shelves alongside his first editions. He firmly drew the line at acquiring a cat, but agreed to consider a goldfish, if I promised to look after it.

New York had been different. I had known from the outset that living together would be temporary, because Dominik was renting just for a few months to fulfil his scholarship obligations. I'd thought of the loft much as I would consider a hotel, which had perhaps been part of the problem.

Even when I moved in with Simón, though we were together for two years, I hadn't made any changes to the place, bar shifting my clothes into one half of his enormous built-in closet and putting my toiletries in the bathroom. I hadn't added so much as a photoframe to his apartment, and I had always thought of it as his apartment, never ours.

My newly found domestic status was highlighted when I received an email from my old friend Charlotte, the girl I had been close to when I first met Dominik and who had introduced me to the London fetish scene. I hadn't seen or heard from her in more than two years, not since I had left London the first time in such a rush and moved to New York.

She had seen a review of the Groucho Nights gig at La Cigale and wrote that hearing about me again, after all this time, had prompted her to get in touch. She was now living in Paris, and had married Jasper – the male escort she had been casually seeing when I knew her in London – after falling pregnant with their first child who was now eighteen months old. A second had followed only a year later.

Jasper was one of the few men I'd known who could satisfy Charlotte's voracious sexual appetite. But it seemed their casual affair had run to something deeper and Jasper had apparently given up escorting and was now at home looking after the kids and studying psychology, while she worked in the finance department at the British embassy.

I wrote back to tell her that I was now together again with Dominik, and Charlotte and I became engaged in a back and forth, discussing the whys and wherefores of relationships, and what it was like to settle down when you never planned to. For as long as I had known her, Charlotte had been resolutely single, even preferring to engage the services of a man of the night rather than pick someone up at a bar for a short-term fling. She had said at the time that she found it easier, and more honest, and that falling for Jasper, the escort who had become her regular paramour, had just been a happy accident.

'Love,' wrote Charlotte, 'creeps up on you when you least expect it.'

The Parisians, though, were much more open than the British about their erotic natures, and while outwardly maintaining a veneer of respectability, Charlotte and Jasper did occasionally book a babysitter and visit Les Chandelles, or Cap d'Agde, the notorious nudist beach.

'Full of swingers. You'd hate it. Stick with Torture Garden,' she replied, when I asked her what it was like.

I couldn't imagine coaxing Dominik into a military uniform or a latex outfit, though I thrilled at the thought of seeing him clad in riding boots and wielding a crop. He had never been one for the trappings of fetish, and preferred to live out his fantasies with the weight of his touch and words alone. Anything else would be a conversation for another time, but I doubted that it would ever include specialist bed linen or any sort of handcuffs, either of the fluffy pink or the thick leather variety.

We had made one addition to our toy box. Viggo had sent us a housewarming present. A Hitachi magic wand. Dominik had pulled it out of the box and held it up with a perplexed expression, and I had gladly given him a demonstration of how it worked.

Simón had also heard, through Susan, that Dominik and I were back together, and he had called me, out of the blue. It had always amused Simón that I hated telephone conversations, so when we were dating he'd made a point of always calling me, never texting or emailing, even if it was something banal, to check what time I'd be home for dinner, or to ask if I could pick up some milk at the local Korean convenience store.

I picked up the call before I'd had time to think about it, presuming that it would be Susan, calling to check how I was getting on in the studio. Viggo was helping me set up my own recording space for the New Zealand album. I'd been down there every day, rehearsing with the Bailly, getting back into the rhythm of classical music again after my rock hiatus. I'd found it impossible with other violins, but Dominik's gift suited me so well it was almost as though the instrument sang as soon as I touched it.

'Hey, you,' Simón said, when I answered. It was the way that he always greeted me, two words that had been a sort of code between us, an entire conversation that meant 'Hello, how are you, I'm home', and a dozen other things in between.

'Simón?'

'You haven't forgotten me, then?'

'How are you?' I asked. 'You're back in New York now? With the orchestra?'

'Almost. Just passing through. I'm moving back to Venezuela though, for good.'

'Conducting in Caracas?'

'Not even that. A government job, believe it or not. Minister for Culture.'

'Wow! Congratulations. So you get to go to lots of bull-riding events officially?'

'Every week. And get fat on coconut and caramel-flavoured desserts.'

'Sounds like a pretty good deal to me.'

'You should come and visit sometime. And Dominik,' he added quickly. 'Susan told me that you had got back together. And I've been keeping up with all your musical adventures, of course.'

'It's been a bit of a wild ride.'

'It would make a good book.'

I smiled at the coincidence. 'Dominik's writing one. Not about me this time, he's promised. But about the Bailly.'

'I figured he would be. So he gives you the music, and you supply him with the words.'

'I'd never thought of it like that, but I suppose so.'

'I always knew you were made for each other. We never stood a chance.'

He said the words with warmth and humour, and I laughed. Simón had a habit of being right. It was one of the reasons why we'd broken up.

Speaking to him gave me a sense of closure. I was glad to hear he sounded happy as, although he'd ended the relationship, I'd always felt guilty that it was somehow my fault.

The more I thought about it, the more fearful I became that moving in with Dominik was a mistake, just like moving in with Simón had been a mistake. I just wasn't the domestic type. I'd felt trapped with Simón, and I was terrified that I'd feel the same way with Dominik within a few months of sharing the same house day after day.

If it worked, then living with Dominik would be blissful, an answer to everything, the relationship that I always hoped I could have.

But if it didn't work, then it would destroy everything we had.

In Dominik's novel he had now written his way past the carnage and folly of the Second World War and reached the late 1960s, where Edwina Christiansen had become the latest in a series of unfortunate, doomed heroines and owners of the cursed violin.

Edwina was a single mother from Hannover in Germany. Her little boy was the result of an ill-advised love affair on the hippy trail when she was still in her early twenties. Following her return to Germany, she had married Helmuth Christiansen, a ship's chandler in Hamburg, but the marriage had not lasted, his staid habits and the significant age difference too much to bear for her free spirits, and she and her young son had returned to Hannover where she worked as a technical manager and union representative at a car plant.

The violin, which she couldn't even play, had come into her hands following the death of a distant relative and no one else in her family had laid claim to it, so it now rested at the back of one of her cupboards, and Edwina was totally ignorant of its worth.

In Dominik's mind, Edwina looked a bit like Claudia, the graduate student he had had an affair with shortly before he had encountered Summer. It always helped him to have a mental image of his characters and there was no better inspiration than stealing from real life. Claudia's hair was naturally light brown but she always dyed it bright red, a gaudy, unnatural colour which left faint traces on his sheets and pillows, and caused her to avoid the rain like the plague to avoid seeing the colour drip across her face, vulnerable as it was to the prolonged assault of water.

He had been writing through the night and a satisfied form of weariness was now spreading through his limbs, every typing finger heavy as lead as he searched for the right words to describe the way Claudia's thighs met at the intersection of her shaven delta.

He had left Summer in bed upstairs shortly after midnight. They had made frantic love until she had coiled up in a ball, spent, sated and fallen asleep with a childish grin of delight illuminating her face. Dominik had tried to sleep, but his mind and body still felt on edge, feverish, and he'd walked out the bedroom and made his way to his study to see if the electric buzz still animating him could translate into his writing. It had and the night had flown by like a dream. But now it was taking its revenge, and he knew that the time to rest couldn't be delayed any longer.

He set the computer to 'sleep' and pushed his chair back and was about to walk upstairs when he heard the sharp sound of the door flap. Checked his watch. The postman was doing his rounds early.

Out of habit, he lumbered towards the front door to pick up the mail.

It was the usual mix of magazines he subscribed to, junk mail, bills and a lone postcard. From Bali.

He turned the card over. It was from those old dissolutes, Edward and Clarissa. Wishing he was there for 'the party that never ended'. Dominik smiled. Some people would never change, it seemed. They would roam the planet in search of pleasure until the apocalypse came, he guessed. There was something endearing about that.

As he put the rest of the mail on the low-lying phone table, he noticed that Summer's Bailly and its battered case was not in its usual place in the corner where she always left it. He knew for certain it had been there the previous evening.

His heart jumped.

He rushed up to the bedroom, skipping stairs in his haste, hoping that for one reason or another Summer might have taken the instrument there. Not that she ever practised upstairs, having shortly after her arrival shifted most of the furniture in the ground floor back room that led to the garden to convert it into an improvised rehearsal space.

All sorts of doomsday scenarios flashed through his mind. Summer had been unusually quiet for the past few days, and more than once he'd caught her staring into the distance with a pensive expression on her face. Could she have had second thoughts? After everything, did she really not think their relationship could work?

He pushed the door open, his eyes getting accustomed to the surrounding darkness.

He looked all around the room. No violin case.

He turned to the bed, expecting to see Summer's shape under the covers. But the bed sheets were thrown aside and the bed was empty.

The world stopped.

Collapsed around him.

In a blind panic, Dominik ran through the house, checking every room, blood rushing to his head.

She was gone.

He was back in the ground floor hall, where he had begun his search. He moved a hand to the door to steady himself. He knew – he had always known – that Summer was a free spirit. That tying her down to a conventional relationship would only drive her away. He had been selfish and stupid, and once again he had lost her.

He sank down, his back against the door. His hand fell to his sides and he felt something long and smooth beneath his fingers. It was one of Summer's bows, lying across the mat. She must have dropped it in her hurry to escape. He hadn't noticed it earlier as the pile of mail had fallen over it and concealed it from view, and he had failed to note its presence when he had distractedly picked up the assorted envelopes and magazines.

He ran his fingers along its length, thinking of Summer. Beautiful, fragile, proud. The woman he loved. The woman he had lost once more. And right there, his fingers gripping the only piece of Summer he had left, Dominik thought his heart might break.

He knew straight away the bow was not in its normal place.

It had been positioned as if it was pointing towards the door.

A sign?

He opened the front door. The road was quiet and free of traffic at this early hour. He checked his watch. It was only seven in the morning.

On the narrow pavement, just a few yards from the house's front door, he noted a dark-brown plastic guitar pick.

He bent over and picked it up.

The logo of Groucho Nights was carved across it, a cabalistic sign that Summer's sister Fran had unearthed in a book of esoterica and that had tickled the imagination of Chris and his fellow musicians.

They'd had a few thousand of the picks produced and had traditionally thrown them into the audience at the climax of their final encores. It was a cheap and effective promo trick.

On the other side of the house, the side turning that led to the depths of the Vale of Health was like a pocket of darkness.

Dominik caught sight of another of the small guitar picks, on the opposite pavement, just a few footsteps from the kerb, in the direction of the towering shape of the Royal Free Hospital which stood at the bottom of the steep hill. He crossed the road, leaving the door of the house open behind him and still wearing the flip-flops he had been typing in throughout the night. A further two minutes down the road he found a third pick.

It was a trail.

A message from Summer?

He quickly backtracked to the house, changed into a pair of trainers and picked the first sweatshirt lying around in one of the downstairs rooms, slipped it on above his top, seized his keys and locked up behind him, and went in search of further guitar picks littering the downward path of the hill.

As he did so, his memory was working overtime. Trying to remember the fairy tale, if it was one, *Red Riding Hood* or *Pinocchio* or *Hansel and Gretel* or yet another, where a trail of small stones – or was it seeds? – had directed a character in the right direction.

At first, I thought it was a ridiculous idea.

I ought to just leave a note for him on the breakfast bar: 'Gone for a walk. Come and find me,' with a map attached and an X marking my planned destination.

But the more I thought about it, the more the idea began to take root in my mind, like an acorn quickly sprouting.

I had woken in the night to find him gone, his side of the bed cold and the covers flung off as if he had left in a hurry. Dominik was eternally neat, and under normal circumstances he would have pulled his side of the sheet up behind him.

I immediately felt a pang of anxiety. Thought that he might have woken up to find me alongside him and felt that the bed was too full and he wanted to be alone. Sometimes, I felt that way, still unaccustomed to us being together. Perhaps he'd gone to seek refuge at a hotel, or with a friend, maybe asked Lauralynn to let him into one of Viggo's guest rooms for the night.

The bedroom, without him in it, had felt suffocating. I had pushed the covers off and quietly padded down the stairs. That was when I saw the light on in his study, and as I approached, heard the very faint clicking of his fingers on the keys.

He was writing.

The door was slightly ajar, and I creaked it open a little further and called his name softly, to check if he wanted a hot drink, or a glass of water, but he hadn't responded.

He had that familiar expression on his face, part joy, part furious concentration, the way he gets when a new idea has dawned on him in just the right way, like an irregular visit from an unpredictable muse, and I thought it best not to interrupt.

I'd poured myself a glass of milk and returned to bed, but I still couldn't sleep.

I sat awake for the rest of the night, thinking about the future, and what it might hold for us.

Whether we would make it. Whether moving in with him so quickly would prove to be a mistake.

Only time would tell.

My eyes had alighted on the Bailly which I'd left in the hall the evening before, and my fingers twitched, longing to pick it up and play it until I wore myself out and tiredness finally settled like a heavy cloak around my shoulders and dragged me into sleep, but even with the door closed, I feared that my music would rouse Dominik from his creative trance like a siren song and bring him back upstairs.

Sometimes I felt like the Pied Piper of Hamelin, because

Dominik always followed the notes of the Bailly. He used the sound of my violin as a barometer of my mood, and I noticed that, out of habit now, he would glance at it wherever I left it to double check that it was still safe and firmly tucked away before turning out the light.

I had listened to the story of the Angelique which he was using as the bread and butter of his novel. I'd always been interested in the history of my instruments. Always wanted to know which hands had held them and what stories they'd told before they came to me. But I wasn't quite as romantic about the whole thing as Dominik was, and teased him for his superstitions.

The person wielding the violin had more power than the instrument, surely?

Even Mr van der Vliet, my late violin teacher, had always taught me that the right player could bring music out of anything, even by rubbing a stick against a woodsaw.

But that got me started, thinking about the Bailly, romantic fairy tales and legends, and once the kernel of the idea had planted its seed, I couldn't escape it. Soon I had a fully hatched plan.

I dressed quickly, in my old black velvet dress that I still used for performances sometimes, the one that I'd bought from Brick Lane years ago, and had worn for Dominik at our first recital. It felt poetic.

Then I'd picked up the Bailly, and realised the first stumbling block in my plan. I had to give him some kind of clue. But what?

I clicked open the case and brushed my fingers over the almost orange-coloured timber, as warm as a sunset, and hoped that the violin would provide me with an answer.

The violin didn't, but the case did. The pocket bulged, and I reached in and found a stash of the Groucho Nights branded guitar picks that we used to fling into the audience to an often frenzied welcome.

Perfect. Like a trail of breadcrumbs that I would drop along the way to the Heath, that would lead to me, rather than a gingerbread house.

To be doubly sure that he would at least have a chance to work it out, I left a spare bow on the doormat, pointing in the direction that I was headed, where he would find the first guitar pick.

Dawn was breaking as I made my way along the downhill road to the open reaches of the Heath. The orange ember of the sun rising over the tree-lined horizon sent streaks of pink into the sky like tentacles. I was rarely awake so early, and having barely slept at all, felt as though I had stepped into a dream, a haze of chilled air punctuated by birds tweeting and the soft rasping of the wind through the trees.

I was careful to drop the picks as I went, in all the places that Dominik would recognise. I followed the same route that he had led me on the first time that I'd walked this trail. Again, I was barefoot, and I smiled at the familiar feeling of spongy earth beneath my feet.

Past the ponds, across the small bridge by the outdoor swimming area and up the path. I winced as the sharp pebbles dug into my feet and was careful to place a guitar pick on a large, black stone that stood out of place amongst the other smaller, pale rocks so that Dominik would find it. By now, he should know for sure where I was taking him. I hadn't walked the same route since that day long ago when

326

I had first played Vivaldi for him here, but the way was burned onto my brain as fiercely as a treasure map.

Finally I reached the soft grass again, and sighed with pleasure as the dew nursed my stone-bitten feet. Then I was under the canopy of trees that blocked the light like a curtain, before emerging out into the open, within sight of the bandstand that sat atop its gloriously green hillock as if it had sprung out of the earth like a tree made from wrought iron pillars instead of dirt and wood.

I hadn't bothered with the guitar picks for the last few hundred feet. Dominik would be able to hear me by now.

If he came.

And I was sure that he would.

I stepped gingerly onto the stone steps that led to the bandstand's small stage, and turned and looked out onto the open field, and the line of trees from where Dominik would soon emerge.

It was just me, the Bailly, the birds and the Heath. No doubt at least a few early morning joggers would appear soon, disrupting my solitude, and that thought nearly put me off the next plot point in my plan, but I resolved to do it anyway.

What was the point in playing a recital for Dominik, on the bandstand on the Heath, if I wasn't nude? It was my final message to him.

Maybe it was just the sleepless night talking, but by the time I reached the Heath, I had made up my mind.

If he appeared, if he noticed the violin, and me, missing, and followed my clues to the bandstand, then I would take it as a sign that we were meant to be together, and I would banish my doubts and commit to making it work.

If he didn't, if he carried on writing for the rest of the day, or found me missing and presumed I had gone for a jog and left me to it, then I would move out, and put the whole thing behind me. Start again. Single.

One final roll of the dice. Putting our fate into the hands of fate. It seemed a very Dominik thing to do, the kind of thing that he would recognise and approve of. But that was the very reason why I thought it would work, because I proposed to meet him halfway, by appearing naked, and playing Vivaldi.

Just like the first time.

I kicked off my dress, closed my eyes, and launched into concerto number two, 'Summer'. It was out of order, but I planned to finish on 'Spring', because it felt like a beginning, which suited my purposes. Ending on 'Winter' would be too depressing.

The notes flew from the Bailly as soon as I touched my bow to the strings, and I was gone with it, flying across the Heath on the wings of a song.

I was playing the final notes of 'Autumn', when I remembered my purpose, and opened my eyes again, scouring the tree line for any sign of him.

Maybe he hadn't come after all, and this was all a stupid idea. Maybe we'd made a mistake and this was fate telling me to leave, to run away while I still could, before either of us ended up getting hurt. But as I played on, I knew that in my heart I wanted him to come to me.

My bow hand shook slightly as the enormity of my feelings surged, as I whispered a silent prayer to Dominik. *Find me. Come for me. Don't give up on us.* I felt a tear escape, sliding down my cheek and landing on the smooth

surface of the violin. And I knew, right there, as the swee.
notes of Vivaldi rose through the morning mist, I could not
live without him.

I saw a silhouette, emerging from the canopy of trees, about
a hundred yards away. It was impossible to identify anyone
at this distance. My heart began to beat wildly, as I thought
I recognised the old university athletics team sweatshirt, but
I pushed the thought out of my head, closed my eyes again,
and let the violin take over.

I thought I felt his presence hovering nearby, tiny shifts
in the air around me, as I launched into 'Spring', the end of
my recital, the first movement. Watching me, planning his
next move, or maybe just listening to the music.

He grew impatient in the end, and disrupted my song.

First I felt his hot breath on my neck, as he leaned in as if
to kiss me, but he didn't.

Instead, as I reached the final chord, his hand gently took
the violin from my grasp and he lowered me onto the cool
stone stage of the bandstand.

I opened my eyes.

Dominik, grinning from ear to ear, with that familiar
dark glint in his eyes.

'But I haven't finished,' I whispered.

'Vivaldi will forgive us,' he replied.

And then we made love. In our own way.

Acknowledgements

We would like to thank our agent Sarah Such at Sarah Such Literary Agency, who did such a wonderful job in getting Eighty Days to market. A deep vote of thanks also goes to Jon Wood, Jemima Forrester, Susan Lamb, Emma Dowson and everyone at Orion, who have done so well in getting us onto the bestseller lists. A tip of the fedora to Tina Pohlman and Allison Underwood at Open Road Integrated Media. We also owe a debt of gratitude to Rosemarie Buckman at the Buckman Agency for all the foreign sales, and to all the countless foreign publishers who have taken the series on, as well as Hamish and Junzo at the English Agency (Japan), and Carrie Kania at Conville & Walsh. A final thank you to our eagle-eyed copyeditors, proofreaders and translators who worked tirelessly and at great speed.

Much of these books were written on the road and heartfelt thanks must go to our respective partners, family and friends whom we had to singularly neglect as we devoted our time to Summer and Dominik, as we roamed London, Paris, Bristol, Rome, Berlin, Edinburgh, New Orleans, New York, Chicago, Avignon and Sitges, with laptops and iPads in overdrive.

And a final thank you to Matt Christie for photography,

to Vina's employer for her support and encouragement, despite the many writing-induced absences from work, and to all the necessary anonymous sources who helped us with our research.

It's been an exciting ride . . .

The turbulent romantic adventures of Summer and Dominik may have reached their conclusion, but the Eighty Days series continues with *Eighty Days Amber* and *Eighty Days White*, in which both Summer and Dominik will make an appearance, alongside Luba, Viggo Franck, the girl with the teardrop tattoo, and many other acquaintances, both old and new.